THE TANNER'S WIFE

A PEMBROKE STORY

Other titles by Freda Davies

Published by Allison and Busby, London
LET HEAVEN FALL   (1995)

Published by Constable and Robinson, London,
and by Carroll and Graf, New York.
A FINE AND PRIVATE PLACE   (2001)
BOUND IN SHALLOWS   (2003)

THE TANNER'S WIFE

A PEMBROKE STORY

Freda Davies

Published by
CAERIW PUBLISHING Ltd

Caeriw Publishing Ltd
Glanafan, Hundleton, Pembroke SA71 5RD, UK

Copyright © Freda Davies 2004

A catalogue reference for this book is available from
The British Library.

ISBN 0–9546676–0-3

Typeset by Photoprint, Torquay, Devon

Printed by Antony Rowe Ltd, Chippenham, Wiltshire

For Sara and John

Chapter One

Mist rolled up from the sea and by first light the town was covered and filled by its dense whiteness. The wood of houses and hovels loomed solid, indistinct, and even the castle and its palisades were hidden. The presence of the Franks there was given away by the neighing of horses, shouts of men, clanking of iron and the smoke of cooking fires. Elsewhere figures appeared and menaced, causing fear with the threat of a raid until they were near enough to be touched and recognised as neighbours.

Air moved and the mist began to thin. The day warmed and a breeze rustled, the damp miasma dispersing as the slight wind strengthened. By the time the first farmers reached Pembroke and began to set up their stalls, the only sign of the white invasion was tendrils of it still curling and wisping in the tallest trees.

The tall Fleming listened to abuse being screamed at him by an old man contorted with rage. He had tried hard to understand the tongue used in this far corner of Wales but words coming from the bony gums defeated him, except for one. Outlander. As he moved to escape dottle spat at him he wished he could do as he was bid and go home but that place was denied him. It had been invaded by an enemy more deadly than any army and all he had held dear was buried beneath the sea.

7

Ugo strode the roughness of the road. The houses and shops on either side of him had been built soon after the castle rose on a crest of stone above the river. It was a market day and the crowd through which he walked had every type of face and clothing, colour and smell. Weather beaten farmers and their women trudged past him on their way home and he saw sailors from the hot lands of Greece and Africa mingling with seamen from the frozen north. Urchins scavenged as best they could and traders stood at the doors of their shops, eagle eyes searching for a customer with coin in his pouch.

"Ugo! Good day to you," was shouted by a big, broad man descending from a laden cart. His head was capped by gleaming black curls and a full beard jutted cheerfully as he grinned a warm welcome at the Fleming. "When will you come and eat with us as you promised? I want to hear more of your travels."

"Gerwyn, it is good to see you." Ugo thought yet again how his new friend, a tanner, brought smiles to the faces of all he encountered. Unlike any others of that trade Ugo had encountered, this man of Pembroke did not carry the reek of his work.

"Gerwyn!" From behind roped firewood the Fleming was being glared at by a large woman dressed in black. She was like Gerwyn, apart from the beard, but fiercely unpleasant. "I am waiting."

"Coming, Non," the tanner assured her and held out his hands to help her descent to the roadway.

"We will meet again," Ugo said quietly. With a salute he was on his way, reflecting Gerwyn was a kindly man and the rest of the day would be hard for him in the home behind the leather shop.

"Where is that wretched girl? Manon! Where are you?"

Stupified with sleep, Manon wondered if she was enduring a nightmare. "Please God, let it not be Non," she prayed but the voice came again and she knew she was awake.

8

"My brother away from home, she should have been in charge of the shop – certainly the kitchen – and yet she is nowhere to be seen. Does she expect to hold on to all this imaginary wealth of hers if she is so slovenly in her ways? A chit of a girl at the cooking fire and an outlander who speaks not as we do selling in the shop? Manon is mad! Gerwyn, you should not let it be so!"

Manon lifted her baby son and hurried down the ladder from her sanctuary. Dybion's eyes were open and unhappy, his lips puckering as he drew breath, ready for an indignant bellow. When the massive black figure of his aunt appeared, the baby screamed until his cheeks were bright red.

"Must you let him bawl so? This is scarcely your first child, Manon, so you should know how to make him behave. I see I visit not a moment too soon."

Gazing at her husband's sister, Manon kept her expression pleasant, her mouth fixed in a smile of welcome as she prayed Non could not guess secret thoughts. Of that there was no danger. Non was too busy deciding how to alter all she saw wrong in the young family's life.

In a tunic of black wool and a matching kerchief of the finest linen wound around her throat she might be mistaken for a holy sister but for her expression. It was not serene, her skin thick and dark around the chin as well as above a mouth thinned to a slit by displeasure. Non's nose had bone and flesh a man might envy and under hairy brows dark eyes were prominent and missed nothing. Only her hands had any grace. She held them folded on her stomach, her fingers not coarsened by hard work. That was left to her unceasing tongue.

Nudd shuffled in with a basket of the guest's belongings. She barked at him and he dropped the load, scuttling away in the direction pointed by an imperious finger.

"Why is that creature still here? I told you last time I was in Pembroke he was to go. You ignored me!"

Manon struggled to remain calm. It took time, time in which she remembered Gerwyn bringing home the frail

9

scrap of humanity which was Nudd. Born deformed he had developed growths on his face as he grew, rendering him hideous even to his mother. Abandoned as little more than a baby he survived alone in the woods, eating roots, nuts, berries. Gerwyn had come upon Nudd as he watched men cleaning and curing hides beside the river and had carried him home as he would a dying dog. It was Gwen, the servant girl, who had taken the unloved boy to her heart and, with care and good feeding, he had grown to be useful, playing with Manon's babies as he learned to be a child and then a man.

"Nudd –" Manon began.

The black menace glared at her. "His name is against all our mother church approves."

"Because Nudd was brother to Halfgan, the king of the underworld in our legends?"

"There you are! Even his name is of Satan – and you still allow him the freedom of your dwelling? I have warned you before, he will be a curse on you all."

Three years old, Heledd was small enough to hide behind Gwen but the child was so frightened she ran to clutch at her mother's skirts and bury her face there. Manon cradled the child against her leg as she stood tall and faced the woman who had invaded her home.

"We have demons in our lives, as does everyone, Non, but Nudd is not one of them. He has a purer soul than many who step through that door to sup at my table."

The older woman ignored Manon's defence of Nudd. "While there is still light I will decide where I sleep. My pallet must have enough space to be unrolled fully and my blankets shaken and freshened. I may as well have that child's bedspace, as I did before."

"Heledd," Manon said, determined her daughter should not be as naught. "She sleeps soundly there and it would not be wise to move her."

"Heledd. A fanciful name for a brat. More sensible to

have named her after someone who could have been of use to her should she be orphaned."

Manon caught her breath at the suggestion. "Such as yourself, I suppose?"

"It would have been the least courtesy you could have offered."

Dybion, sensing misery in the air, whimpered and breathed the familiar skin of his mother's neck, his hands clutching at the softness of her tunic.

"Do you plan to spend longer than this night?" Manon asked, then glimpsed Gerwyn, laden with Non's bundles. With his eyes he pleaded for his wife's forbearance.

"Why do you ask?" Non's brows were a thick, angry line as she frowned her displeasure.

"I know how greatly you prize your home. How could you bear to be absent from it for more than a day?"

"Duty to my young brother and his family has always been of importance to me – indeed I gave up my home to look after Gerwyn and raise him when his mother died."

"As you have told me many times."

"Clearly, not often enough. You are too young and feckless to understand such an obligation."

Manon was annoyed but she held her head high and proud. "You forget my brothers, mistress. My father asked me to ensure their share of his wealth was kept secure for them and I have done so. Indeed the farm you inhabit is in your stewardship until they return and claim it as their own."

For a brief moment Non was speechless but she recovered quickly. "Land should never be left untended – certainly not until some mystical time when slaves return from their captivity."

"But they will come one day," Manon said softly. "Both of them."

Passing through fortified gates Ugo entered another township. Pembroke's castle crowned the heights of a cliff, caves below it storing water and prisoners, the grass of its outer bailey home to grazing sheep, goats, geese. Palisades rose higher than a man on horseback, the ditch in front of this outer ring supplying an advantage to the defenders as well as earth to shore up the wall and allow archers the height from which to shower down their arrows.

The main gates were surmounted by a gatehouse, guards on call at all time to fight any enemy to the death. Equally ready were the men in the gatehouse to the inner bailey, busy now with preparations for the evening meal. Joints of butchered sheep dripped fat on to cooking fires and in the great hall of the castle stewards hurried with slabs of bread to hold meat, flagons of wine and goblets of silver and of earthenware.

Ringing the great hall and dwarfed by it were the sheds housing soldiers and horses as well as store houses, cells for prisoners and a mews for hunting birds. In a corner near this smaller gatehouse were the stone walls of a chapel, its wood and thatch roof drawing Ugo's steps towards it and he knelt in quietness where his thoughts and prayers rose undisturbed. Memories had him almost smelling the home he had known until he reached out to touch his wife, his children, finding only the cold air of Pembroke.

"You are wanted," a soldier told Ugo as he made his way to his quarters in the stables.

"Sir Gerald?"

"Aye – and in a hurry."

Ugo smiled. The Constable was not known for his patience and the Fleming walked faster towards the warmth and noise of the great hall.

"Ugo! The horses – enough?" Gerald de Windsor was tall, lean, greying. His dark eyes were shrewd and missed nothing while the lines graven in his strong beardless face marked him determined.

"Yes, sir," Ugo answered in the Frank's tongue. "They will stay on the farms and be grain fed until you are ready for them to be moved – two more than you asked for."

"Good. You have done well. Get to table while the food is hot."

It was not a bad life, Ugo thought as he sat at his place at the long trestle in the great hall. Fresh meat in front of him, wine at hand, the grunts of men as they ate. There was not the softness and promise of home but in his bed later he could leave that to his dreams.

Non had descended like a cawing crow in a nest of songbirds and Manon paid dearly for her defiance. She endured dark glances, silences, long sniffs of disapproval and criticism of her every move, not knowing the calm expression which she fought hard to present to her detractor only added to Non's fury. It was not the younger woman's fault the skin of her oval face was flawless, large eyes under the fine line of her brows sparkling with health. Nor could Manon be blamed for having a small nose above a generous mouth but blamed she was.

The evening meal was an ordeal for all who sat at table. With dry crusts to eat Nudd and Old Twm had been banished to the yard, Kamal to the workshop. Non only allowed family members to sit with her and even Gwen must go hungry as she skivvied.

"Most peculiar," Non declared the stew, the herbs flavouring it strange to her. Rhodri and Heledd must be forbidden meat as it only resulted in waywardness in the young. Then the bread was too fresh, too plentiful, Non decided, such habits encouraging the sin of gluttony. Milk from the goat should not be drunk so freely, it must be saved for cheese which might be sold.

Manon was even followed to where she sat in peace, feeding Dybion. It was Non's opinion the baby should be properly swaddled and not allowed to wriggle and kick.

"This is your third healthy child," she reminded Manon. "Now you have borne two sons it is time for you to deny your husband your body. Too many children will lessen Meurig's share of his father's businesses."

13

The young woman fought down her fury. She had always known Meurig to be Non's favourite, indeed when Gerwyn's first wife had sickened and died she had helped raise the boy until Gerwyn had sighted Manon and not rested until he wed her. Whatever Non had done in the past, Manon was convinced there was no excuse for her interfering in the life a husband led with his wife. Gazing down at her suckling child Manon silently recited every remembered prayer. The English king's priests insisted Latin be used for all services and for once she was grateful. In an extra language she could petition the Almighty to relieve her of the burden of Non and her spite.

The unpleasantness affected them all. Gerwyn kept out of the way, Gwen muttered what sounded like curses from the old ones and Heledd was a quiet mouse running to her mother's skirts whenever Non loomed near. Even Dybion became fractious, sensing unease in the milk he drew from his mother.

"Why is she here?" Manon asked her husband when they were at last in their bed.

"God alone knows. She was in the cart with her bundles when I was ready to start for home."

"Something must have happened to make her come. What have you said to her?"

"Nothing! I swear."

Heledd, disturbed by her parents, whimpered in her sleep and Manon rolled away from Gerwyn, her curled back a protest.

"Cariad," he began and would have pulled her to him but Manon thrust his hands away. "I tried to persuade her not to come but she had made up her mind – you know what she is like."

Manon would not be persuaded. "You must have given her a reason."

"Never! Believe me, cariad." There was a long, uneasy silence. "It might have been something Meurig said."

"Meurig? When was he at the farm?"

14

"Yesterday, late. He left to ride home again before curfew."

All who lived in the shadow and protection of the castle were under the law of couvre feu and must be indoors before nightfall, their fires covered. Manon recalled the boy coming to the kitchen, hungry for food and with an excited glitter in his eyes.

"I thought he had been with a girl."

"Better if he had been." Gerwyn loved his eldest son but was wise to his ways.

Manon had a long experience of Meurig's attempts to belittle her. "What can he have said to Non to make her want to come to Pembroke?"

The youngest wolfhound was restless, sniffing at strange feet before settling next to his dam in front of the fire. It was quiet in the room behind the great hall of Pembroke's castle. The Constable sat at his ease in one chair facing the fire, his good friend, Odo de Barri, in another. Between them and on a table was a large flagon of wine and silver goblets. The most important men in the shire, their tunics and boots were of the finest quality but plainly cut and unadorned.

"Your lady is well – and the new child?" Odo asked.

A moment's smile enlivened Gerald de Windsor's features. "Thank you. They both thrive."

"You are very fortunate to have another fine son to ride with you."

"Indeed I am but Nest has this one dedicated to the church. He is lusty and when he is grown her decision may not sit lightly with him."

"There is time," Odo said cheerfully. "Now, what of the castle the king has given you gracious permission to build?"

"Palisades are in place and the earthworks behind them. As for the outbuildings, the stables and mews await their rooves. The great hall, is well fortified and it is to have a

15

series of rooms on two levels behind it – Nest was most insistent."

"Nest," Odo said and poured himself more wine. "She will miss her home at Carew."

Gerald waved a dismissive hand. "No doubt – but at last I have land of my own," he added softly.

Odo realised anew how deep was the hurt in his proud friend, the gracious life he had led these past years because of his wife's dowry from the king. He savoured his wine, then drank deeply. "The shire of Pembroke will see many changes when you go north, to Emlyn."

"Little should alter. Geoffrey is the best of shire reeves and he will continue to serve Pembroke well."

Odo cleared his throat and looked hard at his friend, at ease and stretching long legs towards the fire. "Perhaps not, Gerald," he said carefully. "Gilbert de Clare needs a castellan for one of his castles on the English border. He has asked the king for Geoffrey."

The Constable frowned but did not allow himself to appear annoyed. "And what the Clares want, the king will see they are given. I see I must find and train a new shire reeve." The idea was clearly unwelcome.

"One has already been selected for you. The Bishop of London has an interest and is despatching a young man connected to him by the mother's blood. Roger fitzHugh."

"If the family is of such good standing at court why is he to be sent to the furthest point of land away from Windsor and Westminster? What is wrong with the pup he must cut his teeth on my townspeople?"

"Over-indulgence, I fear."

Gerald was well-known to be quick tempered but he had learned control. He would not rail at his good friend, who saw his lips tighten and his nostrils flare.

"I have been chosen to help a spoilt child grow to manhood? The bishop is too kind to give me the task but what of Pembroke? Does his grace not realise we are a border town? There is the sea as well as the land and we have two-legged wolves who can ride or sail here to rob us of the fruits of hard work and good trading – Welsh, Irish, Danes, take your pick!"

"The bishop stands in lieu of the king," Odo reminded him. "Both men have faith in you, Gerald, and I agree with them – if anyone can make a man out of Roger fitzHugh, it will be you."

His chair creaking under him, Gerald was restless, uneasy. "In this part of Wales all men – aye, and women too – are used to certain standards of justice, of security. This mother's boy could destroy all that in the wink of an eye."

"Come, Gerald. We have both been in this shire long enough to know its men and women for what they are. They will not allow young Roger to wreck their peace."

In the home behind the leather shop only Non flourished. Gerwyn trod carefully, his broad, handsome features twisted with concern for his family, suffering because of his sense of duty to a difficult sister. Again and again he would run fingers through the strong black curls capping his head and sigh, gestures copied faithfully by Rhodri, a seven year-old miniature of his father.

Unlike the men the womenfolk were tied to the house and regularly lashed by Non's tongue. Heledd drooped and paled like a gentle flower bud and Gwen became tight-lipped as she defended her brood with glowering stares at Non's back. She slipped what extra bread and meat she could to Nudd and Old Twm. Kamal, with his bronze skin and dark eyes was already slender, his frame toughened by his time as a slave. He gratefully accepted what Gwen could sneak away for him but shared it with the other men, as his eyes followed the curve of Gwen's hips whisking away to yet another task at the bidding of the bird of prey in the shape of a woman.

Laws of hospitality were binding on all who shared the blood of the Britons in Wales, no matter where they lived. For centuries their customs had ensured the survival of the least of guests and Non traded on ingrained habits, driving courtesy to its limits and beyond, especially in the night hours. Those she made unbearable with snoring which shook the wood of the house so only she slept.

When awake, Non always reserved her worst strictures for Manon. The younger woman could not see what excited Non's bitterness afresh each day. It was thick, dark hair curling waywardly when free of its binding, eyes holding the sunshine of laughter and a mouth and body grown ripe with motherhood. All Manon knew was that Non lost no chance to be hurtful.

On the fourth day of Non's visit new blankets were brought by a weaver. With them came a length of fine black wool, enough for at least two tunics. Kamal hurried to Manon, concerned there were not enough coins in the shop to pay the man.

Manon was very annoyed. "Where is Meurig?" she asked.

Kamal rubbed a spot on his hand, the action demanding all his attention. "He had to go somewhere, mistress."

It was a habit of Gerwyn's son by his first wife to leave trading to others when he was bored. Manon followed Kamal back to the waiting weaver, a stranger to the town, his manners and features honest enough, his clothes hard worn but tidy and unstained. Behind him a boy little older than Rhodri, guarded a handcart with the goods for sale. Manon lifted a corner of the clean, old linen in which they were wrapped and saw the blankets were soft, the weaving expert.

"I have not asked for any of this."

"The lady who lives here did so. She said the tanner's wife would pay – she could afford it."

Holding rising fury in check was not easy but Manon knew the weaver was not at fault. "Is there another who would buy what you have brought here?"

The man hesitated, shuffling his feet and not happy to be in the middle of a row between two women. "I was told of a

18

Mistress Mabli at the castle who is always looking for the best weaving."

"And you have fine goods to offer, sir. Your craft should be enjoyed by those who appreciate it most."

The weaver was soothed by praise but still not at ease. "The other lady?"

"I will speak to her," Manon promised.

The man shook his head slowly. "She was very determined on the purchase."

"I have no doubt she was and I would have no quarrel with that – should be spending her own silver. Be sure when I do need new blankets I will wait for your return to Pembroke."

Meurig came into the shop in time to hear Manon's words. He flushed and would have shouted at his father's wife but waited until the weaver and his lad had gone in the direction of the castle.

"How could you?" he demanded of Manon. "My aunt purchased the wool in good faith and you –"

"Refused to pay for it. Tell me, Meurig, do you take money from the box in the shop whenever it suits your aunt?"

The boy resembled Gerwyn and one day would be tall and handsome. Now the young mouth was sulky, his eyes stormy and hooded from Manon as he refused to answer her.

"At the end of a sale I have seen you put coins in your own pouch," she told him.

Manon had his attention and Meurig was wary of her.

"Your father has not learned of these thefts because I do not want to be the source of discord between you," she said quietly. "As for Non, I will not have her throwing this family's hard-earned money to the winds."

"You have plenty!"

"No thanks to my husband's kinfolk, it would seem."

"It is unfair! You have so much and my aunt so little – after all she has done for this family and no thought of reward."

"Is that what she told you? Without a by-your-leave she and your uncle took possession of the farm near the tannery and there they have stayed. In all that time not even a sliver of copper has been paid in rent."

"Why should she give you money? She gave up everything to care for my father when his mother died –"

"So the world and his wife have been told many, many times. Now, if you wish to be of use to your aunt, go and help Gwen pack her belongings."

"But she is not going back to the farm for another week."

Manon's smile was a grimness which quietened the boy. "Oh, yes she is, Meurig."

The young man who strode into the castle was very sure of himself, in spite of his youth and pimpled skin. The collar of his purple cloak shone with silver thread as did the pale green of his tunic which could be glimpsed as he swung his arms.

"Sir Gerald?"

The Constable had been talking with his shire reeve and was surprised by the interruption, frowning his displeasure at the newcomer. Short and given to plumpness, his features had the curves of youth and only a faint darkness as the chin promised a beard to come.

"I am Roger fitzHugh, Sir Gerald, and direct from Windsor."

With an assurance strange in one so young, the costly cloak was tossed aside as the Bishop of London's protégé inspected the great hall and its furnishings. It was clear from his air of disdain he found his present surroundings primitive after the graciousness of the king's court.

"You must have ridden hard to have arrived so quickly,"

the Constable said after he had surveyed the young man and decided on his worth.

"Not at all, Sir Gerald. On the advice of my uncle, the bishop, I left Windsor some days ago and have been lodging with an acquaintance of my mother's in Carmarthen – a small town as yet but one with great promise – then I visited your lady in Carew. She was most friendly and hospitable."

The Constable almost smiled at the patronage. "You should have been warned when the bishop and your mother decided to place you here. I choose my own men," he said. "You will ride with Geoffrey, my present shire reeve, and see all that must be done. Only if I am satisfied by his reports on your progress will I confirm you as shire reeve when Geoffrey must leave Pembroke." He turned to walk away.

"But I am to be your shire reeve, sir. My uncle assured me –"

Gerald swung in mid-stride, glowering at the pimply youth. "Do I choose the bishop's priests for him?" he shouted. "In time I may agree with your illustrious uncle. Until then you should know Geoffrey rises early and works hard as long as there is light. If you are not able to match him, then be prepared to return to your host in Carmarthen."

Roger fitzHugh was not used to being spoken to so harshly but he knew he was finished if he allowed his fast rising temper to be seen. "Of course, Sir Gerald." The French was very formal and echoed in the Constable memories of King Henry and his courtiers. "May I go to my chamber and arrange for an early start in the morning?"

The Constable's formidable eyebrows were raised. He pointed to the floor of the great hall, its rushes well-trodden. "There. Wrapped in your cloak."

"Sir! I protest! I am of noble blood and should not have to lie with commoners."

21

Gerald de Windsor had also learned smoothness in the royal presence of Henry and his kin. "Then you have my permission to persuade them you have the privilege of sleeping nearest the fire."

The storm burst when Non returned to find her bedding and clothes being tossed up into the wagon used by Gerwyn to carry raw hides and sometimes dung to the tannery beyond the monk's town, west of Pembroke. His sister would have screamed abuse at Manon in the public roadway but the younger woman stayed in the kitchen, ready to fight on her own ground.

Non's cheeks were purple with fury and her eyes bulged in their sockets. "What do you think you are doing?"

"Making sure you return to your husband who must be missing you by now."

"I am not going back to the farm for some days yet – I have too much to see to here."

"And buy with money you think I have? How often has Meurig had to steal from the shop to pay for what comes within reach of your greed?"

Non did not even have the grace to blush. "The shop is my brother's property."

Manon lifted her chin. "The tannery is Gerwyn's and always will be. The shop from which you pilfer through your nephew was bought with my share of my father's silver."

"And we all know how he came by it." Spite made Non's lips a thin line of hate.

"Do you, Non?" Manon asked softly. "It was a reward for loyalty – something you expect to grasp but never give. My father was loyal to Rhys ap Tudor from a time before that great man became king and held the south of Wales in his strong and caring power. He was a good judge of men and favoured those who showed courage."

"Courage? Your father was but a ringyll, the like to be found in any village. All he did was make sure his lord's dues were paid by starving people – and you call that courage?"

"Our community fed well and my father served King Rhys truly, more than once, hiding and protecting the king's family from raiders from the north who would have taken his lands and condemned us all to slavery."

"Slavery? You live here a rich woman and begrudge your kinfolk a pittance which barely keeps skin and bone together!"

Angry as she was, the idea the bulk of Gerwyn's sister could ever be thought of as mere skin and bone almost made Manon chuckle, until Non took a step forward and Manon expected a slap. Instead, Non breathed deeply and almost smiled.

"You are far too young to know the best use of wealth," she said in her most condescending manner.

"At least I do not squander it as you do. At your great age you should have learned to be careful with such silver as you have acquired and keep it safe in your pouch or under your hearth."

"How dare you! I am the thriftiest person you could ever know!"

"So, it is just my coin you would scatter?"

"Your money! Your wealth!" Non's sneering features measured the depth of her jealousy.

"No," Manon said and shook her head, "not mine – my family's. Then I must also keep in mind what my brothers will need when they come home."

Non was incensed. "You stupid, senseless little bitch! No slaves return from Ireland! Even if they do get their free-dom, the chance of a ship bringing them back here is beyond their means. Face up to God's own truth. If your precious brothers still live and are free, they will have settled across the sea and sired families by now."

"All the more reason to have good farmland waiting for them when they come – and come they will, Non. Be sure of it," Manon snapped at her and then called loudly for her husband's son.

Meurig was ordered to drive his aunt home. He would have protested at Manon's treatment of her but he saw a new hardness in his father's wife and held his tongue as he assisted Non into the cart and drove her out of town.

Behind them, Gwen bustled around, restoring everything which had been moved under Non's orders back to their rightful places. Old Twm hummed at his bench, Kamal twitched the leather apron he wore and whistled as he cut and stitched calf's skin. Free of Non's tight binding, Dybion wriggled and kicked as he smiled. Heledd's cheeks grew pink again and she ate fresh meat from the pot while Rhodri skipped and ran about the workshop and the yard, teasing Nudd and being chased as they both squeaked and laughed.

Gerwyn was consumed by guilt when he learned the manner of his sister's going but even he was seduced by the peace she left in her wake, as well as by his wife turning to him once more when they were in bed.

Two days passed before Manon could once more be inwardly serene. Non's abuse had released memories which flooded and drowned her, although a few brought secret smiles. Running barefoot through the woods with the daughter of Rhys ap Tudor. Manon and Nest laughing and splashing each other in streams, returning home muddied and happy to their mothers in the shelter of the village deep in the valley of the Gwaun.

Harder for Manon to relive were the upsurging fears when King Rhys died after a fierce battle at Aberdare and his grown sons were killed or captured. Despair governed his people then and gruelling taxes must be paid to the English king and his men from France who built and held sway in their castles as raiders roamed free across the south of Wales, robbing, raping, burning.

The grown Manon sobbed again, remembering her

24

mother's body covering and saving her when all in her village were hacked to death or whipped and dragged to the waiting slave ships. When Manon's father returned to the devastation which had once been his home and his life, he found Manon barely alive. In those days there were many desperate people seeking safety. Like them, Manon's father brought her to the protection of Pembroke's palisades and the fearlessness of the castle's guardian, Gerald de Windsor.

Chapter Two

With the armed might of Dyfed centred in Pembroke, Gerald as its Constable had great influence. His men and his allies used a wall of iron to deter raiders, whether they were from the north of Wales, Danes from Ireland, or even Norsemen from the colder lands beyond the Celtic people of Scotland.

Trades of all kind were encouraged by him, wherever ships could sail. Craftsmen came into the town to work alongside honest journeymen, as well as sellers of beer and wine, money lenders, thieves, cheats, and all manner of women. Farmers and their families brought food to be sold at a market in the town and great ships, carried in by the tide at flood, anchored below the cliff on which stood the castle. Unloaded were oil and fruits from hot countries, furs and jewels from colder climes, spices, silks, tapestries and damascened swords. The tip of the far west of Wales was at the heart of commerce from around the world.

It was early morning, the first fingers of dawn stroking the sky above the castle.

"Geoffrey, are you ready?"

"Yes, Sir Gerald."

"The men you have with you can be trusted?"

"With my life, sir."

"Be sure it is." The Constable's expression was dark,

forbidding. "If this spy's rat hole is not sealed for good, we could all die by fire and sword in our beds. Get on your way lad, and may God go with you."

Slim and dark, Geoffrey swung into his saddle with an ease belying the weight of armour he carried on his helmet and jerkin. Like his men he wore no hauberk and was able to move quietly. Riding to the head of the troop he gave the order to mount, leading the men from the inner bailey towards the main gate. At a word from the shire reeve huge masses of wood opened and the riders urged their destriers into a steady canter along the road leading through Pembroke. It was deserted at this hour before couvre feu ended but the curious peered out at the armed men and wondered.

Once clear of the town the pace increased and was held to a steady gallop by Geoffrey until the track narrowed before descending towards the sea at Stackpole. The shire reeve raised a hand and every man walked his horse quietly along the grassy edge. When the roof of a farmhouse was in sight between the trees, a silent order was given, men dismounting and tethering horses before spreading out to encircle the farm and its outbuildings.

By this time Roger fitzHugh's gleaming stallion was breathing noisily, its rich coverings spattered with foam and sweat. In contrast the shire reeve's loose-legged mare drew breath easily as it tossed its head and watched its rider stride away.

A tired girl came from the house, swinging a milk pail. She saw the ring of men and there was a clattering and a screaming before the shire reeve, his sword drawn and ready, pushed his way into the homestead. From a barn a man ran wildly towards the safety of the woods, seeming to escape until a massive figure stepped from behind a tree and felled him with one blow from a massive fist.

With quiet efficiency the farmer, his woman, two workers and an unconscious man were loaded into a cart. Bread and cheese from the kitchen was shared out amongst the soldiers and the cavalcade began its slow trek back to Pembroke Castle. As the last rider was lost to sight, the servant girl wiped tears from her dirt-streaked face and went in search of the milk pail.

Someone was shouting. Manon dropped her knife and hurried to help Kamal, groaning as she went into the shop and saw the massive back and broad belted tunic of Drydwen, wife to Gwgan the pig farmer. Beside her a sour smelling boy held a limp piglet.

"Kamal is not deaf," Manon said quietly.

Drydwen turned, an ungainly movement. Her tunic might once have been blue but now it was colourless with age and badly stained. A grubby kerchief was pulled around her face and knotted, no headband to add a touch of grace and colour. She glared at Manon.

"What did you say?"

Manon almost equalled the woman in height and stood erect, trying not to smile. Gwgan was so used to pigs he had even chosen a wife with the same thick pink skin, tiny eyes and broad, upturned nose. There was even a suspicion of bristles on her chin.

"Kamal understands what you say and there is no need to shout. Is there something you wished to buy?"

The slim, dark-skinned man was anxious, tugging at the edge of the leather apron her wore. "Meurig go to castle. He take Sir Gerald cloak with hood for rain."

"And you have done well in Meurig's absence, I am sure," Manon said.

Drydwen was at the back of the shop, pawing at caskets covered with tooled and painted leather.

Manon smiled at her. "They are beautiful. Was it one of these you wanted?"

Her customer pointed to the largest of the caskets, then beckoned forward the boy with the pig.

28

"I would need several good sized pigs for that casket."
Manon forced herself to sound regretful.

"I must have one as big as that," Drydwen insisted. "You
sent such boxes to the castle here as well as to Carew, I am
told. The Lady Nest can choose as she pleases where she
will store her valuables – and so will I."

"Princess Nest also has many armed men to protect
her."

Heavy eyebrows met as Drydwen frowned. "What do you
mean by that?"

"News of such a large casket filled with gold and silver
would race through Pembroke like a fire and you know well
whispers go north to Ceredigion faster than a man can ride.
If Owain ap Cadwgan does not come for your treasures, be
sure his men will."

The ugly woman hesitated, nodding at the sense of the
words but she coveted the casket. Kamal had been enslaved
in far off Arabia where he had learned skill with leather
unseen in Wales. When his ship had tied up at the quay in
Pembroke he had escaped his masters, hiding near the
tannery and its familiar smells. It was there Gerwyn found
him, clothed him warmly, fed him well.

Kamal wanted to repay such kindness and showed the
tanner secrets he had learned, strange ways of finishing off
skins to make them soft, supple and immensely strong. The
young man was gifted with brushes, pigments, fine instruments. Before long his artistry was for sale in the leather
shop and Kamal's home was with Gerwyn and his family.

Drydwen caressed the surface of the casket on which she
had set her heart and Manon guessed it had a gentle beauty
totally lacking in Drydwen's home. As Kamal hovered,
concerned the sweat and dirt on the woman's fingers would
stain the perfect surface, Manon picked up the smallest
casket and held it near the piglet to frail to squeal, shaking
her head at the comparison. Kamal could not watch his
work so misused and fled to the workshop.

Behind him in the shop Drydwen was annoyed. "No!" The casket is not big enough. The animal is from good stock."

Manon stood her ground. "If the piglet is as valuable as you say it would have been sold off at market. Left over at the end of the day . . ."

Drydwen clenched her jaw, teeth noisy as they ground together. She scowled at Manon and her small eyes almost disappeared in the folds of her skin.

Manon smiled sweetly. "I will ask Kamal what is suitable."

She made sure Nudd was at the door to the roadway and guarding all the goods for sale before escaping to the peace of the workshop. Kamal was at the bench where light came in through an open shutter. A tool in his long fingers impressed lines in leather which drew the eye to the intricacies of the design.

"That woman, Kamal. A very small pig for a casket?"

He sighed and lifted his shoulders in resignation, then reached below the bench. Lifting something wrapped in a rough cloth, he unveiled it to reveal a casket with an arched lid. Two hands in length and narrow, the wooden frame was covered with leather tooled in a simple pattern, its paint-work bright, crude.

Manon was surprised. "This is not your work?"

Kamal grinned at her. "Rhodri. He learn well. This buy small pig and Gwen cook?"

Surprised by her son's craftsmanship, Manon was still smiling when she returned to the shop. Drydwen was delighted by the size of the casket and its startling colours but she was still determined to haggle.

"Please, Mam," the boy begged.

His head was smacked hard for him. He had broken the first rule of bartering.

"Add something," Drydwen insisted to Manon. "After all, you profit greatly from the castle trade. Pass some of it on to folks like us."

"Of course, Drydwen – when your husband does the same. He breeds good pigs. They have excellent flavour and are tender. What is it he says? 'The best taste deserves the best price'. I have heard him with those words many times."

Drydwen glared at the younger woman but her fingers reached for the gaudiness of the casket. "You drive a hard bargain, mistress. May you not live to regret it."

Returning from the castle, Meurig had pushed his way through the last of the scavengers and stood to one side of the shop door, making way for Drydwen to leave. She did so with the casket in one great hand and her son's ear in the other while the piglet nestled in Manon's arms.

Meurig approved the sale price. "When that is roasted we will eat well," he said and licked his lips.

"No!" Nudd grabbed the little animal and ran, his strange gait made more awkward by his protection of the small weakling.

"He has taken our pig!" Meurig shouted and would have chased after Nudd but Manon stopped him.

"You will eat well, I promise you." She took a coin from the pouch at her belt. "Cynfan has been roasting meat in his bakeoven. Get the best he can offer – your father will be hungry when he returns."

It was a serving maid who first spread the news in town of the spy's capture. The farmer, Gollwyn, and his wife had been questioned by the shire reeve and then the Constable. When they were released townsfolk surrounded them and demanded to know what had happened, why they had been dragged in by the soldiers. Exhausted by their ordeal and facing a long walk home, all they wanted was peace. They were allowed none until Gollwyn repeated the story he had given Sir Gerald. Gollwyn did not know the man suspected of being an escaping spy, guessing he had been a vagrant looking for a dry bed in a barn. The poor wretch had been so terrified by the soldiers' arrival he had tried to run deep into the woods.

Gollwyn's air of injured innocence convinced most of his listeners but he did not hear what was Sir Gerald's decision when he was alone with Geoffrey and the bishop's protégé.

"There is no way we can link him to Gollwyn. As for his wife and the labourers –"

"Should they not be tortured? Beaten at least, Sir Gerald?" Roger fitzHugh asked indignantly in the French used at court.

The Constable turned to the young man. "This is not Westminster," he answered in the same tongue. "Here, in Pembroke, we conduct our business in the language of its people. You will learn, if you please, and quickly. See to it, Geoffrey. This boy is no use to me if he speaks only in French."

The shire reeve nodded, then pointed to the labourers. "What do you want done with them?"

"Send them back to work – and their master. They are more use to us growing crops and attending the animals. As for the so-called spy, pour beer and wine into him until he releases the truth. We will have what we want from him more speedily than with a whip."

"Of course, sir. If Gollwyn is proved to be involved –"

"Then you know where he is to be found."

Three days passed after Geoffrey's order had been given and ran wild through the castle. Only native Welsh was to be used when Roger fitzHugh was present. From kitchen to mews, stables to barracks, the idea was carried through with enthusiasm. Courtly French was ignored and Roger suffered hunger, thirst, frowsty shirts, until he begged for help and was taught enough words to help him survive. From then on he must listen at all times and sometimes speak when he felt able. Occasionally he was greeted with a smile but all too often it was with raucous laughter.

The pampered child in him burned with an unquench-able fury but the shrewd man in Roger fitzHugh kept it hidden. To return to court and the bishop at this point would be failure and would invite ridicule amongst the highest in the land. Whatever the strictures placed upon him, Roger knew he must stay in Pembroke and become successful in the God-forsaken place.

He assuaged his misery with a promise. When he became shire reeve, those who despised him would endure the torture of the damned. As for the uncivilised ulcers mas-querading as men and women inhabiting the castle and the town, they would learn to bow the knee to his nobility and his will. About him he would gather men who were not afraid to deal harshly with cringing peasants.

Gwen was in a scolding mood. "Must you go? You know how rough it can be out there on a market day," she reminded her mistress.

"Gwen, you are an old worry-pot. Heledd needs to walk in the fresh air and it is little enough, going the length of the town. Think how you and I could run in the woods when we were three years old."

The servant girl was not to be assuaged. "That was long ago and wherever we lived there was always someone keeping watch for raiders."

"Aye," Manon said and sighed. "Even in the peace of the woods there was risk." She smiled at Gwen who was standing with her hands on her hips, concerned for her mistress.

Younger than Manon, Gwen's body was shorter, more solid in her worn tunic, its red colour dimmed with time and washing. Thick fair hair was covered and twisted out of the way by an old kerchief, leaving exposed kind grey eyes and plain features which came alive and comely when she was merry.

"You think us protected with the castle up the hill and soldiers trampling all over us?" Gwen shook her head. "I might be thought of as nothing but a woman like you, mistress? You have too much beauty and silver coin for men to leave you alone while your husband is out of sight. You here, her up in the castle, I ask you? What is the difference?"

Manon was shocked at the comparison. "Princess Nest? Gwen, are you mad? She has royal blood, come to her from her father, King Rhys – aye, and her mother too, who was daughter to King Rhiwallon."

"What of the money she had from her lover, the Frank who calls himself King of England? He may have dowered her with Carew but where is the husband he found for her? Going so often far from home to build himself a new castle in Emlyn. How wise is he if he leaves behind a wife all men envy."

Manon was bemused. "What has all this to do with me going to collect sewing Buddyg has ready for me?"

"Everything. You have a husband with strong arms to fight for you – when he is here."

"And when he is not?"

"Then the wolves and raiders we risked as children were as nothing to the men out there in Pembroke who lust to get into your skirts and your money bag. You mark my words!"

Manon laughed at the idea, hugging Gwen's shoulders and pushing her towards the shelves of food. "Fill a satchel for me to take to Buddyg and her children."

"Aye, willingly, as long as you remember today is a market day. There are those who bring only their fingers for trading and feet fast enough to carry them out of sight quickly."

"Then I will carry the satchel under my cloak."

Pembroke was market day noisy but there was underlying order. Geoffrey fitzWalter's men patrolled the crowds on horseback and on foot, carrying on the traditions installed by time and the Constable. Fair trading was expected and thieves knew what they risked if they tried out their skills in the castle's shadow.

Boys, some still barely weaned, with ambitions to take the hard-earned goods or wealth of others were dealt with swiftly. A public beating until they cried served as a warning as well as a punishment. As for their elders, if the merchants who had been robbed had no use for their labours, Sir Gerald did. Roadways and alleys were cleared, so were runnels and ditches, dung pits and hedges, each man watched and helped by a well-placed boot until he had paid for his crime.

The workshop was quiet, only Old Twm in his corner. He stitched with a steady rhythm in the dimness, his fingers feeling where the needle must go.

"Rhodri, where is he?" Manon asked.

Twm looked up and Manon saw him as not really old, just tired and worn.

"Meurig sent him out back to help Kamal sort the hides and stack 'em tidy-like."

Meurig. Gerwyn's son was still losing no opportunity to make life as unpleasant as possible for Manon and her children. Heledd came running, dressed like her mother in clean blue tunic and russet cloak, a kerchief about her hair and tied under her chin. A pretty child, she had her father's bold, dark eyes and her mother's soft mouth and skin as well as her small tilted nose, all blending into delightful mischief under hair like silk which had a reddish lustre to the curls.

With Heledd hanging on to her cloak, Manon walked towards the shop and noise from the busy township beyond. Meurig had just finished selling a leather bucket and as its new owner carried it away, Gerwyn's son secreted the coins earned in a fold of his short tunic. Only when Manon disturbed a pile of soft boots did he turn, refusing to meet her eyes. Heledd was absorbed in stroking the outside

35

of a small pair of boots, the warm wool curling white and clean over their tops.

Meurig pointed an accusing finger at the child. "She had new boots a sennight ago. Does she need another pair so soon?"

Strange how the sound of his complaint reminded her of Non, Manon thought. "No, Meurig, there will be no new boots for your sister, that would be a waste. These are for Buddyg's daughters."

"Who will pay?"

"They are payment, part of what I owe Buddyg for the new shirts she has stitched for your father and which I go now to collect. May your father always have such a good return for the copper and silver he does not have in his hand at the end of the day," she said sternly and watched the redness of guilt blossom in Meurig's cheeks until the boy turned away and fiddled with a stack of leather buckets.

On that clear, windy day mother and daughter began their walk along the roadway leading away from the castle. Heledd was as dainty as Manon, lifting the edge of her small tunic high above the filth. Manon thanked heaven for a dry day as they walked over dried mud mixed with cabbage stalks and onion skins. Any scraps of meat, however rotten, had been snatched up by beggars and hollow-cheeked children. Hidden in the rags which were their clothes, the garnered food would be in a pot that night, boiled into a semblance of broth. A wretched dog ran growling past them, all that was left of a sizeable number which had grown through the previous summer.

"Winter must be almost over," Manon told Heledd but did not explain how she knew. When humans were hungry many a stray dog ended its days in the cooking pot of a starving family.

Manon pulled Heledd to one side of the road as a sledge passed them. It was being pulled by a scrawny boy, his mother and two young sisters pushing from behind. On the sledge was a heap of goods from which protruded legs of a stool and the handle of a battered pot.

Shouts and a clattering of iron made the destitute family struggle to get their treasures to the side of the road. A troop of Franks cantered along the centre of the highway, the huge destriers and their riders leaving little room for others. Manon saw a nearside horse raise its tail and she swung Heledd into the doorway of a shop as she sheltered the child inside her own cloak.

"Good day to you, Mistress Manon. Have you come for a sweet roll for your little princess?"

Cynfan, the baker, lifted Heledd and pulled her close. She knew the man and he had never harmed her but the nearness of his bearded face with its coarse skin and bulbous eyes terrified the child. Heledd, her own eyes huge and pleading, squirmed and held out her arms to her mother. As Manon took her from Cynan the child clutched safety so tightly she pulled aside her mother's kerchief and revealed shining hair.

The baker's lips slackened, were licked, as his gaze lingered on Manon's oval face with its full mouth, large eyes under winged brows, and creamy skin framed by a fall of soft curls. His eyes followed the line of her throat to the swell of milk-full breasts pushing at the cloth of her tunic. Manon was used to men's lusts and always discouraged them as courteously as she could. Standing Heledd on the dusty floor the mother tightened her kerchief and gathered her cloak about her then bent to her daughter.

"Come, cariad," she whispered. "We will go to Buddyg and you will play with her girls." She knew Cynfan had no harm in him. He loved children above all but three wives had died childless and Manon understood how much he coveted her sons and her little daughter. Clucking like an old hen at Heledd, Cynfan had the boy who scurried after him to bring a basket of sweet rolls for Manon to carry in her satchel. She tried hard to dissuade him but the baker was insistent, urging Manon to accept and give pleasure to Buddy's children.

At last Manon escaped the heat of the bakeshop and drew in the fresh, cool air of the town as she held Heledd's hand and they continued their errand. It was not a long walk along the wide ridge of rock, high between two rivers and surmounted at its crest by the castle. The first narrowness was where permanent shops had been built, serving the occupants of the castle at all times. It was there had been built imposing homes for those who wished to be near enough to the castle gate, able to run with their valuables inside the fortified outer walls when danger threatened.

A dip in the road, a rise, and Manon was looking at the widest part of Pembroke town edged by small cottages and gwennies. On the beaten earth between stood the market stalls of farmers, their wives, itinerant traders. Heledd would have lingered at each stall, whether it was a proper trestle with a cover or a pile of baskets woven from reeds. Eggs so fresh the hen dung was still moist, butter, cheese, great cabbages and dried peas, onions of all sizes, fish fresh from the river, tempted townsfolk as did honey cakes and small loaves. The child was puzzled as every stallholder pleaded with her mother to buy and Manon constantly smiled pleasantly and shook her head.

"Why do you not buy, Mama?"

"Everything we need Gwen chooses at first light. The food then is at its freshest and no one makes Gwen pay too much."

"Why?"

Manon's smile had a touch of mischief. "Because Gwen wears her oldest clothes and shuffles her feet. If I come along with my beautiful daughter they will say, 'There goes a rich woman with her little princess. We will make her pay double'. And they do."

Gently tugged by her mother Heledd was pulled past a tray of embroidered ribbons, leather goods too badly made to have come from her father's workshop, a crafty, smelly man selling tiny stoppered pots as he persuaded men to give him coin for a way of satisfying wives such as they had not known. For the women it was drops to make a chosen man their slave day and night. Heledd was fascinated. She listened as the peddler traded the smallest pot for silver, whispering to the buyer to have care how it was used, the contents beyond price. "Your enemy will trouble you no longer, master," she heard him say.

Heledd would have stayed but Manon gently pulled her away. "Come, cariad. Meinir and Nerys are waiting for you."

Buddyg had lived on a farm nearby, working for Idris and marrying him when his aged wife died. Their daughters, Meinir and Nerys, had been the old man's delight until he had died a year ago, the farm inherited by his son, Griffin. The new owner's wife had been afraid of Buddyg's gentleness and serenity, insisting she and her children leave the only home they knew. With her stepson's help Buddyg had found a ramshackle cottage in Pembroke and transformed it into a warm sanctuary. Good with her needle, Buddyg earned what she could in the daylight hours and had become a good friend to Manon.

There was no need to knock on the wood of the door, they had been seen wandering around the market. Excited little girls greeted them, dragging Heledd through the house and into the long garden which went all the way down to the palisade around the town. It was a lovely spot, as Manon's garden could have been were it not covered by a workshop and sheds piled high with tanned leather. Here, vegetables grew in abundance for Buddyg, their greenness promising good stores for the winter. Near the wood of the wall a nanny goat grazed with its kid, her bag heavy with milk. Buddyg brought two stools and she sat with Manon in the sunshine while their daughters played and chattered like small birds in a nest.

Beyond the palisade the river was a narrow stream fed by others before widening into the waterway flowing past the new quay. It was peaceful in the garden, sunlit and sheltered from the wind. There was no sound of creaking oars, flapping sails, shouts of sailors. A cormorant dived, emerging with a flash of silver in its beak which disappeared down the long throat as they watched.

"Ceinwen!" they heard a man call.

Through a gap in the fence they could see Buddyg's neighbour. A tall man, the way he held his body hinted at pride, even arrogance, at odds with the shuffling steps and a wrecked face hungry for sight.

"Ceinwen!"

"I am coming, cariad."

A homely woman reached him and took his face in her hands, kissing him as she would a child who had been lost.

"Where were you?" He grasped her wrists tightly. "When I woke the house was empty."

"I was tending the peas. We should have a good crop to store for the winter."

Together, they walked back into their home as Manon and Buddyg watched.

"It always hurts to see King Rhys' son brought to that," Buddyg said.

"Aye. Robbing a man of his eyes and his manhood so he lives only to hate. Can an enemy rest easy because Hywel ap Rhys will never again lift a sword in anger – nor sire sons to take their revenge?"

"Franks have much for which they must seek penance on their knees."

"It is the way of war, Buddyg, and you know it. Even the priests say it is more Christian to blind and castrate than it is to kill. Why, my father told me our own people had the same kindly treatment for prisoners, long before the Franks came."

"It was the Franks captured and held Hywel. Have you forgotten it was Sir Gerald had him here, in the castle, as a prisoner, long before he married Princess Nest?"

"I was told he always treated Prince Hywel well and not as an enemy. A Frank Sir Gerald might be and as tough as any, but he had respect for a brave son of King Rhys."

"Aye, he had courage. Poor Hywel. A fine family he once had until the great battle at Aberdare. His brother, Cynan, lost in Neath's great bog and the other, Goronwy, killed by prison fever in England. Thank God Hywel came to Pembroke. Ceinwen cares well for him. She loves him dearly and his sister, the princess, makes sure he wants for nothing."

"Except children – and the eyes to see them."

"True, Manon," Buddyg sighed, "and Hywel is good with children. Princess Nest's young ones spend time with him when they are living here, in Pembroke, and not at Carew. They listen to Hywel's tales of battles – and he is a great one for the singing," she added ruefully, remembering nights she and her daughters could not sleep.

"Hywel will miss Nest and her family when the new castle in Emlyn is ready for them."

"Aye, that he will. Constable of the shire would be important enough for most men but Sir Gerald has always looked for more than he had. A good woman he had in Joan, Ninian the silversmith's daughter, but no, he must take to wife a princess."

"The Constable is a proud man, hungering for land of his own. Remember, Nest's estates will go to her children, not to Gerald's firstborn."

"You mean Joan's son, the other William? The one the Franks call the bastard?"

"Aye. Mistress Joan was greatly in favour and she had given him fine children – until Sir Gerald must do the English king a kindness and marry the most beautiful woman in the whole of the kingdom. Then, Nest was always different," Manon said softly.

"You knew her well when you were children."

Manon nodded. "When she and her mother sheltered in our village. Nest was already as tall as some men – and

41

more handsome than any of them. It made no difference Nest was of the blood of Hywel Dda and Queen Gwladus royal in her own right, they lived as we did, shared what we had. Queen Gwladus was not good at the cooking," Manon remembered, "but she was magical with the needle. Nest was more daring than the boys in our village and there was no way she would sit quietly and sew as her mother wanted."

"You miss those days?"

"We were happy and safe as children, then King Rhys sent for his family when the danger to them had passed. Nest was gone and must be a princess again."

"It is something she does well," Buddyg said and nodded to herself, "but we will all be sorry to lose their custom when Sir Gerald takes his family north, to Cenarth Bychan in Emlyn."

"We will all lose but trade has been good," Manon admitted. "Boxes for travelling, new saddles, jerkins, hooded cloaks for the rain – the list is endless. Gerwyn is busier than he has ever been at the tannery, getting hides ready for the workshop. The men burn many candles to keep up with the cutting and stitching. It is as well Old Twm can sew with his eyes shut – and him half asleep," she added with a laugh.

"Here too," Buddyg admitted. "For me it is sheets to be hemmed, cases to cover goose feather pillows as well as night shifts for Sir Gerald and the children."

"Mistress Mabli still decides who sews what the princess wears?"

"The needlewoman in Carew does it all." Buddyg's gentle features clouded. "It is said she has long headaches in spite of all the potions Mistress Mabli can concoct."

"Her eyes?"

Buddyg nodded. When you earn your food by the needle, the thought of losing to use of your eyes is a constant fear."

The friends chatted on in the sunshine, and on occasion

42

there was laughter until three little girls ran towards them, soil clinging to face, hands, tunics.

"These little monsters need water to make them clean again," Buddyg said as she herded them towards a basin and a pitcher. Manon began to rise. "Sit there. You need all your rest before young Dybion attaches himself to you and drains you dry."

It was a relief to sink back on her stool and dream in the soft air moved by a gentle breeze. Small birds chirruped in a nearby bush and Manon wished she could stay longer in the quiet garden. She had laughed at Gwen's idea of droves of men besieging her but a shiver crawled over her skin in the warmth of the sun. As a woman she was only safe and happy because Gerwyn stood between her family's silver and the greedy ones.

The castle by the river at Carew was a place of peace, Odo de Barri decided as he rode towards its gatehouse, Nest casting over the fortress and its inhabitants her particular charm. He remembered her first day in the place, seeing for herself every corner, the servants she met enchanted by the flood of childhood Welsh from a woman renowned for her beauty throughout the kingdom and beyond. The child who had been a hostage and imprisoned in the stiffness of a foreign court had endured exile and come home.

Gerald came to greet his friend. "You are welcome, Odo."

"I am for Cardiff after the Sabbath and the bishop will there, needing news of his protégé's progress," the visitor said as they walked towards the hall.

Gerald's expression hardened. "The boy has been too long at court and is become accustomed to devious ways."

"You are a hard taskmaster, my friend. Have you forgotten so soon such a view of life is the only way to survive amongst those who surround the king?"

Laughter was quiet, bitter. "As ever, Odo, you are right – but it does not help him to play the courtier in this shire.

We need its people with us if we are to drive away from our lands the likes of Owain and his kin."

"Owain! Always Owain! His father tried often enough to burn you out of Pembroke. Let us pray the king's bounty in sending Flemings to live and work in Rhos will halt the young devil."

"Only if they are prepared to fight to the death," Gerald said quietly.

"Well, they have all been seasoned by hardship." Odo de Barri looked at the calm order of the bailey, then lifted his head to the woodlands sweeping down to the width of the river. "What if a great tide came up one evening and buried all this under a mountain of water? Given rich land in its place, would you fight?"

"To the death," Gerald admitted.

"Aye, and so will the Flemings. Now, what news of the spies who pester us from Ireland?"

"There is no doubt the farmer, Gollwyn, is part of the route in and out of Pembroke. He has been earning silver from the trade in men." Gerald smiled, his eyes cold. "He will earn more and save his neck."

"As an informer?"

"Aye, and a good one if he wishes to live."

Odo shook his head. "Gerald, you complain of young Roger but you have not forgotten how to be devious."

"No, but Roger fitzHugh does it for himself alone. The boy is a fool who chooses his companions unwisely, I have been told, and his struggles to learn the local tongue bring him only contempt."

"Was it not so with you?"

"No," Gerald said softly. "I only listened to those I knew I could trust."

Gulls swooped on any scraps left behind as the stalls outside Buddyg's home were emptied and packed away. The sun was still high but most of the traders were on their way home, heading out of town in carts, on horseback, on foot, to farms large and small. Most lived in gwennies, quickly built huts of wood and thatch sheltering labourers and their kin as they slept. Manon had no doubt there were men who would snore the night away on the filth of the floor of a beershop before returning to their families, just as there were families who would spend their night in the haven of a copse, no better place to call their home.

Heledd was tired as she walked with her mother. A boy playing a whistle diverted the child and she pulled Manon towards him. His father was packing up bundles of carvings as he listened to the lilting sound of his son's music. It reminded Manon of evenings in the village in the Gwaun valley, a travelling bard enthralling everyone with his songs and tales of heroism and beauty. She reached into her pouch and found a coin for the boy, a grateful smile enchanting in the grime of his face.

Manon carried her daughter the short distance to their home. The child was heavy and Manon could feel milk seeping from her breasts into the linen binding under her tunic. It would be good to be home, she thought, Dybion suckling her into comfort as he fed.

Boys were running from the quay. They were being chased by angry sailors and Manon guessed food from across the seas had been 'freed' from sacks destined for the castle or for traders supplying the wealthy. As the last boy passed Manon a big golden ball fell into the dirt of the road. The young thief hesitated, wanting to pick up his treasure but the sailors were near, their shouts making heads turn. The urchin ran on and the unfamiliar object disappeared in the sleeve of a wall-eyed stranger. Manon wondered if the strange ball was food, or some plaything for the rich but she was tired and all her thoughts turned to the peace of her kitchen, her steps quickening as she neared the leather shop.

Nudd was sweeping into the roadway dust and dirt tramped into the shop during the day. He lifted his head and saw Manon coming home, dropping his besom and

45

running to lift the sleepy Heledd, then carrying her with the greatest care.

"Has it been a busy day here?" Manon asked.

Nudd, always sparing with words, nodded rapidly. Manon could see there was still a customer inside the open stalls, talking earnestly to Meurig. As Nudd carried Heledd past them the stranger was startled, turning his face away from Manon. She was surprised and saw there was no sign of a sale being made, no articles lined up on the trestle for the man to inspect. The stranger kept his arms wrapped in a short cloak of a weave unfamiliar to Manon. She was intrigued, aware there was no rank smell about him and he seemed clean enough to her, what she could see of him. Shorter than Meurig, the man had little hair on the crown of his head but wild dark curls fell about his shoulders. He was no Frank or Fleming and the few words of Welsh she had caught as she came in had only a faint whisper of the north in them. The man sensed her scrutiny and darted out into the road, still keeping his face turned away from Manon.

"Who was that?" she asked Meurig.

The boy busied himself with buckets and boots to be stacked away for the night. "No one I know. He was asking the price of a jerkin."

"Was he minded to buy?"

Meurig shrugged away the question and Manon heard Dybion begin to cry, hunger in the sound.

"If the stranger is interested in our goods he will return," she said but found herself wondering at the encounter as the baby fed and was content.

Chapter Three

Spring began to warm into summer and Manon was happy. Her children thrived, there was no Non to embitter and Gerwyn wore his new shirts on Sundays for mass in the priory church. After service the prior talked to those who attended, pleased to see so many worthy men with sound businesses to call on for alms. He did not approve of the old Welsh church, Christian though it might be, the idea of married vicars with families filling him with indignation. He was firm in his opinion the Bishop of St David's should not be of Welsh stock, wanting him replaced by a well-trained Frank who could set all believers in the righteous way.

The prior did take some consolation from the arrival of Roger fitzHugh. The newcomer was clearly unsuited to the monastic life if the stories of screaming servant girls were true but there might come a time when the connection to the powerful Bishop of London proved useful. Yes, the prior decided, Roger could be trained to act as he was bid by an officer of the rightful church.

It concerned father prior that the shire reeve, Geoffrey fitzWalter, had been too zealous in following the example of Pembroke's Constable. Both of them had been eager to learn the native tongue and listen to complaints from men and women who were little more than conquered slaves. Young

Roger might be struggling to understand what was being spoken around him but he did have the true spirit of the men who had come from northern France with the Conqueror. Disdain was all the cleric had for the Britons in this shire of Wales.

Father prior had great skill in bending young men to his will. With Sir Gerald resident in the north of the shire and Geoffrey fitzWalter far away amongst the mighty Clares, Roger fitzHugh as the new shire reeve would hold all secular power in Pembroke. He was a vain boy and easily turned by an astute mind. The prior was content.

After her prayers Manon sensed Gerwyn was awake and lying so still she was afraid.

"What is amiss, cariad?" she asked. Gerwyn's breathing was heavy and her fear clutched at her. She had heard of men who worked with raw hides sickening and dying almost overnight. "Are you ill?"

He tossed and turned as he made up his mind to speak and Manon must be patient. At last he confided his worries to her. They were all working so hard in the tannery mistakes could be made when the men were tired.

"Even Myrddin loses count," he said.

"Myrddin? You surprise me. Is he too old for the work?"

"No! I trust Myrddin – indeed I would trust him with my life. If he says there is a cause for unease then it is so."

In the safety of her home Manon shivered. Gerwyn felt the tremors and pulled her close, cradling his wife as he would Heledd.

"At the end of the week," she said slowly, "you have the skins you expect?"

"Not so many."

"How many do you think are missing?"

"At least one or two in any week."

"Have you any idea where they could be going?"

"No," he said and sighed. "I have listened in the town and there is no word of any hides for sale except from me. I

48

know the trade and there are no signs of extra leather reaching any journeymen skilled enough to fashion it."

"Surely any good workman could cut and stitch even rawhide to shape shoes and buckets for his family?"

"Indeed they could," Gerwyn agreed, "but who besides Kamal can work leather fine enough for a lady's glove? Those are among the skins we miss."

It was Manon's turn to lie in the dark and chase thoughts in her head. "So, someone knows which hides to steal."

"Only the best," said Gerwyn bitterly. "There are no secrets in a town like Pembroke. We know, you and I, every piece going to those who can afford the quality of good craftsmanship. Not even a whisper."

"Then the skins must be going far away from Pembroke," Manon reasoned. "Tenby? Carmarthen?"

"I have listened to journeymen. Nothing."

It was quiet in the bedspace, rain spattering the roof with a regular thrumming. "If it is impossible to catch the culprits when they sell, let us catch them stealing at the tannery," Manon said slowly.

"How?"

"I was thinking. Myrddin is getting very stiff at the walking."

"He is indeed, poor soul. Nudd takes him herbs to stew and drink the liquor from them. It helps a little."

"Why not tell everyone Myrddin will no longer work with the hides in the pits and sluices – the dampness being bad for him. Because you are such a kind-hearted master you have decided he must stay wrapped up warm in sheepskins and keep account of every hide, now you are so busy."

"He does count – by marking a stick for week's work and he still says the sticks in the shed are wrong. If Myrddin is to be believed, someone must be replacing his tally sticks with new ones – and fewer notches."

"It is simple, cariad," Manon said. "Let Myrddin make his mark for each skin on his sticks and make a copy of each

49

one which he hides in his sheepskins. At the end of each week you can match up Myrddin's sticks with the ones in the shed. Then you will know how many have been taken by the fairies."

"Fairies!" Gerwyn snorted with disgust. "Damned thieves, more like, and I will have the skin off them before they go in my dung pit." He allowed his temper to simmer for a while, listening to the rain until it stopped. "But you are right, cariad, in what you suggest. Tomorrow, I will talk to him."

When Gerwyn moved from her and slept, Manon's thoughts gave her no ease. Someone smiled each day at the tanner and his wife, yet stole from them in such a crafty way, even as they spirited the skins far away from Pembroke.

Who was he?

It was the boy's laughter which reached Manon in the kitchen. Gerwyn had left early for the tannery, leaving Meurig in charge of the shop.

"What trouble is he causing now," she muttered as she hurried towards the sound.

Meurig was almost crying as he roared his amusement, while the redness of Roger fitzHugh's fury made him almost glow.

"Meurig!" Manon's voice was quiet but it was stern and the boy sobered.

"He says he wants a fat lady."

Manon turned to the angry Frank. "Monsieur – " she began, struggling to find more French words.

It was enough to release a flood of words from Roger and Manon could only hold up her hands in protest. She recognised one word she had heard before.

"Pluie?" was hard for her to say.

A nodding from the customer had her hurrying to the workshop, returning quickly with a half-stitched leather cape and hood, the kind Kamal treated with his oils to keep

50

the wearer dry in foul weather. There was another torrent of words which Manon stemmed with a gesture. She held up the garment, using its name carefully and waiting for Roger fitzHugh to repeat it. When he had the words exactly she smiled and called Kamal to come with his measure. 'Three days' took a little time to explain but the Frank was satisfied as he left the shop and walked back to the castle.

The exercise did little to lessen Roger's foul mood. It helped that the garment he needed would be delivered and he relished the idea of the servant girl who had taught him the wrong word getting the beating she deserved. Never, he decided, would he forget the embarrassment he had endured at the whim of the peasants in the leather shop. One day, he promised himself, there would be a chance for retribution.

"You drink alone?"

The stranger was courteous in the darkness of the beer-shop but Meurig lived in a town and was wary. He had seen the man before, interested in the goods stacked on the trestles in the shop. He was small, not threatening, his tunic and cloak of finely woven wool and clean. The belt and boots he wore were almost new and of good leather but not of Old Twm's stitching. Meurig shrugged his shoulders and the traveller sat facing him, drinking deeply from his pot.

"That was good! Your roads are tiring," he told the boy who could see little of the man's expression, hidden as it was behind the whitened curls of his beard. With a deft movement the cloak was shed and dark curls streaked with grey tossed away from his shoulders. "You are no farmer's boy," he said and smiled disarmingly, then waited for Meurig to speak.

It took little encouragement, the boy angry to be dismissed always in his home as a child. With understanding nods and Meurig's pot kept filled, he talked of his frustrations as well as his pride in the shop he thought of as his, the quality of the goods they sold.

"Your father is often away from home and leaves you in charge?"

Meurig told his new friend of the tannery, hides soaking in the dung pit, washing and scraping of skins, Nudd and the barks for tanning, Kamal and the oils to make sliced leather strong and supple.

"This Kamal is not one of us?"

The boy was contemptuous of the quiet, dark-skinned outlander but man enough to admire his skills. Eyes shining with beer and pride, Meurig's gestures became increasingly extravagant as he described caskets only the cracach could afford to buy.

"Many for the castle, no doubt?"

"Here – and for the new one," Meurig boasted to his new friend. "The biggest are to carry the Constable's treasures when he sails north to live in Emlyn."

"Cenarth Bychan, I am told he has land?"

"Aye, The castle must be big, all that is being ordered from us, from weavers, the silversmith." Meurig knew the gossip of the town and talked of carvings, furs from ships, perfect sheepskins as well as horses being gathered in from farms, cooking pots and all kinds of herbs being dried through the summer.

Soon, the boy's eyes were heavy with sleep and Elystan, as he had learned to call his new acquaintance, helped him outside into the fresher air of Pembroke. They walked this way and that until Meurig's legs were steady and he could go home to his supper and his bed.

It might have been Gerwyn's questioning, or the sight of Myrddin noticing every move at the tannery as a hawk watches unblinkingly for a vole. Whatever the reason, the cunning mind behind the thefts decided to wait. Neither Gerwyn nor Myrddin relaxed their vigilance, pleased none of the hides tanned in the ponds beyond the monks' town had disappeared.

Gerwyn was a happier man, wrestling with Rhodri, raising Heledd in his bear-like hug, tossing a hiccupping Dybion high in the air. Manon smiled each night as she prepared for bed and was not surprised when the flow of her milk lessened. Dybion was growing fast and already too big for the cradle she now knew must be used by the next baby.

Only Meurig gave cause for concern. He was surly when his father was at the tannery and as often as he could he left the selling in the shop to Kamal and Rhodri. When Manon confided her unease to Gerwyn he could see no wrong.

"The boy is cheerful enough, cariad."

"When you are here, he is."

"It will be a lass taking his wits – you mark my words."

"I wish it were so."

"What do you mean?" Gerwyn turned to her a face with its strong brows drawn together below deeply furrowed brow. "You suggest –?"

"No, he likes girls," Manon hastened to assure him. "Very much."

"So? He is almost a man."

She shook her head. "It is the company he keeps –"

Gerwyn grabbed her and danced her around the kitchen until she was breathless. "Cariad, soon he must come to the tannery and learn all its secrets. Let him have fun while he is still so young."

Later, Manon's thoughts returned to haunt her. She had been warned Meurig had been seen deep in conversation with strangers in quiet corners of the town or where men gathered to drink.

It was Gwen who had heard the rumours. "They have the tongue of the north," she told Manon.

"Gogledds from Powys? Gwynedd?"

Shrugged shoulders had been Gwen's reply. "Ceredigion, beyond the Teifi, is far enough away when men plot and scheme."

"What is there for Meurig to talk about? And why are men from Ceredigion risking their necks in Pembroke?"

"Necks? More like their eyes and balls if the Franks seize them!" Gwen had said with a throaty chuckle.

Manon's worries were not eased. "If there is to be trouble, Cadwgan must be the plotter, his son is too hot-headed. I wonder if ever in his lifetime Owain waited to make a plan?"

"In the market, early in the day, there is talk of Cadwgan," Gwen had admitted. "They say he would host an eisteddfod – all the best bards and harpists in Wales invited to his manor at the mouth of the Teifi."

"When?"

"At Christmastide, so it is said. Cadwgan wants such a gathering to show the Franks who really controls the hearts of the people."

Manon's mouth had had a bitter twist. "And while Cadwgan listens to the bards, will Owain do what he always does to the people his father would rule? Take all the souls and bodies he can and sell them to the Irish?"

A voice was raised in anger in the shop, loud enough for Manon in the kitchen to hear what was being said.

"Not again!" She despaired of Meurig as she cleaned flour from her hands, straightened her kerchief and fixed a pleasant expression on her face as she went past the workshop.

"Driving good men from their homes and taking their land – you should be ashamed!" Meurig shouted at the only customer.

A very tall man was being patient with Meurig and Manon recognised him. She did not know his name but Gerwyn had told her he was the Fleming in charge of Sir Gerald's horses.

"Meurig! You are needed in the yard." Manon tried to hide her anger but she could not mask the sudden blaze in her eyes. "Hides have been slipping – there could be damage."

The boy was annoyed but he knew not to argue with Manon in this mood. As he turned and scuffed his way slowly to the slipping hides, Manon began apologising to the Fleming.

"There is no need, mistress." His Welsh was simple, strangely accented and not fluent. "Since my fellow-country-men have been moving to Rhos, I have become used to such words."

"We have heard much talk of Rhos."

"Of Flemings who have gone there with grants from King Henry and made good Welshmen landless?"

"Are the stories true?"

Ugo smiled and looked younger, the bones of his face and his deep-set eyes no longer heavy, serious. "There is truth in part. Many Flemings have gone there at the invitation of King Henry."

"Why would he do so?"

The man turned away as he fingered the leather of his jerkin. "Many of my people lost all they had when the sea rose and covered our country," he said quietly.

Manon realised from his controlled anguish the Fleming still suffered. "Sailors told us of the great flooding and taking to England all the survivors they could carry."

He nodded, not looking at her. "Too many Flemings lost their lives. Those who survived and sought sanctuary from King Henry were fortunate."

"One of the brothers at the priory is Flemish and has taught many in Pembroke to weave in special ways," Manon said.

There was a rueful smile for her. "It was not so elsewhere. In one ear the king heard murmurs of rebellion from English weavers losing trade to Flemings and in the other ear news from this part of Wales of land being wiped clean of all workers by Owain, son of Cadwgan."

It was Manon's turn for sadness. "Too many of our men and women – aye, children too – have put Irish silver in the moneybags of that devil!"

He bent to her, concern in his eyes and his demeanour. "You have lost kin?" he asked gently.

Manon straightened her shoulders, facing yet again a reminder of her loss." My mother and sister were killed and brothers taken, sir."

The big man stifled a sigh. "Then you understand why no Welshmen in his right mind lived where Owain found such rich pickings and why their fields and homes stood unattended, waiting for men and women who would farm and fight. Be sure Flemings will keep the land prosperous as well as be a difficult enemy for the devils north of the Teifi," he assured her.

The shop seemed empty after he had left it. Manon was thoughtful as she studied the silver and copper in the money box, deciding it was safer in her keeping.

"Meurig!"

He came at last, dragging his feet and avoiding her gaze.

"It is not our business to judge the people paying for our goods."

"Why not?" the sulky boy snapped at her. "It is men like that Fleming who take from us what is ours by right."

"Ours, Meurig?"

"Yes – our land and our tongue. Why must we be slaves to the Franks and try to speak their damned language?"

"The Fleming spoke to you in Welsh and can you of all people talk of slavery? You are free to come and go each day as you please. The couvre feu keeps you at home at night but it also saves you from being beaten senseless and robbed of everything on your body. Your belly is filled with the best meat and you have money to spend, money earned from such as the Fleming you despise."

Meurig made no secret of his disgust. "How could you take his silver from him?"

"The same way as you take it from me," Manon said quietly. "Willingly."

Red flooded up Meurig's neck and suffused his face, boyhood spots marbling the colour. "I am going to my aunt," he flung at her. "She is wise and does not think like you."

"So be it. Were you the slave you think you are, you would not be free to go and you would have no kin to comfort you. It is what my brothers must endure."

In the distance children played at the river's edge, a tall beauty lifting her skirts to run barefoot with them in the water. Seated on the bank a sturdy figure kept the sun from a baby as it slept in the sweet air.

"A precious spot, Gerald," Sir Odo said, nodding towards the happy little group.

"It is. Nest always insists on being here when she can. 'Easier for Mabli to keep harmful humours at bay' she tells me."

"And right she is to do so. We have met many mediciners in our time, you and I, but few could match that woman's skill."

Gerald threw back his head and laughed. "I heard it was near to getting Mabli burned as a witch when she was at court. Only the king's intervention saved her."

"The king," Odo said slowly. "His agents will be in Cardiff when I sail there next week. What news can I carry to them of the spies?"

"There is little trade through Stackpole. For some reason our Irish friends are keeping busy their own side of the water."

"And yet?"

"There is talk of strangers in Pembroke. Welsh words come naturally to them and they have plenty coin in their pouches to loosen men's tongues in the taverns but they are unremarkable in other ways. Little is spoken by them, instead they watch, listen, then disappear back from whence they came."

"The north?"

Gerald nodded. "Without doubt they are from Cadwgan."

"You are certain it is him and not the son, Owain?"

"That whelp of Satan seldom bothers with spies. He raids on rumours – word of a township after a good harvest is all he needs to have empty ships waiting for grain and slaves."

Odo was little older than his companion, yet seemed to age as his eyes narrowed in a frown. "Cadwgan holds Ceredigion with royal consent and he is grown wily. He resents the king's strength at Cilgerran and now you go nearby to garrison a fortress of your own."

Gerald's strong chin jutted. "We show our power and he will show his, you mean?"

"This gathering?"

"An eisteddfod. The old kings of the Britons revelled in them, bards of all kinds meeting for a feast of music and words as they competed for crowns of their own."

"And you believe this is his answer to you?"

The Constable smiled. "Cadwgan does not like our garrisons so near Ceredigion, you say? Perhaps he chooses to do battle for the hearts of men with his bards."

The two of them watched as the tall woman lifted her little daughter from the river, swinging her round and spattering water on the brothers.

"Gilbert will be in Cardiff. What can I tell him of young Geoffrey fitzWalter?" Odo asked.

"Let him leave Geoffrey with me until it cools in the autumn. By then we should have young Roger trained to our ways."

"Roger – does he advance? His patron, the bishop, is certain to ask."

"You can tell his grace the brat begins to speak a kind of Welsh – now we have dissuaded him from choosing servant girls as his tutors. The prior sends one of the brothers to the castle to help Roger. By St Michael's mass he should understand what is being said of him in Welsh – and be able to answer in kind." Gerald's smile was wry.

"And as your shire reeve when Geoffrey has gone and you are living in Cenarth Bychan?"

The smile vanished and Gerald's expression hardened. "He will be ready by then – if I have my way."

Sited by the tidal river and so near the jagged and beautiful coast, winds were part of everyday life in Pembroke. Through the winter they scoured the mire from roads and alleys. In spring and autumn gales were less frequent but they could still rise and whip skirts, caps, tempers, into dancing frenzies. In summer there were days when everyone gasped in the heat, not even the slightest breeze to move air almost too warm for comfort. Without any wind to clear and clean the air of odd humours and with flies thick in every corner, Pembroke that summer was flooded with ailments which swept through the town.

Manon watched her children, Nudd aiding her with fresh garlic which could be stewed into liquids helping young bodies recover and be well again. As did many mothers, Manon was relieved when cool weather succeeded hot. Rain washed the roadways clean and flies disappeared, taking with them their constant buzzing and annoyance.

Beyond the town, trees bent by the harshness of winds had begun to show autumn's colours. Days were shorter, the signal to cover fires in the town coming fast on the heels of earlier sunsets. In the tannery Gerwyn and his men worked hard all the hours of daylight. Cattle, calves, goats, were being killed and salted for winter meat and their hides turned into leathers to grace the bodies of the cracach as well as jerkins thick enough to protect fighting men and farmers.

With the sighing of the year after summer's end, Sir Gerald sailed his family from the airy beauty of their home in Carew. They came along the River Cleddau to the new quay below the castle and Princess Nest and her family were once more in their Pembroke home.

"You make progress, my son?"

Father prior was a tall, austere man, years of privation and denial scoring deep lines in his cheeks yet his question was kindly to the young man still troubled by the pimples of youth. It pleased the cleric to see Roger fitzHugh no longer resembled the fabled bird of paradise. The colour of his tunic was muted and there was little silver embroidered at neck and sleeves. Even so, the cost of his clothes would have made an acceptable donation to the funds of the priory.

Roger had bent his knee to the prior, remembering the strictures from his kinsman, the bishop. Isolated in the furthest corner of the kingdom he might be, but the prior was held in high esteem.

"Brother Paulinus has been diligent in his teaching, Father," the haughty young voice told him. "Daily, he has me speaking as do the lesser men around me."

"I am pleased, my son." The unconscious arrogance in the young man's manner would not help his days in the shire of Pembroke, the churchman decided, but it could be a handle by which the youth might be turned to benefit the priory. His fingers described a benediction. "Go with God, Roger. Sir Gerald has done well in these parts for the king and for the church. May you follow him in all his ways."

With long, slow strides, the prior swept away towards his chapel, the young Frank barely nodding to the lowly monk at the gate who released him from the priory's bounds. Roger was sure, thanks to Brother Paulinus, should the day come when he needed formal Welsh he would be eloquent enough for these peasants. As for a man's needs, Brother Paulinus had spent so long on his knees he was useless.

The youth's step was lighter as he thought of the serving girl come newly from Carew who could teach him the words of the bed and of the body. By the time he reached the coracle waiting at the foot of the steep slope from the priory, Roger had planned what speech he must learn from the girl, becoming quite cheerful and licking his lips as he anticipated just what she would learn from him.

*   *   *

"Mam!"

Rhodri's cry made Manon look up from her cheese-making. Coming towards her was a tall, beautiful young woman gowned in a tunic of sky blue linen almost as fine as silk. Her cloak was of such tightly-woven wool it was uncreased, the hood of it lying on her shoulders and edged with the redness of squirrel fur. Embroidered blue was the colour of her headband, the kerchief swathing her hair and throat a creamy silk dulled only by the glow of her skin.

"Manon, you look well! You must be happy," the vision declared.

The tanner's wife began a deep curtsy but was stopped, lifted, kissed on both cheeks.

"As I always tell you, never bend the knee to me, my dearest friend. We have been in trouble too often for there to be such formality between us." The woman's laughter was rich, mischievous.

Manon searched the lovely face. The wilful child was still there, the blue of her eyes ringed with darkness and set wide apart under the winged brows. Skin envied by count-less women had a cobweb tracery of lines and the once-full lips were shaped in a sterner line, passions flooding Nest contained and held in check so often. She chuckled and was a child again.

"Well, do I bear your scrutiny?"

"As ever." Manon caught the hands reaching towards her. "You are well and for that I thank God."

"Do not forget Mabli, with her medicines and her scold-ing. With their aid she keep's me in God's good health and I thank her for it. That reminds me. She asked for the boy who knows the plants she needs –"

"Nudd."

"Of course, Nudd. He has more herbs growing here for her? She is most respectful of his knowledge and would have him come to the castle as soon as possible."

Manon hesitated. "The armed men at the gate frighten him."

61

"Then I will make sure he is properly welcomed at all times. Mabli must not be disappointed."

"Few risk that," Manon said, remembering Mistress Mabli was the only child of King Rhys' mediciner and as such, twelfth in importance at court. He had taught his daughter well but as a girl Mabli had not been allowed to take her rightful place among the courtiers. Only when her husband had been killed saving King Rhys did she become part of the royal household, medicining the king's family and having charge of Nest when the princess endured exile in England.

"Now," Nest declared, "I must see your children, Manon."

Rhodri was stiff with shyness and Heledd had to be coaxed from behind her mother's skirts, while Dybion gazed up at the woman holding him and pulled at the softness of her kerchief.

"They have grown so sturdy. You have great cause for pride," Nest said quietly. "Gerwyn has sired on you the fine children I always thought would be yours. When is the new baby due?"

Manon was startled, thinking her tunic hid her condition. "How did you know?"

Nest laughed and tapped the side of her nose. "Mabli. She taught me all the signs. Day after day in those foul-smelling hovels they call castles in England it was a game we played, deciding which of the ladies around us was carrying – and who might be the father! Praise be to God you are happier and healthier than any of them."

"As you were fortunate to be back home in Wales when your husband's children lay beneath your heart."

Nest bent her head to the baby on her lap, hiding her face from Manon with the fall of her kerchief. "It was always my wish to bear little ones in good Welsh air."

"They are well?"

"Thanks be to God, they are free of the sickness as they grow in to fine fitzGeralds to please their father." There was

62

a glint of tears as Nest lifted her head. "Oh, Manon, we never dreamed what our lives would be when we were together in the haven that was your home. So much has happened to both of us, yet we draw our real strength from our children."

"The king's son?" Manon asked, almost fearful of her daring.

"My baby – Henry? Gilbert de Clare ensures I have messages from his foster mother." The beauty was wistful as her thoughts were with her firstborn. It had torn her apart to leave him behind at the king's insistence when Nest returned to the safety of Wales. Like all good Frankish boys he must learn from the cradle the manly arts in a home which was not his mother's. "The past is gone, the children are our present – and our future." Nest sighed. "I often wish my little brood knew the freedom and happiness that was yours and mine when we were together. Waking to the smell of cooking fires, running – always running. It is how I remember us, Manon. Did we ever walk anywhere?"

"Your mother, the queen, tried to make you," Manon said, relieved Nest was making such an effort to be happy.

"And I tried her sorely, even to the last day I saw her." Memories overwhelmed the princess. "It was so long ago."

The sadness in her friend's voice took Manon to her knees beside Nest, cradling the tall, bowed figure as she would a weeping Heledd. "Is Queen Gwladus well?" she asked at last.

Nest nodded and Manon felt the shoulders in her grasp stiffen as a strong will brought the proud head erect, lips firm in a smile which did not quite reach her eyes.

"In the last message I had, my mother made no complaint but I have heard she finds difficulty in walking and must needs use a staff. I pray she has someone like Mabli near her, with drops to ease the pain and help her sleep."

"Your brother?"

"Gruffydd? He is eighteen years old – can you believe it? I am told he has grown tall and strong, like our father. My mother has ensured he speaks the Welsh and learns all he can of his bloodline from Hywel Dda but he is interested only in battles and can recite them all, then name the enemies of our family who still live."

"Will Gruffydd ever return?"

Nest bent to Dybion and played with his fingers until he chuckled. "One day. When he is ready."

Manon heard a strangeness in her friend's voice. "You fear for him?"

"Of course. He is the son of King Rhys, his heir, and will expect the kingdom of Deheubarth when he sets foot on this soil again. Henry will never agree to such a change."

There was always talk of the English king who had been Nest's lover, a man who held tightly what he took by force. Manon knew just how firm were the invisible chains still binding Nest to the youngest son of The Conqueror. Henry might be king but he would never be Nest's enemy, as he would be for her younger brother.

"The Franks who have made their homes across the south of Wales will not welcome Gruffydd," Manon said softly.

"No," Nest whispered. "It would be good to see Gruffydd again, yet when he comes the hearts of our people will be anguished as their men fight and die. Oh, Manon, why can there not be peace?"

"One day," Manon promised as she soothed Nest. "The new castle of Sir Gerald's, is all ready?"

"Not as he would like," Nest said and sat erect. "Men are still clearing the land nearby for the park Gerald has promised me. He will encourage deer and I will be able to ride as long and hard as I choose. Ugo, the Fleming, has been finding horses for us. The stables are complete, as are the barracks for the men who will protect us. The hall and its rooms have a roof so carpenters can work in the dry but Gerald is mostly concerned the palisades are high enough and ditches wide enough to keep out Cadwgan."

"Surely that man is too busy with his Christmas eisteddfod?"

"When all the great and good of our people gather on the bank of the Teifi? You know the men of our blood, Manon. When they are together and tell each other stories of the past it takes little beer or mead to madden them enough to fight."

'Oh, dear," Manon sighed, "and Owain ap Cadwgan empties this shire of Pembroke to stock with our men and women that God-forsaken country they call Ireland. To fill the farms and fields the king sends us Flemings, angering all true Welshmen, not one of them dreaming of taking their own families to live there. Then Sir Gerald must build a new castle in Emlyn to keep all safe and secure."

Nest threw back her head and laughed, a rollicking sound which had the children around her wide-eyed.

"Manon, you have the same way of seeing things as that good man, your father. Now you see why my own father trusted my mother and I to his care when there was danger."

Manon shared the laughter, then sobered. "When do you go north?"

"Gerald has determined to celebrate the feast of the Nativity here, in Pembroke, as is the custom. He would be in his castle at Cenarth Bychan to welcome the New Year."

"The eisteddfod! You will sail past Cadwgan and Owain at the mouth of the Teifi, drinking with their cronies. Who will protect you then, Nest?"

"My husband."

The women were silent, thinking of the Constable defying his enemies yet again.

"You are fortunate he has power and is fearless." Manon hesitated but she knew she must warn her friend. "There will be many nearby envying Sir Gerald his claim to Welsh land because of you – and even more jealous of all the silver and other valuables you take with you to Emlyn."

65

"As long as Gerald draws breath he thwarts any ambitions others might have through me and my blood so I will be safe from harm – my children too."

Manon shivered. Her fingers made the sign of the cross on her forehead and breast. Beauty and wealth. They made a dangerous coupling.

Chapter Four

The Constable stood beside his shire reeve, the early morning of the castle bustling around them. "You will be missed in Pembroke, Geoffrey. I have come to rely on you greatly but Sir Gilbert is important to the king. You will do well."

The two men walked from the great hall, their long strides matching.

Geoffrey was dressed for travelling. "I am grateful for all your training, sir. You set an example which is hard for us lesser men to follow."

Sir Gerald smiled, warmth for the younger man gentling his expression. "You speak kindly but by the year's turn I will be on my own land and this town and shire will have to rub along without either of us."

The younger man hesitated to speak, was doubtful. "The bishop's kinsman must work hard to be ready to take control when you finally sail north. He does not use the Welsh easily and I fear he is still not wise to the danger of spies in the town."

"Spies! It should be the one quarter in which he is already expert. Remember, Roger has been about his mother's skirts in court. Since he suckled he has learned all there is of plots and schemers."

Geoffrey grinned. "Of that I am sure, sir. It does not inconvenience you I take Gan and Maslin with me?"

"Not at all. Roger must select his own ansels. How he judges men will help me decide his nature."

"Is that why the Bishop of London takes such an interest in this small town and shire? Roger fitzHugh – have we been have we been on trial, you and I, sir?"

Gerald's hand was large and firm on Geoffrey's shoulder. "No, lad. To the bishop we are as falconers training a fledgling. This little bird we call Roger had been going astray in the strange breezes fluttering the silks at court. Mark my words, when Roger fitzHugh rides away from Pembroke he will fly straight and true."

Winter slowly tightened its grip and the flow of goods to the castle became a torrent. Beds, chairs, stools, coffers, all carved by the best craftsmen in Pembroke joined bowls and cooking pots, mattresses of the finest wool and pillows stuffed with goose feathers. Flemish tapestries were unloaded from ships and waited to hang on the walls of the fortress in Cenarth Bychan.

While the sea was calm, fully laden ships sailed from Pembroke along the River Cleddau and around the coast to the mouth of the Teifi. From there captains used tides and oars to help the weighted vessels reach Cilgerran and its castle, the highest point tides could reach. Once the cargoes were unloaded the goods were hoisted to the top of the cliff and carted along paths to Cenarth Bychan where there had always been a stronghold of some kind in the beauty of green woods and pastures.

The goods moved seemed unending and were but a part of the wealth and artistry in Pembroke, as much as a measure of the man whose wife could pay for it all.

It was a market day. There were many men and women with silver and copper hidden in their clothes as they thronged the town, each eager to spend some of their good fortune earned from the Constable and his lady.

Beershops were packed with thirsty customers and in

dark alleyways and decrepit hovels women eased men of their lusts and their money. Most of Pembroke's visitors that day had been hard-headed and spent money wisely on new tunics and shirts, dried peas for the winter, a new leather belt or boots, buckets to replace worn ones or even a leather jerkin and a hat to keep out the rain and cold to come.

Meurig had been away from the leather shop for a sennight and in the two days since his return he was making an effort to be civil to his father's wife. He worked steadily, for once leaving Kamal and Rhodri free of the viciousness of his tongue and feet and when Gwen hurried everyone to the washbowl, there was an air of feasting. Even Old Twm smiled and showed his gums as he chewed his roasted sheep while the children laughed and ate their fill.

Warmed wheaten cakes and honey were fast disappearing when Manon retched with a sudden nausea and ran to the privy. It was a place she could not leave, her supper shot until she was dry. Even then the sickness continued, with barely rest enough for Manon to catch her breath. Long into the night violent cramps began and Manon cried out in her distress.

Gerwyn was distraught, begging God and everyone else for help. Nudd was more practical. He heard Manon's anguish and disappeared, braving the wrath of the soldiers to break curfew, as he called it, and fetch Mistress Mabli from the castle.

The guards above the gate knew Nudd but wondered if he was being used by spies or raiders. The boy persisted, calling for Mistress Mabli in his strange tongue. One of them finally relented but Mabli was allowed out of the castle as long as a small troop of men accompanied her to Gerwyn's home.

Once there she gathered Manon in her arms to console her. "Is it only you who ailed?" she asked the young woman.

"Praise be to God – no one else should suffer this," Manon whispered.

"You are right, child," Mabli said gently, then called to Gwen for hot water. "Enough to stew herbs quickly," she added so forcefully Gwen ran to rekindle the dying fire.

"What is wrong with me?" Manon whispered.

Mabli's broad face with its twisted cheek was grim. "I have a suspicion, nothing more, but I have seen the princess in such a condition."

The girl remembered her friend as she had last seen her, cheeks full and flushed with health, her eyes bright. Manon was heartened until fresh cramps caused her to bend and cry out.

"We must get you warm in a bed," Mabli decided and with smooth haste had Heledd's pallet laid in front of the fire which was beginning to throw out a fair heat.

The goodwife pounded rue, stirring in warm white wine and waiting only until the liquid was cool enough for the invalid. Manon endured spoonsful of Mabli's liquid, every dose making her vomit. This was repeated through what was left of the night, the mediciner inspecting the bowl used until she was satisfied with what she saw. Manon was wrapped in blankets and skins, too exhausted to sleep as Mabli mixed and brewed more herbs.

The next liquid Mabli must swallow tasted and smelled very strange but she was assured it would ease her throat and she obeyed Mabli's gentle command. There was no more vomiting and Mabli smiled her encouragement as she spooned wine mixed with poppy juice into Manon. As pain lessened and exhaustion took its toll, Manon leaned back on her pillows and for a long time knew no more.

When she woke she was safely back in her own bed, realising a day had come and gone and with it her new baby.

Gerwyn held her as if he would never let her go. "Please God, no! Not Manon," she heard him whisper against her hair.

Mabli dosed her again and almost at once eyelids became too heavy to keep apart.

"I have given her the strongest poppy juice," Mabli told an anxious Gerwyn. "Manon will sleep well and I will return in the morning." She was a big woman and almost matched Gerwyn in height as she put an arm around his great shoulders. "I am sorry for the loss of your babe."

"Thank you, mistress. It was part of me – my child with Manon. Our son."

His tears told Mabli all she needed to know. Manon would be cared for with tenderness. "I was puzzled," she said when he was himself again. "You kept saying, 'Please God, not again!' What did you mean?"

"I remembered my mother ill as Manon was, just before she died. It was like a ghost come back to haunt me. If it had not been for you –" He could say no more as tears flowed and ran down his cheeks.

"So be it," she said softly. "Yes, you could have lost Manon but Nudd fetched me and my medicines did their work again."

"Again?"

"Aye. Once in an English castle the princess suffered as did Manon but I was watching for her and had the rue and wine ready. She recovered fully, as will Manon. Now," she patted the big man, drained by the agony he had endured, "sleep with your wife and let your arms be round her when she wakes."

It was many hours before Manon floated up from the depths holding her. Gerwyn snored at her side, one arm heavy across her. She kissed him and turned with a sigh, seeing Meurig's face in the half-opened door and lit by the new day's light.

"Are you well?" he whispered.

She was surprised. "Praise be to God, I am but the child is gone. It died before it breathed and was unshriven except

71

for my prayers. My trust is in Christ and in his mercy. He will guard the new soul from harm."

Meurig sniffled and wiped eyes and nose with a sleeve, much as he had done when a small boy. Manon doubted Gerwyn's son had slept, he looked so haggard.

"Before God, I am truly sorry for your illness, Manon. Believe me – please believe me!"

"I would like to Meurig – for your father's sake."

The boy crept into the room and knelt beside her. "My father was so burdened. He said he had seen such sickness before and thought you must not live."

"My baby did not," she reminded him. "He would have been your brother."

Meurig bent his head, making the sign of the cross as he whispered a prayer, asking for God's blessing on the soul of the fresh little corpse. After a moment he added a prayer for Manon's continued health. He looked at her, his face distorted by his agony. "I must go."

"No, Meurig, your father needs you."

"He is better without me," Gerwyn's son said through more tears and fled.

After he went away Manon lay in the half-world of poppy juice. Her body and most of her mind was numb but some things were sharp and painful. For once Meurig had looked straight at her, his eyes begging for her forgiveness. Did the boy really have no idea what he had been about? If that were indeed so, some other hand must have given him the poison, for it was Meurig's fingers Manon had seen hovering over her cup at supper.

Awake, Gerwyn could find no peace. After God and Manon he prized his children above all else and in one lightning strike he had lost his firstborn and the child to come. Discovering Meurig had taken money from the shop and a satchel filled with the smallest and costliest of the painted caskets, added to the father's misery. He roamed the house and shop, disrupted the workshop and the yard, searching for yet never finding peace. Manon could do little to help him but at night he cradled her and drew strength.

A day passed, two, and colour began to return to Manon's cheeks. Gerwyn knew he must go back to the tannery but was unwilling to leave his wife. She smiled, kissed him and made him go about his business.

"Get on with you, cariad. You are under Gwen's feet all day and as for Kamal and the others, they are of a mind to be angry with you. Have no fear for me. Thanks be to God, I am stronger with each passing hour."

At last Gerwyn was persuaded to go to the pits and pools beyond the monk's town and for a blessed hour or two Manon could rest quietly until she had visitors asking for her. With Mabli that morning came Princess Nest, anxious her companion in the mischiefs of youth was returned to good health. They found Manon sitting by the fire in the kitchen warmly wrapped and with her foot on the rocker of Dybion's cradle.

"May God be thanked indeed," Nest said as she gently kissed Manon. She searched her friend's face. "It is over."

Manon put out a hand and Nest grasped it, her warm, firm flesh encouraging the stricken young woman.

"Mabli told me you endured the same affliction in England."

"The poisoning, yes," Nest said. "It was the loss of the babe, coming as it did, put you in such grave danger."

"Yet it was because of the harm done to you, Mabli knew what poison she was fighting. I thank you for that."

Nest chuckled, a joyous sound. "I am glad to have been of service, lady! When I was the one to suffer at court it was because jealousy wanted me out of Henry's bed. Who have you upset so much they want you dead?"

Manon did not speak for a long moment. "I do not believe he wanted me dead."

"No? Mabli told me Gerwyn's eldest boy has fled, thieving as he went. Was that the escape from guilt?"

"He may have given me the reason for my illness but he was as frightened as his father by the suddenness and strength of the vomiting. He was not the one wanted me a corpse."

"You think the plan not his?"

Manon shook her head and was dizzy for a spell. "He is a wilful, moody child – not one who could think ahead or make any plan which could succeed."

"Is that all you have in his defence?"

"Gerwyn kept saying I was ill in the same way his mother had been before she died," Manon said softly. "He told me, after Meurig left, the boy kept questioning him, determined to know who had been in the house when Gerwyn's mother became ill. Gerwyn said it was hard to remember but Meurig persisted and made his father relive those days. It was after that Meurig came to me and begged my forgiveness."

"Without Meurig we can never know whose hand guided him but the greater puzzle is why?" Nest was frowning. "Have you no idea?"

"No, nor why Meurig was so discontented – until Gwen talked to Old Twm."

"The shrivelled little being who sits and sews, pulling his lips tight into where once his teeth had been?"

Manon laughed at the description and Nest was relieved. Her friend was almost herself again.

"He is not so old, poor soul," Manon said. "At supper, the night after Meurig left, Gwen wondered aloud why the boy left us. 'Hated the tannery', Twm told her."

Nest nodded and smiled as she understood. "I see. Meurig is Gerwyn's eldest son and must expect to work with his father and then inherit from him."

"As did Gerwyn."

"But your Gerwyn is not only a very good man he is also a very good tanner. His work is respected in the whole of the shire – and beyond."

74

"Bless him," Manon said with a fond smile. "He delights in a new leather and is so proud of all he can do."

"While Meurig prefers to dress like the Welsh cracach and sit with his elders as they condemn all things Frank."

"And Flemish," Manon added, thinking of the tall horseman.

"Did Old Twm say what had been Meurig's hopes?" Nest asked.

"The farms."

Nest's eyes opened wide in amazement. "Both of them?"

"So Twm said."

"Surely the boy knew they were for your brothers?"

"It has been said often enough. Perhaps Meurig believed others and thought me foolish to expect their return."

Nest stared into the fire as her thoughts raced. "With you out of the way, Gerwyn might have been persuaded to let him take over the land."

Manon was tired. "It is not the land which interests Meurig, of that I am sure."

"What, then?"

"The silver land can yield if it is well-husbanded."

Nest was scornful. "Meurig had ambitions to be a man of leisure – living off his estates?"

"Why not? He is young enough to dream."

"And old enough to poison! By God's good grace you escaped the wicked death prescribed for you. If the farms are the reason, what have you done to ensure they do not fall into the wrong hands?"

Manon was puzzled and could not answer.

"Have you assigned those farms to your brothers – or left to your children should Emlyn and Ossian not return from Ireland?"

"Should I have done so?"

"Of course. Come to the castle when you are well and I will see our own scribe does that service for you. Bring Gerwyn to make his mark and show he agrees with your wishes."

75

"No! If I do that it will be obvious to all I hold Meurig guilty."

"And you think he is not the moving force in all this? I understand your fears. The scribe will bring the parchment here for you to sign – but make sure Gerwyn agrees and it is noted. Now, tell me exactly what it is you wish to happen to all these riches of yours?"

Manon was suddenly shy. "They are so little compared with all you have, Nest."

"Are they indeed! They are quite enough to earn you your death if you are not careful."

Days were filled with long hours as Manon regained her strength. From the castle kitchens came cuts of freshly killed deer, livers wrapped in leaves in a basket. Mabli visited daily and spooned the juice of wild rose hips, eventually getting Manon to her feet and in to the hubbub of workaday Pembroke.

"Time you were about your business again, my lady," she insisted. "You need not fear your enemy will threaten you again – not while the Constable has us all in his firm grip. He is a fair man," she said more gently, "and his justice is swift and strong. Any cowardly enough to poison you through Gerwyn's son will be too afraid to try again and earn the wrath of Sir Gerald. Now, Gwen is worn to a shadow. I will see to Dybion while you go as far as the bakeshop for bread straight from the oven. It is not far and the walk will do you good."

Manon would have protested but it was never wise to argue with Mabli. She managed a shaky smile, surrendering to the mediciner's will. A few breaths later, cloaked and mittened against the cold, Manon started on her way, leaning against the doorway of the shop before she forced herself erect and struggled into the heaving crowd which was usual on a market day. Slowly, she walked the short distance to Cynfan's store, surprised by how many stopped to ask for her health and give God's blessing for her safety.

Their goodwill made Manon walk straight and tall, colour flying in her cheeks from the cold air but not hiding the gauntness of her face and body.

She was thoughtful as she returned with warm bread in her basket and the memory of Cynfan's pity for her state. She looked at her home with eyes opened to the reality of what was there. The shop lacked its proper order and needed sweeping. Manon walked around the trestles, tidying them and seeing dust. Kamal heard boots being moved and came running, anxious and then relieved to see her safe.

"Rhodri?" she asked.

"He sew buckets. Now good."

Manon found her son, head bent over his work, a blood-stained cloth nearby to wipe pricked fingers. Rhodri looked up at his mother and she was ashamed to see the misery in his face. Old Twm nodded from his seat as he ran needle and thread to and fro in a rhythm which never altered. In the kitchen Heledd was a listless shadow, plucking at the wool of an ancient fleece. Even Nudd ran and hid from Manon, leaving Gwen to take the basket of loaves.

"What has it all come to?" Manon asked Mabli. "Have I been so blinded by my own grief I no longer see what I should?"

Mabli smiled and put into Manon's hands a cup of warm, spiced beer. "Just drink that. It will put heart in you for what must be done."

Like a child Manon did as she was told, each sip sharp, stirring. Mabli would not leave her until the cup had been emptied, then beckoned Gwen to bring Dybion to his mother. The infant wriggled and would have escaped had not Manon tightened her hold. She saw the wariness he had of her and was ashamed, crying in her weakness. It puzzled the child to see tears and his fingers played in the stream.

"Thanks be to God," Mabli said quietly and Gwen sighed her relief as she wiped her own eyes with a sleeve.

"The baby I lost was a boy," Manon whispered at last.

77

"Aye, I know," Gwen said. She had carried the tiny body away.

Mabli stirred the fire. "What name did you give him?"

"Had he lived he would have been Gwion."

"Then call him that now. Let him be one of the family – and let the little soul sleep in peace," Mabli said.

"Gwion," Manon said quietly, then, "Gwion," she said loudly.

Gwen was smiling. "There you are, he is with you here in your home – and always will be."

"How did you . . . ?" Manon began.

"My mother, God rest her soul," Gwen said "She lost a baby. We were all so hungry after a raid and the old vicar was dying but he talked to her and made her see the baby was safe in Christ's keeping. Unshriven, made no difference. It was a girl and she never lived to commit sin, so what was there to pardon?"

Mabli swung her cloak about her. "You will do well now, all of you and I must return to my duties. Getting all the herbs and medicines necessary for a new castle in the back of beyond taxes even my wits, but it must be done. I must remind Nudd to bring me all the hazel twigs he can. How could we keep our teeth clean and our mouths fresh without his help?" She accepted Manon's thanks kindly but brusquely and was gone.

Heledd crept to her mother's side and Manon's arms tightened about her and Dybion. Neither child was restless. These were the embraces they had longed for and were content. Only when Dybion's wetness reached Manon's legs did she stir and hand the baby to a smiling Gwen. The mistress of the house was prepared to take charge of her home again.

"Nudd!"

The little man came scurrying at Manon's call.

"The shop floor must be swept and the roadway outside is a disgrace!"

Nodding and smiling, Nudd scampered away to the

besom as Manon cuddled Heledd and persuaded the child her face must be washed and her hair combed. With the little girl in a clean tunic and her cheeks shining almost as much as her eyes, Manon let her daughter's dark curls hang freely.

A new spirit was flooding through Manon and she turned her attention to the kitchen. Gwen was sent to market, ample coin in her pouch, to search for and bring back any foodstuffs which could be added to the winter store. Manon lifted the lids of pots and baskets, cleaning the wood of shelves, Heledd helping where she could. Then it was the shop, Rhodri giggling with excitement as Kamal moved caskets, boots, jerkins, belts, and arranged them as temptingly as possible on newly-washed trestles.

By the time they all gathered for the evening meal anything which could be stacked tidily had been neatened and anything which could shine, gleamed. Dust had been banished, the fire burned brightly and from a pot hanging over it came the smell of food prepared with skill, good meat blending with vegetables.

Gerwyn returned to a home transformed. The heaviness of his face was raised in a broad, beaming smile as he kissed his wife and daughter, tossed his youngest son in the air and cuffed Rhodri with a gentle hand.

"Which men will you take with you to search the woods by the river?" the Constable asked in fluent but heavily accented Welsh.

Roger fitzHugh's smile was quick, smooth. "Surely, Sir Gerald, we might converse in our own tongue when there is but the two of us?"

The Constable ignored the question, repeating his own but this time with a frown.

"Sir –"

"Tell me, boy, do you understand what I am saying to you?"

"The men are ready to ride, Sir Gerald."

Indeed, four men, their leather jerkins well-studded with protective metal, waited by their mounts. Gano and Vaden were familiar to the Constable, the other two strangers. He noted the massive shoulders and bellies of the newcomers, hair which was greasy and overlong hanging below their helmets.

"I ride with you today," he told Roger, his words in the local tongue but clear and clipped in the polished style of King Henry's court. "When we return you will report to the priory," he continued in French so there should be no misunderstanding. "Father prior will allocate you a cell and a habit and there you will stay, working with Brother Paulinus, until both the prior and I are sure you are fully aware of everything said in your presence – and that you can answer sensibly. Do I make myself clear?"

"Yes, Sir Gerald."

"As for this sortie, we ride in search of spies and their accomplices. If there is any resistance words may be spoken in fear and haste and lead us to their masters but you are of no use to me if they are in the Welsh tongue. Remember, we are at the frontier of the kingdom and its safety depends on our vigilance. Can the two new men you have chosen understand local Welsh and be wise to treachery?"

Roger fitzHugh fidgeted uneasily, his discomfort increased by the coarseness of his shirt, being made of the kind of linen approved by the Constable for working soldiers.

"Christ in Heaven, give me strength!" Sir Gerald growled. "Send those men away, Vaden, and roust out Fulke and Leon. We ride as soon as they are ready – and you, Master fitzHugh, pray we are not too late!"

"Do I ride with you, sir?"

"You do, but keep your eyes and ears open and your mouth shut. As long as you do not have a command of Welsh you are a weakness in the justice in this shire – and I will make sure the Bishop of London knows it!"

Chapter Five

It was Rhodri who showed greatest change and it distressed Manon she had not realised the full extent of Meurig's bullying. Gwen swore Rhodri grew every night he slept and the boy ate as much as any man. His curls were glossier, bouncing around plumping cheeks as he ran about his tasks. Only Gerwyn's spirits remained low.

"Be patient," the Mabli advised as she visited. "It must be hard for him to accept all Meurig did to you. The boy is not here to be ashamed, so his father carries the burden for him."

Manon was not wholly convinced. "It is more than that – almost as though an old memory has returned to haunt him. In his sleep he cries for his mother."

Mabli nodded sagely, having learned from Nest of Meurig's questions before he fled. "Be grateful to God your man can talk of it, even as he slumbers. It will take the Lord's time but he will heal."

The Constable stood, refusing to admit aching joints as a constant part of his life. Straightening his shoulders he turned to lead the congregation from the priory church. The building was of solid stone, wooden roofed and already part of the hill which faced the castle across the river. Going from dimness and the smell of candles and incense, fresh air from the sea was welcome. Sir Gerald bowed to the prior as the cleric processed with his monks from the church.

"You wish for news of our student?" The prior's smile was disarming.

"If there is any, Father."

"You will be surprised with his progress. Brother Paulinus has been most diligent."

"Young Roger now uses the Welsh easily?"

The prior considered the question. "I would say he understands well enough. As for his speech, it will suffice and allow him to perform his duties."

"You are ready to release him?"

The priest's smile was gentle. "I believe that for Master Roger, freedom will be most welcome."

The new shire reeve hid his relief when he faced the Constable next day. Gone was harshest of coarse linen against his skin and the rough wool of a Benedictine habit. The first tunic he chose was a favoured one, its weaving of blue and brown comfortable with wear.

"Your efforts these last weeks have found favour with the prior," Sir Gerald said.

"When may I assume the duties I was sent here to perform, sir?"

"As shire reeve?"

"I have been patient, sir, but in his letters my kinsman wonders at my lack of progress."

"It is good of you to remind me." The Constable was relieved they could at last converse in Welsh, even if Roger unconsciously used a French word when he hesitated. "I have set up a troop of men for you. All are experienced and will be under the command of Kemen."

Monastic living had helped clear the young man's skin but it was marred now by an angry flush. "You assured me the choice would be mine."

"So I did, just as you insisted a month ago your knowledge of Welsh was good. You deceived yourself and I will

82

not take the risk of you appointing men to the guard who may deceive you in turn as to their loyalty and good intent. Tomorrow, I ride north to Cenarth Bychan and will be away from Pembroke for a sennight – if reports I receive during that time are favourable. When I return you should be at home in your position."

There was no need for the Constable to explain what would happen should Roger default in any way.

"Remember, in this shire you can never relax your vigilance. I swear our enemies can smell when that happens and flood us with spies, so – be warned!"

Roger fitzHugh bowed, was gracious, deferent, all that he should be in the company of such an experienced soldier. Dismissed at last he made his way to his quarters, firming his decisions as he went. When the Constable, his family and his hangers-on were living in their eyrie on the border with Ceredigion, the cooks could be taught to slice meat and poach it gently in spiced sauces. New ansels could be chosen, the humourless Kemen and his cronies replaced by men able to discipline the townspeople and the rest of the shire as harshly as they deserved. Spies? They would not come near, too obvious in a shire under the strict control Pembroke needed.

He licked his lips. Roger had hated the bishop for sending him to such a devil-infested hole but in time there could be compensations for all the rigours he had endured.

The roof of the leather shop had been made secure against the coming winter storms, cracks in the walls sealed and wood for the fire stacked high in the yard. In the kitchen grain and peas were safe from rats in wooden boxes, honey waited in earthenware pots large and small and in the nearest shed barrels of salted meat waited to be soaked and stewed while above them were haunches of pork, salted and smoked. Herbs hung in bunches everywhere. They were dry but needed only to be touched by a passing shoulder to waft aromas of wild thyme, mint, parsley, garlic.

Manon was fully well again and surveyed her little realm, content she had done all she could to prepare her family for the worst of the winter. Even hyssop was at hand should an ague strike and coughs succeed it.

However diligently Kemen and his men surveyed the men and women who came into town each day, they could find no strangers who might be spies. Not one.

"Are you certain?"

"Aye, Sir Gerald. We know who stays each night in the town, even if they do hop around different beds when they fancy a change from their wives."

"Outlanders?"

"We watch, sir, as God is our witness. An odd man here and there we follow and listen to him trading. Nothing – except the stories of Cadwgan and his eisteddfod grow daily."

"Tell me what is said," the Constable demanded.

"Well sir, there is talk of old farmsteads being torn down, the wood used for new housing to shelter the bards and the cracach who will come to hear them. Great piles of firewood grow, promising no one will be cold. As for cattle, any still alive in that part of Ceredigion are being herded towards the Teifi. Then chickens, geese, new pens await them while Cadwgan's men carry all the barley and good wheat they can. Some of the grain has been sailed to Cadwgan from Powys, Ireland even."

"All these whispers must have come from men's mouths and those men arrived here from the north. Where are they?"

"Not in Pembroke, sir, I swear it – nor in the farms and settlements around."

Sir Gerald's eyes narrowed and his mouth was a hard line. "It may only be one, Kemen, but he is there, I feel him. He is watching us, waiting for a sign of weakness. When he sees it, then he will slip away to his master with the signal. Whoever he is, he must be stopped."

Kemen was a big, capable man but he was uncertain. "What about the shire reeve, sir?"

"He is new to his duties and a boy." The Constable stared at Kemen, the two men of the same height and build. "Your orders are from me, Kemen, and I rely on you. Do you understand?"

"Mistress! Come!"

Kamal was too excited to say more, pulling at Manon's skirt to speed her into the shop. There, the tall Fleming darkened the doorway. She looked at him but he did not speak.

"What is it?" she asked Kamal.

He pointed to one of the trestles. On it was one of the small painted caskets like the others on display, but shabby, as if travel-worn. She looked at the Fleming, his smile kind, and then at Kamal.

"I know it," Kamal said. "Meurig."

Surprise robbed Manon of breath. "Are you sure?"

Kamal nodded, dark hair flopping with excitement.

"Go, get the master," Manon said. "He is with friends."

The arab ran, guessing Manon did not want to tell the Fleming Gerwyn was in a beer shop.

Manon picked up the casket. "Please come," she said to the Fleming and gestured to her home, suddenly shy.

He shook his head. "Your family – it is the Sabbath."

"Then all the more reason. You have news for us, you are very welcome."

"It is why I came today. No persons in the shop."

Gwen was clearing midday food from the table and Manon filled a wooden platter with meat and bread for the Fleming, sending Gwen with a jug for beer. Ugo sat where he was directed, at home in warmth and comfort. He decided it was good to stretch his legs under a table scrubbed clean above a floor regularly swept. Iron and copper pots gleamed from their sanding and no dust lay on wooden bowls and clay jugs. The big man began his meal, relishing the flavour of the stew he mopped up with his bread as he waited for Gerwyn. He needed little patience.

Without a word, Gerwyn strode into the kitchen, picking up the casket and cradling it in his hands as he would a frail baby.

"You have seen my son, Ugo?" he asked.

"No."

Gerwyn raised the casket against his face. "Then . . . ?"

The Fleming hesitated, searching for the Welsh words which would help him explain. "I was near Cenarth Bychan and the new castle in Emlyn. The Welshman they call Cadwgan is famed for his horses. He breeds true and I was to meet one of the farmers who had a mare in foal from Cadwgan's stud. There was hope of a trade." Ugo shrugged his shoulders. "The farmer was very proud and tells me there will be no trade. He did not want any mare of Cadwgan's bloodline to be owned by a Frank. So, no horse to bring back to Pembroke. I tell him Pembroke is a good place to be and he shows me the casket – from Pembroke. He had seen a boy with it and buys it for his wife. I bargain with him so I can bring it back to you."

"You must have paid dearly for it," Manon said.

Ugo's answer came with a slow grin. "No money. We talk horses. I promise him a foal due soon from a good mare. He is happy to have good Frankish stock and Sir Gerald will not know."

Gerwyn was impatient. "What did he say of Meurig – my son?"

"The boy was well. He was working with the men who prepare the houses for the . . ." Again, the lifted shoulders as Ugo failed in the search for a word.

"Eisteddfod?" Gerwyn asked and Ugo nodded.

The Fleming was eager to talk. "The stables must be filled when Sir Gerald and his family reach their new home. They sail but I will take more horses north for them. The animals must rest before they are needed for the hunting."

"Is it true land has been cleared for a great park?" Manon asked.

"Yes. It will be a fine place for the princess to ride."

"And the people who lived in the woods there?"

"Sir Gerald's lady has ordered new homes for them in the shelter of the castle. They will not go hungry or be in danger from the men of Ceredigion."

"All people are in danger from Cadwgan and Owain," Manon said, her lips twisted in a thin line of bitterness.

Quietly, Gerwyn explained to Ugo the reason for Manon's hatred. The outlander who had lost so much understood.

"Before God, I am sorry, lady. The men in Emlyn fear Cadwgan and his son but they tell me Cadwgan is now the great man. He wishes to be important with the king, as is his brother Iorwerth."

Gerwyn laughed, startling Manon with a sound she had not heard for so long. "Iorwerth and Cadwgan, they are true blood brothers."

"So now they grow old and wise, perhaps?" Ugo asked. "This Cadwgan has bards to sing to him and rides to kill only to hunt for deer and wild boar."

"May God be praised if that is so." Manon made the sign of the cross. "Better still if he had not trained his son so well in his old ways."

Gently, Gerwyn laid the casket on the table and went away, returning with a new one which he handed to Ugo. "Please, take this with my thanks. Because of your kindness I know my son is safe and one day may return."

Ugo saw the hunger in Gerwyn's eyes and bowed his acceptance. He knew how much the father needed to hold the small box carried by his boy.

"When you return to Emlyn . . . ?" Gerwyn began.

87

"I will look and listen and then I will ask questions in my best Welsh," Ugo assured him.

They were not a wholesome pair. Brede stood taller than the shire reeve but was not as broad, his skinny frame moving with lanky ease. A deep scar scored his right cheek from chin to brow although it was almost hidden by thick, black hair. Nothing obscured the coldness of dark eyes set deep, nor the way his thin lips curled.

Rolf was smaller, quick and neat but just as unused to keeping himself clean as was Brede. Under Rolf's grime was a cheerful smile, marred by the chill of his blue eyes.

"You will pay us now?" Brede asked.

Roger fitzHugh nodded. "As we agreed. Enough for your food and bed. When the Constable finally sails for his castle you will lead the guards to my orders. Until that time I expect you to watch and listen. There are thieves aplenty in the town, as well as those who would cheat us of our dues and have treachery as a bedfellow. I will have names for them all. Understand?"

That night Gerwyn held Manon and breathed a sigh into the curve of her neck.

"Cariad, it grieves me still my kin could harm you so."

"I am recovered," she said, "and Meurig is alive."

"Meurig," he whispered, "God keep him safe."

"Amen to that – and may the good Lord give you ease this night."

Gerwyn slept in her arms until it was nearly morning. As the first fingers of light poked through the shutters he again became restless, calling to his mother in his distress. Manon held him, crooning as though he were Dybion, puzzling as to why he cried so. Good news he had had of Meurig and still he was unhappy. Was there another fear Gerwyn hid from her?

It had rained without ceasing. Pembroke, so near the sea,

knew only bad weather lasting a few days before strong winds gusted in and melted snow or dried floods. This time water cascaded into every crevice on its way to the rivers. Homes were as sodden as the woods and fields. Such cattle as escaped the winter cull and salting stood miserably in thick mud. Sheep were weighed down under fleeces heavy with water and humans fared no better. Wood for fires was never dry and in the thin heat and steam, diseases took hold and killed.

A coughing sickness spread through the town. New babies who could not vomit away the thick mess from their lungs, choked and died. Older children weak from hunger and neglect did not have the strength to cough or breathe and lay in the graveyard or charnel house beside the old ones who had succumbed.

Manon's children fared as did those of any family feeding well and staying warm and dry. Days and nights of coughing needed constant watchfulness but they lived, broken sleep the legacy of the evil. She heard Buddyg's daughters had sickened and prayed the good meat and goat's milk their half-brother supplied would give them the strength to wake each morning.

The castle fared no better than the town, small coffins leaving to join those in the town being blessed and buried. All four of Princess Nest's children were afflicted but they had Mabli to physic them. The older boys, William and Maurice, quickly recovered, Angharad too, but the baby, David, gave cause for concern. He was young and needed very careful nursing. All this Manon learned from Buddyg when she walked through a quietened town to visit her friend.

"Are your girls well?" Was Manon's first question.

"Thanks be to God, they are – and thanks also to Nudd. The ground ivy and garlic he brought me was not to their taste each morning and night, pounded up in milk but they suffer less and the choking phlegm comes away easier." Buddyg swayed on her stool, tiredness and relief claiming her. "My little ones will do well now – although I come to beg more garlic from Nudd. I can stew it in their food."

"Who is with them now?"

"Ceinwen. She has been a Godsend, persuading them to swallow what they thought was poisoned milk, cleaning them when they were sick and sitting with them so I could sleep. Such kindness – and her with no children of her own." Buddyg was a kind woman, fortunate to be able to rejoice in so good a neighbour.

"It is so sad," Manon said. "Ceinwen would have been the best mother in the world."

Tears welled up in Buddyg's eyes. "Which she is to Hywel, poor dab. Enemies take so much from a man and what is left in his skin but a child?"

"You are right. When he is well and strong it is easy to remember he is a prince of the blood and then comes the knowledge he is unmanned and blind. Helpless – but for Ceinwen. He did not suffer the coughing sickness?"

"No, nor Ceinwen. Bless him, Hywel was willing to manage on his own, difficult though that be for him, so Ceinwen was free to help me with the girls."

"Like Nest he was raised to care for the children. Queen Gwladus can be proud of her teachings," Manon spoke fondly, remembering the dignity and kindness of the royal lady.

"All this trouble in Pembroke and yet Sir Gerald will not alter his plan," Buddyg said and frowned. "He will leave for his new estate at Cenarth Bychan as soon after Nativity as the tides and winds are favourable."

"Surely he will not force the children to go?"

"No? He ignores illness in himself – sees it as a weakness of the flesh which must be overcome. Mistress Mabli is greatly angered, so I have heard from Ceinwen. The princess is to go – and all her children with her."

"The baby, David?" Manon asked.

"Aye. His father would risk his newest son's life in the cold winds beyond the Cleddau – all to show Cadwgan and his merrymakers at the eisteddfod who it is rules in these parts."

Manon was unhappy. "The Constable may be a brave man but he is a fool to risk his son."

Buddyg was more practical. "He is a Frank. Men, weapons, huge horses, they mean more than the common sense which is the gift of God."

"And such horses! Franks may despise all the Britons here in Wales but the horses our people breed are better suited to the land in which we live. Tough and small boned they can gallop through the trees and up the hills better than those huge monsters they call destriers."

"To be sure – and yet more monsters must go north to Cenarth Bychan."

"Most of them are already there," Manon said.

"How do you know that?"

"Ugo, the Fleming who brought news of Meurig. He has been filling the stables there for some weeks. He visits Gerwyn when he can."

Buddyg glanced at her friend's face. She had heard the stories but her sharp eyes saw only innocence in Manon. Perhaps the Fleming really did come to see the husband. "Ceinwen says Gerald's son by the daughter of Ninian the silversmith is to go north with the family."

"Is he? Yet what you say does not surprise me."

"Why is that?"

"Carew. It was deeded to Nest by King Henry and will pass in time to her first fitzGerald son, William. By building his castle in Emlyn, Sir Gerald will have property which is his by right, land he is free to deed to his own firstborn."

"The William they call The Bastard?" Buddyg asked.

"If both boys must have the same name, how to tell them apart? It means much to Franks, this business of how you are born," Manon said. "Their old king, the Conqueror, was such a one – a bastard. It is said it is why he fought so hard to take possession of all he could."

"As if Franks needed a reason for war!" Buddyg scorned. "The ways of the Britons in Wales are better. All that is needed for a child is that his father owns him. It gives him all the rights he will ever need."

"And women – they are due what is theirs from their father, as I was, but the Frankish laws will have us lose all that."

Buddyg nodded her agreement. "It is a rare Frank who sees a woman as anything other than a bedmate and a breeding mare. And if, like the princess, she has wealth, he sees it as his to spend on a new estate."

"You must be patient!" Roger fitzHugh thundered.

He had ridden from Pembroke to meet his ansels in a derelict barn close to the road to leading to Lamphey.

Brede's truculence flared. "You promised us work to fill my pockets and all I have done is hang around Pembroke and its farms. We are tired of waiting."

Rolf muttered agreement. His usually expression had slipped, revealing the harsh crudeness of the man beneath. "With Pembroke town so busy before the Nativity and when every man and woman spends all their waking hours stuffing the new castle with goods, prices have soared. The money you grudge us only keeps us starving."

The shire reeve was furious. "So this is the reason for the summons to meet – you demand more coin to fill your bellies in the taverns and bed even more women each night! I warned you. Nothing moves in Pembroke without there being gossip and you have earned yourselves places on the tip of every witch's tongue. What about the work you were to do? Have you the names of all the robbers the townspeople would keep hidden from us? And what of traitors? I doubt you could even smell one if he was right up your nose!"

"There is one," Brede said slowly, "but he knows this town well."

"Name?" the shire reeve demanded.

His two ansels shook their heads. "He is like the mist, creeping round and disappearing when you get close," Rolf said.

"Then how do you know he exists?"

"As soon as he is gone talk starts. Of Cadwgan and Owain, their proud blood, their right to land the Franks strut over," Brede told him.

"And he must talk of life with them," Rolf added, "food always in good supply with no need to toil in the fields. Wine from France as well as plenty of beer and mead."

Roger snorted his disgust. "Does he also talk of how the meat gets to Cadwgan and Owain? Robbed from the fields of our own farmers who should be feeding us? The wine – stolen from ships carrying it to Pembroke, aye, and Tenby, too?"

The men were silenced and the shire reeve mused aloud, almost forgetting they were there.

"He lives with Cadwgan and Owain, yet he can move unseen when he is amongst us. Someone shields him, someone who can pass unchallenged and with him, any companion. Find the spy – and the traitor!"

It was the eve of the Nativity and a cold wet day but the kitchen was warm and filled with rich smells. Manon turned at the sound of a visitor. The bulk of the mediciner filled the doorway and Manon's spirits lifted, her face radiant with a smile.

"Mistress Mabli! It is good to see you again. Come, sit by the fire."

Gwen had just finished milking and the ageing woman was soon settled in Gerwyn's chair, a cup of goat's milk still warm and frothing in her hand.

"Nest is well?" Manon asked. "And the children?"

"By God's good grace," Mabli said and sipped her milk, wiping whiteness from her lips. "David still lingers with the coughing but the fever is broken and he will mend in the Lord's time."

"I heard my mother talk of the hooping cough," Manon said and shivered. "I prayed never to hear my own little ones suffer – but it was not to be."

"They have come through it well, Nudd tells me."

Manon made the sign of the cross as she breathed a silent prayer of thanks. "A dryness in the night when they sleep – the cold air has them coughing then but they are not awake."

"An infusion of hyssop in honey works well then, I have found. It soothes and helps sleep give healing."

"My mother always believed God's hand was in the honey-making. 'Trust it', she would say. 'It never has in it the evil which rots all things'."

"Your mother spoke true – and you are fortunate to have Nudd." Mabli pulled a scrap of a dried plant from a pouch. "I hope he has some of this for me in his little garden. Garlic in any form can be of use. Tell me, have you been rubbing the baby's feet with it as I said?"

Manon chuckled. "I have and his breath carries the smell of the herb so quickly but it has helped him. Nudd brings us some each day for the stewpot so we all gain."

"I am glad to hear it. I would have extra to send with my lady when she sails north. We are gifted in Pembroke with the garlic. Never have I found it so abundant and there is no knowing what the hedges and woods may hold in such a foreign place as Emlyn."

Manon hid a smile as she fed the fire with dry wood. North, Emlyn might be but it was still in the shire of Pembroke. "When does the family leave?"

"The Constable has been told these strong winds will drop in two or three days, then the ships will take passage north."

"When do you take David?"

Mabli's lips thinned, her twisted face adding to the line of determination. "When I decide he is well enough to travel. Ugo the Fleming stays behind to accompany us when I am ready for such a long journey." She spoke as though the

94

castle at Cenarth Bychan was at the edge of God's universe and not on land which was part of Sir Gerald's rule as Constable.

"You do not like to sail?"

"Not at all! I ask you, Manon, how can I be about my business and care for the princess and her children when I am laid flat and not able to move?"

"Then who goes with her?"

"Menna, the girl who came to me at Carew. She is strong with the children and good with her use of herbs. I must see what else Nudd has which she can take north with her."

The birth of the Christ Child was celebrated with great noise in the castle and with thankful relief by many families, the worst of the coughing sickness having passed. Gerwyn lifted Manon and the children into the cart and drove them to the priory church for mass, the Latin words and the chanting of the brothers become almost familiar, even welcome. Gwen preferred to walk the distance to her old church at Lamphey and a service in her own tongue. The vicar had a wife and children and had been appointed by the Bishop of St David's when his grace had stayed in his palace, a bowman's reach from the church. New clerics, approved by Rome, were unable to lie with a woman the night before mass and with mass to be said daily, there could be no wives, no children for Frankish priests.

Such feasting as there was in the town spread from the castle. After returning from a service in the priory, Nest was a hostess welcoming all the dignitaries to the best food and wine she could offer. The Conqueror had begun the tradition of assembling around him all his nobles at Christmas, as well as at Easter and Whitsuntide, so he could hand down his laws as well as smell out conspiracies, treason, rebellion. His sons, William Rufus and now Henry, continued this method of disciplining strong willed subjects. Those who could not travel too far from their estates must needs gather around the kingdom, each group with an unknown king's spy in it's midst. Princess Nest knew well the habits of the English court and was usually aware of her guest who would report back to King Henry.

At the gates were the poor and needy, the beggars and the starving urchins, waiting for scraps from the kitchens. Those came early. Most prized were the large slabs of day-old bread which acted as trenchers for the cracach, juices from the roasted meats draining in and softening the baked barley meal with a rare richness. With Sir Gerald and his princess soon to go and live in Emlyn, such luxury would not be repeated.

A few days later noise in the town bubbled like a spring coming out of a mountainside. Ships at the quay were being loaded with the last of the cargoes for Sir Gerald's castle. Food in sacks and boxes could be guessed at and cause excitement at the provisions going north. The ornate caskets and coffers were gossiped over as they were carried through the waiting crowd, Roger fitzHugh and his men clearing a way for the labourers.

All who could viewed the procession streaming from Pembroke's castle, jeering at some loads, cheering others. Manon was as curious as any. She had Heledd by the hand and both were wrapped in woollen cloaks and hoods, mittens of lamb fleece and shod with boots of toughened sheepskin. Rhodri had long left them, darting with urchins to the front of the crowd and all of them wriggling like eels to see everything possible.

There were moments when Manon could feel eyes on her. Once it was Ithel the money-lender, his white hands hidden in sleeves of thick, fur-trimmed velvet, a pudding of a hat in matching black velvet keeping out the rawness of the morning. He smiled at her and bowed, glancing along her length and down at Heledd as he would pieces of precious silver, gold even. Manon turned back to the activities on the quayside. If this journey of Nest's meant a quieter Pembroke, there would be less profit for the money lender. Trade going to Tenby might cause Ithel to go too.

"Good day to you, Mistress Manon!" It was Cynfan the baker, carrying the smell of the opened oven about him. He bent down to Heledd. "I will bring you a warm cake when we all go back home, young lady. Would you like that?"

Heledd had learned not to fear the baker but she still pushed herself into the shelter of her mother's cloak.

"Come, you sweet thing. Let me lift you high to see what is happening. Such a day when so much richness is to be seen in Pembroke town. None of it is as beautiful as you, my little one – unless it be your mother."

Manon blushed, was heated by Cynfan's eyes and his breath. She lifted Heledd and the child clung to her.

"Thank you, sir, but it is better if Heledd stays with me. She has the cough and it may strike at any time."

"Poor little soul –"

Any more Cynfan said was lost as the crowd surged and Manon, Heledd in her arms, could escape. Nest was coming along the road to the quay. She was walking, her children with her. William, her eldest boy strode in imitation of his father. Maurice, the younger, quieter lad was at his brother's side and close behind came the other William, taller, older than his half-brothers, a boy who looked about him with a keen stare as he heard the rustle of words naming him 'the bastard'. All were dressed in woollen tunics under sheep-skin jerkins, with boots high to the knee and stitched by Old Twm.

Their sister, Angharad, was a little older than Heledd. She was a lovely child and Manon had a moment of memory, seeing Nest when she first arrived in the Gwaun valley. Like her mother Angharad was wrapped in fleeces and what Manon could see of her purple tunic matched that of Nest. The child's kerchief was free under a wide head-band but Nest's white linen kerchief was pulled up around her throat as it must be for a married woman. The veiling did not hide her beauty, the swathe of linen greatly enhancing the creaminess of her skin.

Nest and the four fitzGerald children walked towards the Constable, waiting at the ship which was to carry them to their new home. When they were on board, Manon put Heledd down, once more feeling someone's gaze on her. She let her glance roam over her neighbours and saw a man staring at her. He seemed part of the crowd in worn leathers and a greasy cap, with wild dark hair around his shoulders and mingling with his beard. He continued to stare at her and she could see he was clearly one of her own people and not an outlander. Manon could not recognise him, though he had the look of someone she knew.

When the man moved awkwardly to let pass some of the armed men who would sail with Sir Gerald, Manon saw the back of the stranger and knew where she had seen him before. He had been in the shop when she returned from Buddyg's home, making sure Manon did not see his face. Then, he had been deep in conversation with Meurig.

Her heart began pounding in her breast and she could barely breathe. What did he know of the boy and why was he here now, watching every item, every person, going to the new castle? Had he been one of the men Meurig was said to have been meeting in the beershops? Before Manon could satisfy her curiosity, the stranger was gone.

All the way home after the ship had sailed downriver Manon fretted over the man. What was his business in Pembroke?

Chapter Six

There was little dealing done in Pembroke once the Constable's ship was out of sight down the river. Only stalls selling food ready to eat and shops stocked with strong liquor had brisk trade. As the day drew to a close desperate farmers and their women sold their goods off so cheaply they were able to start the trudge home early. As the day darkened the shire reeve's men were busy, the addled heads of customers reeling from the beershops needing to be smacked until their owners could either walk unaided or be locked away in an animal pen in the castle for the night.

Gerwyn had been at work early that morning, his brisk hammer blows all that could be heard in a town unusually quiet. He tightened roofing, sealed walls, mended shutters, putting his home ready for the winter gales which always raced in from the sea after the New Year. Nudd was at his side, tools and scraps of stout leather to hand, a Nudd who had grown fatter. It was not so much from extra meat and bread as the layers of old clothes in which he swaddled himself.

"I can see no more holes, Nudd, can you?" Gerwyn asked.

Nudd shook his head, his thatch of hair tossed by the wind.

"Then I must be off to the tannery. Even with Sir Gerald and his lady gone, leather must still be ready for sale. Fetch my pack, will you?"

Manon had it ready, bread, cheese and a stoppered flask of beer. She followed Nudd to the shop and Gerwyn caught her to him.

"Soon, I will be with you again," he promised, kissed her hard and was gone.

She followed him with her eyes until he was out of sight in the crowded roadway, imagining him rounding the castle palisades to take the road to the ferry. Coracles waited at the water's edge, shells of wicker covered with hides caked thickly with rendered fat. For a copper coin a ferryman would row Gerwyn across the mouth of the stream leading into the Cleddau, landing him below the priory walls and making the journey to the tannery an easy walk.

Perhaps Mabli was right, Manon mused. Gerwyn's night-mares had gradually lessened as he laid to rest ghosts from the past. A worm of a thought wriggled in her head. Was that the reason Gerwyn had gone so cheerfully? Could it have been he had decided to face his fears and defeat them?

Manon shivered, then shook herself, inwardly scolding such a weakness when there was much to be done. First, Kamal had to be consulted as to what Old Twm and Rhodri should cut and stitch. Fine clothing would still be needed by the local cracach as well as for those who longed to copy the rich ones. Farmers would find coin for well-shaped leathers to keep a man dry in the rain keeping the country-side green and fertile. Their wives needed aprons of leather for the hard work of a farm which was women's duty, as well as boots tough enough to stand tearing by the rab, stone which appeared from layers under the soil and wore out flimsy covers on the feet as it shredded wooden ploughs.

"Gwen? Look to Dybion, will you? I must be in the workshop." Manon was thoughtful as she walked the short distance from the shop. She would miss Nest's visits and there would be great changes in the town, yet she could not subdue a tremor of excitement at what was to come.

The first ship of the Constable's fleet rounded the headland and caught the wind, sailing westward along the broad reach of the River Cleddau. The shire reeve turned to his men ranked at the water's edge and raised a hand in a brief salute.

"When you have seen off the rest of the craft, report to me – and what is his name? The one who is always with you, like a hungry dog?" he asked the most senior of them.

Fulke was used to the Constable's temper and Geoffrey's speed of orders, coming to accept neither man wasted words. This Roger fitzHugh was different in the flash of his kingfisher clothes and the haughty way he held himself. The Constable's ansel ignored the sneer and implied insult.

"Leon, sir."

"Really. Well, with the Constable gone we must deploy our strength where it is most needed. Sir Gerald left strict orders – which I will have carried out my way! Mine! Do I make myself clear?" Roger had meant to sound in command and was annoyed his voice rose in an excited squeak.

"Aye, sir," Fulke said with an attempt at deference, watching the young man strut his way from the quay and back to importance. "What is the fool up to now?" he asked himself quietly, careful no one else heard. Fulke was uneasy. A plain, long-faced man, his brows moved into a frowning scowl. "We will know soon enough," he muttered as he saluted the captain of the last ship to leave the quayside for Cilgerran.

The walk to the castle was a short one but the steepness of the climb had Roger fitzHugh gasping for breath. He waited at the castle gate, apparently watching the town, as he regained his breath and his composure. Anyone who approached him met with a dismissive gesture as he hurried to the kitchens.

"Only the breasts of the chickens," he insisted to a bemused cook. The freshest butter was to be used, Roger licking his lips as he ordered a white wine as the cooking liquor into which would be thrown a little garlic and perhaps wild thyme. "Present the dish when it is ready, with crusty, well-risen wheaten bread."

The prospect of decent food at last cheered the shire reeve as he surveyed his store of clothes. A silky shirt and a green velvet tunic with a wide band of silver embroidery at neck and sleeve edge held his attention and gave him pleasure as he slid them over his head.

Garbed at last as he chose Roger fitzHugh went towards the assembly in the great hall and installed himself in the carved chair Sir Gerald used. He hooked a finger at the leader of the Constable's guard. "Fulke. Carew Castle – it concerns me greatly. With its owner known to be absent, along with many of her guards, it will be a temptation to raiders – far too easy for them to reach it silently by boat at night. I am putting you in charge of its defences and I want vigilance, day and night."

Fulke took a step towards the dais which raised the shire reeve above lesser men. "Sir Gerald –"

"Is no longer here." There was no mistaking menace in the soft, boyish voice. "Take Leon with you. He will be good company in the long hours."

The stalwart soldier flushed and would have defended his friendship but he saw a blossoming of power in the new shire reeve and stilled his tongue.

"Give your keys and your accommodation to Brede. He will need them for the work he is to do."

"Brede? He is no soldier, nor has he had the training the work will demand of him."

Roger fitzHugh's eyes narrowed. "He is most suitable, Fulke. Unlike you he takes my orders without question. Be

102

gone within the hour and mark my words – I do not expect to see you in Pembroke, castle or town, again."

"Mistress."

Kamal was frightened and an iciness squeezed Manon's heart. For two days she had been uneasy for no reason. Something was wrong and she was afraid to ask for the truth.

"Mistress, Myrddin's son. He comes for the master."

"Tell him he is at the tannery."

"No, mistress. They look for him there – and the farm where the black sister lives. Men at tannery need him so Myrddin send son. He must come here and get master to go to tannery."

Manon closed her eyes as terror swept through her, swaying her where she stood. "Oh, God!" she whispered. "Please God, no!"

It was Gwen who moved. She sent Kamal to fetch any friend of Gerwyn's he could find, leaving her to hold Manon tightly, persuade her to sit by the fire, its warmth easing her shaking.

"I must find him, Gwen."

"We will. Now, you stay here and get warm. You are no use to anyone, shivering as you are."

Her mistress was still chilled, rocking in mute misery as one man, two, three, crowded into the kitchen. They clutched caps, twisting them until they could find words for the stricken woman.

"I have a horse," one said.

"And I," from another.

It was agreed they would ride to the tannery. When they left, more men came, groups of them agreeing where to hunt for their missing friend. The kitchen was not empty for long, Roger fitzHugh striding in.

"Mistress Manon, it is grave news I have heard. Be sure my men will do all they can to return your husband safely to you. " His Welsh was hesitant, awkward. "Gerwyn is a fine tanner, very fine. We may not afford his loss, even for one day. Tell me, when was it you last saw him?"

Manon forced herself to speak calmly. "Two days ago he went to the tannery."

"He was to sleep at home that night?"

She shook her head. "Gerwyn was to stay with his sister at the farm nearby. He sleeps there when he is not able to be back in Pembroke by curfew."

"And there has been no sign of him, here in town, since he left that morning?"

"None."

"Were there many hides waiting for him in the tannery, do you know?"

"No fresh ones, he told me. One of the men was to be married and Gerwyn had given all his workers his consent to be at the merrymaking. 'No point expecting good work out of them when they all have thick heads from the beer'. He said they could return after the Sabbath."

"Why would he be there on his own?"

"Gerwyn likes time alone with his pits. He brews herbs for new dyes and rubs seeds and barks to find oils for leathers to make them wear well. It is not easy to do when the men are working. 'Always someone wanting me', he would say."

"When we find him, ma dame, he can say it again."

Manon bowed her head as tears flowed too quickly for her to control. The children had caught the smell of fear and Heledd crept to the shelter of her mother as Rhodri, white-faced and erect, stood at Manon's shoulder, determined to protect her from any further harm.

The shire reeve bowed in the Frankish way to a lady and left Manon, hoping he had sounded convinced of success. Privately, he had his suspicions. The tanner was a handsome, lusty man. He was likely to be bedded with some young girl while his wife grieved for him.

Roger fitzHugh was in need of new boots and only the

missing tanner could produce leather good enough for his tastes. The shire reeve had his weaknesses but he had given his word Gerwyn would be found. Leaving enough men to patrol Pembroke he rode with five troopers to the tannery. There, he questioned Gerwyn's workmen, shivering as they waited in the stench from the pits. Unable to work or be paid in their master's absence, they had hunted through the woods for their master. The shire reeve made them search again, this time aided and driven by his men on horseback while Roger fitzHugh rode to the farm and the unpleasant black-clad shape of Gerwyn's sister. He found Non scolding a serving girl.

"No, I have not seen him!" the sister screeched at the shire reeve, then scowled at him. "My brother was supposed to be here two days ago – I had a task for him in the house. Leather I must have to seal off the wall of a bedspace and he has not brought it! Am I to freeze to death because the stupid girl he married is unable to keep him in her bed?"

"You think he is with a woman?"

"Not if he has any sense – but then what man has?"

Her own man crept about in her shadow and would have disappeared but the shire reeve spotted the movement in the dim kitchen.

"Have you see Gerwyn?" was demanded of Iolo.

"No, sir." It was a quiet voice, careful not to give offence, like the small man in a frayed grey tunic belted around a thin waist. He kept his head bent, his eyes averted, as greying hair wisped to his shoulders and his thin beard quivered. "I was in Pembroke last Wednesday and I saw him in the market."

"And not since?"

"No, sir," Iolo said and his beard waggled as he shook his head.

Roger fitzHugh set his men to ride the paths through the woods between the farm and the tannery, orders to watch for even the smallest sign of a disturbance ringing in their ears. The light of the short day was already beginning to fade when they met again at the tannery.

"Is there anywhere we have not explored?" Roger fitz-Hugh demanded of all the searchers gathered in front of him.

Wherever he looked, heads were being shaken hard, giving him an answer he did not want. The shire reeve was annoyed. Not only must he wait for his boots but when the Constable next visited Pembroke he would expect his expert tanner in his place and working.

"All of you, start again," he shouted. "Gerwyn must be here."

As his men and the labourers moved off in a tired straggle the shire reeve went to an exhausted Myrddin, sitting on a fallen tree.

"You work here even though you are old?" he asked the man wizened with years and the pain of his joints.

"Aye, sir. Gerwyn trusted me."

"Was there anyone employed here he could not trust?"

"No, sir – and yet . . ."

"Explain yourself."

Slowly, Myrddin told of the missing hides, then the copied sticks.

"If we get the sticks from the shed and compare them –"

"No good, sir. I looked for them when I first got here but they were gone. I thought Gerwyn must have them – until I knew he was lost."

"Before this, had the thieving stopped?"

"Aye, sir, when Gerwyn had me sit and watch all that went on. Lately, I have been doing it at night, instead of when the men are working."

"Why?"

Myrddin pulled at his chin, twisting whitened hairs between his fingers. "He thought it was when hides might be taken."

"You have been here every night?"

"Indeed I have, sir. Nothing to see," he said slowly.

"To hear?"

"Maybe. I told Gerwyn there were rustlings in the wood and he made me stay home the night of the wedding, said he would watch here, in my place."

"I begin to see. A thief might have come and been surprised by Gerwyn."

Myrddin was stiff in all his joints but he managed to shake his head. "No way! If that had happened the rogue would be lying somewhere handy, covered in bruises and with a very sore head. Gerwyn is not a man to anger."

"I agree. So, no thief, no Gerwyn." The shire reeve looked around at the dark woods, the sheds of the tannery, the pits for treating the hides. "You have watched the search, Myrddin. Has any place been ignored?"

Myrddin frowned and considered with great effort, pulling at his chin and scratching a scalp thinly coated with white hair. "Only place is the dung pit but it is as it should be. No need for the cover to be moved with no fresh hides last week."

The shire reeve walked towards the unpleasantness of the dung pit. All useable dung was collected from Pembroke and with a small boat, one of Gerwyn's workers regularly moved all the ordure from privies and roadways to the tannery, resulting in a stew of decay which offended the nose and caused eyes to water.

Roger fitzHugh hesitated before he gave the order. The wooden cover which kept out rain was lifted and put to one side. Holding his breath the shire reeve peered into the murkiness of the reeking liquid which held the hairs and wool from hides soaked in its vileness. As he watched, the mess stirred. There were bubbles and a hand floated into view.

"Here!" he shouted, stepping back from horror.

Myrddin limped towards him, men came running, gasping with the fear of what they must soon see. All had hoped to find Gerwyn alive and many already wiped away tears. They stood round the pit, keening their grief as they saw what was left of Gerwyn float upwards. With great gentleness the men who had worked for him lifted his body from the pit. Some ran for buckets of water from the river to wash the corpse clean and as the freshness sluiced away the mess they could see the dung pit had done its job well. Thick, springing curls had gone, only small patches left in odd places. The bare face was of a man asleep.

The shire reeve cleared his throat of its choking. "Turn him over," he ordered quietly.

Again, there was gentleness and more fresh water as a kindness to a man so well regarded.

"You, with the light," Roger fitzHugh pointed. "Bring it here."

A flaming torch illumined the dung pit, its recent inhabitant lying in a pool of water, his sodden tunic twisted high about his chest. Gerwyn had been a good tanner. His methods ensured the dung pit exposed how he had died, the back of his head crushed and crackled like the shell of a hen's egg.

With so much talk of Gerwyn's death, few in Pembroke noticed the changes occurring in their lives. They came slowly as Brede and Rolf strolled the road from the castle during the dark hours of couvre feu. Any man or woman they met was stopped, handled roughly and searched. Coins found were 'confiscated' and tucked away in Brede's pouch. Rolf smiled at the victims, punching them about the body where no bruises would show as Brede promised worse to come should any word of the encounter slip out.

All that did trickle into the town was a growing sense of unease and the beginnings of great fear.

Manon was as a sleepwalker, eyes wide, seeing nothing. The unknown terror gripping her had become a reality in which only her children had any meaning. Slowly, so slowly, she held out her arms to Rhodri and Heledd and they crept into a familiar shelter, too frightened to speak or even to cry. On Gwen's shoulder Dybion smiled for a while, then whimpered quietly to himself.

The kitchen was crowded, more men and women trying to push their way to Manon. A tearful Buddyg hugged her. Ceinwen was a grasp, a gentle whisper, while Kamal and Nudd stood in the doorway, fingers tugging at their clothes. They were silent yet Manon understood their misery. Still in his sheepskins, Myrddin knelt to tell her in a gruff voice the loss he and Gerwyn's men shared with her. Countless faces she did not know loomed in front of her, spoke and disappeared again. Ithel took the chance to stand near enough for Manon to smell the mustiness of thick velvet. He leaned close yet she barely heard his words or felt the touch of his hand.

Grief was foreign to Roger fitzHugh, convinced the tanner's wife must have answers to his questions. Manon was bemused by the strangeness of his Welsh words, doing the best she could to be courteous until Gwen's voice, harsh with her own sadness, challenged the shire reeve to let her mistress grieve in peace.

"Gerwyn was struck at least one blow from behind. It was murder," he shouted at the fiery servant.

'Murder' was the only word Manon heard. It added to the horror in her mind, echoing again and again, becoming louder, until she put her hands over her ears to shut out Hell's tocsin. It's ringing deafened her as darkness whirled and encroached.

"Come now, Mistress Manon. A sip of this will help."

She knew the husky sounds. They held kindness yet she struggled to escape the supporting hands. Gwen's anxious face swam in front of her and Manon reached out.

"Do as he says," Gwen urged. "The spirit may lose men their wits but it surely helps a woman keep hers."

Obediently, Manon sipped from the cup held at her lips by Cynfan. The liquid soothed at first, its cold trickle welcome. Next moment she was gasping, struggling to breathe.

"It would seem I have come in time," a loud voice declared. "My brother newly-dead and his wife drunk in the arms of another man!"

Cynfan stood and faced Non, his fingers curling into two huge fists he held rigid with difficulty. "Hold your tongue, woman! As you say, your own brother is killed and all you can do is berate a loving wife when she is widowed."

"I can smell the spirits!" Non insisted. "Yet another filth brought to us in abundance by the Franks!"

"Then you have my word, lady. Should you swoon lifeless as did Mistress Manon, I will never try to rouse you."

Non's upper lip twisted in a sneer. "It is as I thought. You are one of her men."

Manon gasped and Gwen put a hand on Cynfan, his reddening cheeks and rising fists warning of the threat to Non.

"Thought?" Cynfan spluttered. "You old witch! If you have any thoughts at all be sure they have come straight from Satan's own privy!"

The insignificance who was her husband moved towards Cynfan but Non was calling on God for strength and making the sign of the cross with such extravagant gestures, Iolo was buffeted backwards and into silence by flailing black wool.

The baker bent his head to Manon. "Do you want her here, mistress?" he asked so softly only she heard. He saw the slight shake of her head and was satisfied.

Cynfan glared at Non. "Get you gone from this place! Gerwyn was a good man and should be mourned with decency. His wife and children need peace in the loving home they shared with him."

Murmurs of support for Cynfan's words swirled around Non and for once, she hesitated.

"It is almost time for curfew," she said, unable to say the Frankish words properly. "Where am I to go?"

Cynfan was implacable. "If you are courteous to the

110

reeve's men they will let you find space in a pot-house. Pembroke has many."

"Allow me to help," a quiet voice said in smooth Welsh from a distant part of Deheubarth.

Non turned to Ithel, the sheen of his sable velvet gleaming in the firelight. Her eyes widened, were cunning. She knew this man had wealth. "How can you?" she wanted to know.

"I have properties in the town. One came my way this very day and has no occupants. If the reeve is willing I will send a woman to make it ready for you – and your husband."

"I see," Non said and nodded, her mouth tight and smug. "Another of her men."

"I do not have that good fortune," Ithel told her, "but I had great respect for Gerwyn and I would like to think of myself as a friend of this sad family. If I can add a little comfort for Gerwyn's sister . . ."

Non had heard stories of Ithel's way of trading. She suspected him of wealth second only to that of the Lady Nest and had no hesitation in accepting his offer, not seeing the slightest of acknowledgements passing between Cynfan and Ithel. Manon would have her peace.

It was not to be. The shire reeve bowed Non away from Manon and her children, waved his hand to clear the room of unnecessary people, then began his questioning again. When had Manon last seen her husband? Was he concerned about his shop? His tannery? The men he employed?

Haltingly, Manon spoke of the thefts, notched sticks, Myrddin's vigils. At last she whispered the unease she had sensed in Gerwyn.

"You think he believed the tannery was to be robbed again?"

"Perhaps."

"Did he have reason to fear the robbers?"

"I do not know – there was something." She shook her head to clear its confusion. "He never spoke of it."

111

Manon was exhausted and the shire reeve knew she could be of no further help. He bowed over her hand as he had been taught and Roger fitzHugh's sense of loss was real. He might associate Manon with the ridicule he had endured when first in Pembroke but Gerwyn supplied fine leather-wear at such reasonable costs an ambitious man could easily be of good appearance.

Mabli came and she was strong arms and a warm bosom against which to surrender. Her murmurs soothed Manon but even Mabli must leave. "The curfew," she whispered, "and David has a fever. It is lessening but I must return to him."

Before Mabli left she gave Gwen two small vials. There were strict instructions as to the number of drops. One for Dybion, two for Heledd, three for Rhodri from the tiny stoppered flask tied with a wisp of linen. The other held oblivion for Manon, as much as she needed.

"Mind you get sleep yourself," Mabli insisted to Gwen. "You have your own sorrow and you will be much needed in the morning."

"How will she manage?" Gwen whispered. "He was her life."

"As is the good Lord. To lose as she has done is to be out in a storm naked, not even a shred of skin to keep off the worst deluge. Only God and time can allow the growth which numbs the pain. Your mistress has already endured much hardship, she is used to growing new skin. Just let her sleep all she can."

When the doors had been barred for the night, Gwen brought Dybion to his mother, Rhodri and Heledd standing close. The warmth of their little bodies was of this world and solaced as Manon fed the baby his sops, her tears making it hard for her to see him clearly. Heledd pressed her little face against her mother's and Manon felt the child's wetness on her own cheek. Rhodri tried hard to be a man, as all the visitors said he must, but he cried too and Gwen was glad. Grief without tears took too long to heal, she thought as she poured Mabli's liquid into Manon's cup.

Decently washed and shrouded, Gerwyn lay coffined in the castle chapel, a mark of respect to a man regarded so highly in Pembroke. Manon and her children prayed beside him, winter greenery culled by Nudd lying on the wood above him. In Manon there was no life, exhausted as she was by crying and watching everlasting nights of darkness turn to light but Mabli's drops had achieved their purpose. Gerwyn's family faced the agony of his funeral with mute acceptance.

The journey to the graveyard was slow, Gerwyn carried through a host of mourners who had valued him when he lived. The priest was a man grown old in the ways of the native church and for Manon there was the comfort of her own language only the Franks and a few Flemings could not understand.

Escorting the mourners was a troop of men led by Brede, each with his bow slung and his hand above his sword. They behaved decently but when the men from the tannery had buried their master, they were marched under guard, back to the confines of Pembroke's castle.

"What is happening, Myrddin?" Manon asked in a voice little more than a whisper.

He alone had been permitted to be free. "The shire reeve is sure one of our men killed Gerwyn."

"God in heaven! Why?"

"It must be one of them stealing, so he reckons in his wisdom, and that man must have done for the master. All are to be kept locked away until the bastard son of fitzHugh has the truth."

"Could he be right?"

Myrddin shook his white head, wincing with pain as he shuffled from one foot to another to ease his joints. "No, mistress. Your man had me watching them like a hawk. Mind you, someone knew the best hides to take, and when to take them, but I swear on my life it was a stranger. All the men the shire reeve holds were at the wedding and half Pembroke ready to bear witness."

"If it is so, the men should be freed. When will the shire reeve release them?"

"God only knows, mistress! He is driving everyone hard and says he will have answers soon. Every day he rides to the tannery and searches the ground, the bushes, the pits."

"He has found nothing?"

"What is there? The day we found Gerwyn the tanners still had sore heads from the wedding. They were stumbling all over the place so it is of no use for the reeve and his men to look for tracks. Then we sluiced the master with bucket after bucket of water and all around the dung pit was a quagmire. If there had been any signs we washed them all away, Gerwyn's needs coming first. No, Roger fitzHugh is determined he will have the name of the killer – and soon."

"Gerwyn always said of the man he was very eager to improve his lot."

"Aye, he is that, and it is in him to do it the Frankish way – have every man suspect and beaten senseless, then declare some poor soul guilty and hanging at the end of a rope before Sir Gerald returns."

Manon put out her hands to the old man and he gripped them tightly, imbuing her with his warmth and strength as best he could. "Oh, Myrddin, our lives changed the day the Constable sailed away with his family. I pray nightly for his return."

"Amen to that, mistress."

Days were an unending succession of miseries. Friends came and went, even Non, at Ithel's urging, forcing herself to be pleasant when in her dead brother's home. Mabli walked daily to the leather shop to inspect Manon and her children, trusting Gwen to dose her mistress as directed. Manon knew they conspired but was too weary to resist, even grateful for the calm they induced in her which in turn helped the children accept their loss.

Gradually, Mabli lessened the strength of the potions and Manon turned her mind to the work which must be done if they were all to survive. It did not happen quickly but Mabli and Gwen nodded with satisfaction and relief as they saw her natural determination emerge from the shadows.

Not all were as patient. Roger fitzHugh fumed and strutted about his business. He had been unable to name the murderer and it became necessary to release Gerwyn's men. He was not so much obeying King Henry's law as realising Pembroke, and in particular the castle and himself, needed a continuing supply of stout leather. The shire reeve shrugged his shoulders and Manon was asked to keep the tannery working.

Ready at last to accept the extra responsibility, she decided Myrddin was to be in charge. The men went back to the pits, grateful their families need no longer starve with money being paid again. It was enough to tempt thieves and one attempt to get a pouch of coin to Myrddin ended with the messenger robbed and nursing a broken head.

"Let me do this small thing for you, Mistress Manon," the baker said as he offered to carry the men's wages. "Rogues round Pembroke know to leave me alone."

"You are kind, Cynfan, and mean well but I do not want you in danger."

"Have no fear. The good Lord keeps me safe and my cudgel sees God's will is done. Gerwyn never had trouble, did he?"

"No, God be praised. He always said any who stole from him would end up in the tanning pits with a sore head."

The words had been spoken lightly but Manon gasped, her face paling, as she realised what she had said. The air echoed with her words until Cynfan bent to her.

"Did Gerwyn have anyone in mind?" he asked.

"I did not think so when he said that . . ."

"Yet he might have seen someone in the trees on such a journey?"

She nodded slowly. "There were times since St Michael's mass I knew he was troubled but he would never tell me, however much I tried to persuade him. Gerwyn did not want me to worry when he was away from home."

"Should you tell the shire reeve, mistress?"

"Why? So he can gather even more men into the castle and beat them until their wits are gone? It is all he understands."

Manon trudged wearily through each day of endless, empty hours. Gwen tried hard to persuade her mistress to eat, only succeeding when the children were at table and Manon must show them a good example. In time sorrow sculpted flesh from her bones, exposing a woman even lovelier than before.

At last Manon heeded Myrddin's advice and when Roger fitzHugh came to the shop she spoke to him of Gerwyn's unease before his death. It made little difference to the shire reeve. He assured her every possible idea had been thoroughly investigated. "Indeed," he told her, "hardly a man in Pembroke has not been brought to the castle to be questioned."

It was well known many had been thrashed into unconsciousness and yet there was still no hint of a culprit. Gossip fed and grew in the cold town and the beershops, Ithel learning of Cynfan's journeys to the tannery. The usurer determined to be of assistance to the beautiful widow and made his way past the leather shop and into her kitchen.

"I have had many talks with your sister, Non," he told her as she stood with Heledd clutching her skirt.

"It was generous of you to give her shelter, sir. I trust she has made you aware of your gratitude – as I do mine?"

"Of course," Ithel said and smiled, trying to remember if Non had ever used a word of thanks. "She did give me a notion. As you can imagine, she talked long of your plight – a husband gone and children to raise alone. She also talked much of the farm near the tannery and how insecure she feels there."

Manon bent her head to hide her surprise and straightened Heledd's kerchief with great care.

"Is that why you have come? On Non's behalf?"

No, mistress. It is you I would aid – as much as it is in my power."

Manon heard something in the man's voice which made her wary. "You are well-meant, sir."

"It came to me I should buy the farm from you – for a good price, of course. You would have a reasonable sum to keep your children in comfort, although you would not have the rent from the farm."

For the first time in the dark days Manon smiled. "If it were just the rent, sir," she said and felt mischief begin to bubble.

"What do you mean?"

"Non has always refused to pay rent. She believes she may make the farm her home, without payment or dues of any kind and whatever the land earns is hers and hers alone."

In the warmth of the kitchen Ithel was deadly pale and it was some time before he could trust himself to speak. "You said 'If it were only the rent'?"

"Of course. Were that so, I would gain much silver where none had been forthcoming before but I am not free to sell the farm."

"Not free? Surely it is yours, to do with as you please?"

"The farm by the tannery and the other near Lamphey are for my brothers."

Ithel hesitated for a moment, then assumed an expression of sympathy. "I was told you have no kin now but Mistress Non."

117

Manon sighed and told him how she had arranged her father's money, the parchment on which she had made her mark. "I regard only the leather shop as my share."

"If your brothers are dead?"

"I do not trade in 'ifs', sir. Until I have proof they no longer live I will keep the farms ready for them."

Colour began to return to Ithel's cheeks and he laid fingers firmly on his lips to end their quivering. It had been a very narrow escape for his silver.

"You are right, mistress. With your belief and with the farms, your brothers still have breath in them and are in God's good care."

The weather changed, clear skies ending the rain and a steady, bitter wind penetrated every chink, drying all it reached. Early one market day Manon watched Gwen feed the fire, flames lighting the tiredness in a woman already exhausted before the day had properly begun.

"Gwen, you sit by the fire and sleep there if you can. Dybion will not wake for a while so Heledd and I will do the marketing and Rhodri can come with us to carry the basket."

Manon would listen to no argument, Heledd running with an old cloak of her mother's to wrap around Gwen while Nudd stood at the door of the kitchen, ready to keep out any who would wake his friend.

Outside in the roadway the early air was bracing. Manon shivered in the weak sunshine as she wrapped Heledd's cloak tightly about the child and bid Rhodri hurry. They had been out of the house so little since Gerwyn's death it was a strange walk to the stalls at the end of town. Heledd chattered as she helped her mother choose the best of the dried peas, onions loose in a basket, a big cabbage. Only when the child's steps slowed and she yawned did Manon give in to her own weakness. Smiling at Rhodri who was struggling to be the man everyone said he must now be, Manon and her children walked home. It was quiet in the town that early in the day until men came running from the castle end of town.

Manon drew the children into the shelter of a shop deserted for the winter. She shivered but not from the cold, sensing danger. Had it happened already or was it to come? The men ran past, shouting as they went and Manon's blood froze. One man was slower than the rest. He saw Manon, her face familiar, and bellowed his dreadful news at her, tears streaming from him as he spoke. When he had gone Manon picked up Heledd and grasped Rhodri's shoulder as she hurried her children to the safety of their home.

Gwen woke as they tumbled into the kitchen. She saw Manon's awful pallor and fear on the children's faces.

"In the name of God, mistress!"

Manon made the sign of the cross and prayed a moment before she turned to face a dazed and frightened Gwen. "The new castle."

Gwen shook her head to clear it of sleep. "Sir Gerald's? In Emlyn?"

"Aye, burned to the ground," Manon said and sank on a stool, Heledd crowding in against her.

Gwen was horrified. "Please God, no! Are they all dead?"

"Better they had perished," Manon said and her tears began.

"What could be worse?"

"It was Owain. He and his men attacked the castle at night. They are gone off with Nest and the all children."

Sleep still held Gwen and she was slow in understanding the terrible news. "Sir Gerald?"

"Escaped. It is said his wife insisted."

"You mean he left her to face his enemy while he saved his own skin?" Gwen could not believe it of any man, above all the Constable.

"No, Gwen, you do not understand. I know what Nest must have been thinking as the fire took hold. Her children were only safe if their father lived."

119

"Never! How can that be? After all the tales of his courage the Frank is a coward!"

"Nest spoke of such a thing happening and I knew she was right. When we talked we never dreamed it might happen – nor so soon."

"There is no sense in it."

"Oh, yes there is," Manon said softly, bitterly. "Sir Gerald dead, what might happen to Nest? She could be married out of hand and against her will to any man who wanted her body, her blood line – and half Wales. Remember, she is the daughter of King Rhys and Queen Gwladus. Any child sired on her must command loyalty from us all."

"At least she would still be alive," Gwen said.

"And her children by Sir Gerald? They would be a hindrance to Owain – he might claim they were in his way. You know Owain, Gwen. If you were him what would you do with the young ones Nest has already birthed? Think of William and Maurice! Little Angharad! What would happen to them?"

"God in heaven! What are you saying? Owain would kill them all?"

Manon had no doubts. "We have heard no good of the man and murdering children is no new sport for him. With Sir Gerald dead, his sons would soon follow him, but if the Constable lived, no forced marriage to Nest would be a true one in the eyes of the King's law – or God's."

Gwen was horrified. "You say the princess talked of all this?"

Manon sighed. "Yes, Nest did. It was light-hearted at the time but I understood her fears." Her own man gone, she realised she, too, was vulnerable to other men's ambitions.

"Then may the good Lord keep her safe."

"Amen to that!"

The two women fell to their knees and prayed, Heledd looking to Rhodri for reassurance. Manon and Gwen were silent, their pleading to God fervent. They had known too many women whose lives had been ended by a careless sword or a ravaging fire started by raiders.

"Sweet Jesus! One of the children is not of the princess' blood," Gwen whispered.

Manon had forgotten the boy. "William, called the bastard." She made the sign of the cross and mouthed a prayer for his safety.

"What will become of him?" Gwen wondered.

Manon wept as she thought of Ninian's grandson. "God only knows, Gwen – and only God can know."

Chapter Seven

The earth shook. There was shouting, screaming, a sound as of thunder and Manon covered with her cloak the food she had bought at market. Almost deafened, she felt the rush of wind as a troop of hauberked horsemen galloped past on their way to the castle. The leader was not a young man, the features Manon could see under his helmet were grim, angry. Sir Odo de Barri, the Frank who had built a castle at Manorbier, was a familiar sight in Pembroke. Behind him was a solid body of men on the finest destriers, knights to the fore and soldiers at the rear, each of them helmeted, armed and wearing a surcoat with the emblem of the de Barris.

Her basket undamaged and free of dirt and stones flung up by flying hooves, Manon returned home.

Gwen was worried. "You are pale, mistress! What was amiss?"

"Did you hear them? The horses?"

"Those great beasts the Franks ride? Enough to wake the dead! Were you harmed?"

Manon shook her head and Gwen lifted the basket on to the table for her.

"You found some good butter, then. From the farm out towards the warren?" Gwen asked, referring to the ring of stone encircling a patch of green grazing for the plump hare-like creatures the Franks had brought with them to breed for winter food.

"It is sweet grass so near the sea." Manon watched Gwen unpack the eggs, and leeks. "Sir Odo and the men with him, they scared me, Gwen."

"Then you were in danger from them?"

"No, not me. Owain is the one with cause to be afraid. They are ready for war and did not look the men to settle for less than his head."

"The fool deserves it!"

"Maybe he does, Gwen, but when men like Sir Gerald and Sir Odo ride out who else will die besides Owain?"

The women were silent, mourning deaths to come then Gwen became brisk. "We have become soft living here in the safety of Pembroke. There has been time for us to get used to living in peace."

Manon did not move, uneasy thoughts still holding her. "Until Owain failed to curb his lust and cast aside peace as a spoilt child discards precious food," she said quietly and found it hard to hide her trembling from Gwen.

The sight of the armed men determined on battle had raised such fear in Manon. Now more than ever she longed for the strength of Gerwyn's arms about her. He should be here, protecting his family, making each day safe for Dybion and Heledd and Rhodri. With unrest in the town the shop could be attacked and stripped of all its goods.

Bereft, Manon yearned for Gerwyn but she was alone and there was no comfort.

Sir Odo was not the only Frank to ride to Pembroke with his men. From castles at Carew, Tenby, Narberth, horsemen drove spurs into the sides of their mounts. Gerald de Windsor was a man of battle and would need an army behind him in his search for the man who had wantonly ripped his wife and children away from him. Unless an example was made of this callous raider, no man, woman or child would be safe in its bed.

Pembroke was seething with armed men, travellers, traders, as well as the curious wanting news or seeking an opportunity to steal. Daily, Gwen stood guard in the shop while Rhodri ran like a mad thing, carrying harness to be stitched, fresh gloves with stout gauntlets, capes to keep out the rain. In the workshop Kamal cut and Old Twm stitched long into the night, Manon keeping candles and flares alight for them to see as best they could and helping Gwen feed them bread and meat which they ate at their benches.

Everyone walking into the leather shop had a different tale to tell, rumour feeding on gossip and flying in the wind. It was Ugo who brought them true word of Sir Gerald.

"He has already gone north. A second troop of knights and soldiers follow in the morning."

"Rhodri saw horses being carried across the river by ship," Manon said.

"It is the quickest way and I must get another cargo of horses on their way as soon as I have the strongest leather for their reins, mistress."

"Sir Gerald?"

Lines in Ugo's face had deepened with exhaustion. "He is a man possessed of one thought – the death of Owain."

"Then the stories are true? It was Owain who raided?"

"The princess herself recognised him when she rose in the night to the children – one was coughing badly. Two days before the attack the hellhound had been to the new castle. He told Sir Gerald he must see for himself his cousin who was said to be the most beautiful woman in Wales. Then Owain returned in the dead of night to make away with her – and all the children."

Manon shuddered. "Nest and Owain are close kin and both claim descent from Hywel Dda. They have his blood."

"Blood? It was shed in plenty at Cenarth Bychan." Manon had never seen the Fleming so grim. "Many friends of mine died there by the sword and by fire, even the monk who was with the family."

"Yet Nest made sure Sir Gerald got away with his life," Manon said softly.

"His lady would not have him stay and fight and her reasons must have convinced him. I have fought beside the Frank. He has great courage. Here, in Pembroke, his defence of the castle against Owain's father, Cadwgan, is witness enough to his bravery. Times without number he withstood attack, I have been told."

Manon nodded. "His daring acts are already part of the town's legends."

"Can you believe such a man would be willing to leave his children – four of them, remember – to the likes of Owain? And his wife? He has said he heard her screaming as Owain took her in her bed, there in the middle of the slaughter."

"Where was Sir Gerald?"

"In the sluice leading from the privy. It was the princess who thought of it and he must slide through the ordure to get outside the castle and away."

Manon had heard the stories and now knew them to be true. How desperate Nest must have been to send from her the one man prepared to fight to the death on her behalf.

"You say he has already gone north?"

"Aye, mistress. To find Owain and every man who was on that raid. They will all die."

In the emptied castle Roger fitzHugh sighed with relief and was glad he had freed all the men who could possibly have had a hand in Gerwyn's death. By sending them back to their work in the tannery and elsewhere he had helped speed the Franks, Flemings, Welshmen, who were going north to find and release the Constable's wife and his children. Busy in the north, Sir Gerald could spare no thoughts for Pembroke and its inhabitants.

Manon's days were filled with her children as well as work in the shop and the house behind it. Only at night, in the privacy of her bedspace, was there time to grieve for her murdered husband.

One thing cheered Manon. Ithel had become weary of Non's possession of his small property at the edge of the town. With the very air of the country around Pembroke heavy with unease he could rent out the shack for a good sum to a farmer and his family anxious to be near the safety of armed soldiers. Ithel had walked to see Non.

"Your home must sorely be in need of your good offices, mistress," he said as soon as the compliments of the day had been exchanged. "The beasts in your barn – they have been so long unattended by your husband. Who knows what disease has them in its grip?"

Iolo said nothing, his wary eyes following every tiny movement the usurer made. As always, he left the talking to Non.

She never failed him. "It is winter and little to be done, sir. There is time for me to visit my brother's grave and see his wife and children do not weaken and fail."

"Mistress Manon has many friends in the town who are anxious for her every need. I am sure she could spare you to your own duties."

"Never will I desert my brother's family in their hour of need, sir!" Non declared in a voice which made most men flinch. Certainly Iolo crept against the wall, trusting it strong enough to hold him.

"Need, mistress? You are wise to talk of such a thing. Cai ap Gwilliam is urgent to move his wife and their children to Pembroke and I have promised this house to him – when it is free."

"Rash of you," Non said and glared at her unwilling host. "You made it clear this was to be my home for as long as I chose."

Ithel could be smoothness itself. "Indeed it was, mistress,

but the day has come when these walls must earn their keep in rent."

The idea of paying out her own coin unnerved Non, almost as much as the thought of being distanced from Manon's money. "What is it you are trying to say?"

"Cai has silver ready. If you can better what he would give me –"

"Say no more!" Non shouted at him. "I leave this miserable hovel today! Iolo! Get the cart. We lie in our own bed this night."

Talk in the town still echoed with the name of Princess Nest, many licking their lips as they repeated the stories of her rape and kidnap. There were those who condemned the Constable for deserting his wife but wiser heads and mouths knew every fitzGerald, however young, would have died instantly by the sword had their sire stayed to be defeated.

Gossip flowed through Pembroke like a raging torrent, leaving fighting in its wake. As shire reeve, Roger fitzHugh controlled the town and its surrounding lands and was unwilling to allow violence to erupt at anyone's will but his own. He had his men patrolling every alleyway during the hours of daylight and taking the worst offenders they encountered to the stew of a prison in the castle. At night after couvre feu, the tramp of soldiers kept many awake as they achieved an uneasy peace. The shire reeve may have been satisfied with the efforts being made but he could not stop tongues wagging. Behind closed doors the arguments were bitter, fomenting like a boil readying itself to burst.

From all the whispering and shouting few facts emerged. Buddyg was a good source of information and Manon welcomed her visits which brought calmness and sanity.

"Mistress Mabli ensures Hywel knows all that is true. The baby David's health improves, thank God, and when Ceinwen goes to the castle to help with him she learns what news arrives there."

127

Her friend was relieved. "It will make more sense than we hear in the shop each day or among the stalls as I go to market."

"Aye, idiots are abroad in plenty. There is no doubt the Lady Nest was raped when she was taken and with Owain the man we know him to be, she has suffered every night since. To you and me such behaviour is a victor's sin against a helpless woman but to the men in the town . . .!"

"I know! At every turn you hear a man declaring it is no rape if it is by a Welshman. Owain is of good family and as such he has his rights, they say. How often I have heard it said it is the way of nature and far better than being bedded each night by a Frank? Who has the right to decide how and when a woman is to be violated?"

"Men! Not one worth the name needs to rape to get what he wants."

"Oh, Buddyg, you and I, we know what it is to be loved and by a real man, as has Nest. What must her life be like now? In fear for her children all her waking hours and under Owain each night. Is there no sign of her being found?"

"She and the children are supposed to be somewhere in Ceredigion, in a manor of Cadwgan's – at least it was Cadwgan's. Ceinwen heard King Henry was so enraged by what Owain has done to Nest and the insult to Gerald, his liege man, he has stripped Cadwgan of all his holdings."

"All?"

"Aye, every one. His manors and estates, the stud he prizes, even a town from which he draws much of his money in taxes. Cadwgan's present wife and mother of his two youngest sons is a Frank but that makes no matter. The father loses all because of Owain's crimes against the king and all those he holds dear."

Manon had her doubts. "Will his father's sufferings and loss be enough to make Owain release his captives?"

"Owain is a fool and Cadwgan clever, yet even he will

need time to persuade Owain to a sensible path if he is as besotted with the Lady Nest as everyone says."

Manon thought over what Gwen had said. "You know, Gwen, Cadwgan losing all his money and his precious horses – it will be urgent for him to discipline his son and get him to safety. Should he fail and Sir Gerald get to Owain first, the Constable will not sheath his sword until his enemy's blood reddens its length." Manon's lips tightened and her gentle eyes were angry. "May God give his arm the strength it needs."

Buddyg nodded her agreement as she watched her daughters play with Heledd and the baby. Dybion was growing fast and struggling to walk as did the girls. "The children who were taken, how can they survive?"

"I wonder." Manon pulled at her lower lip. "If Owain hurts even one of them I think he will find Nest's knife between his ribs."

"The princess? She would kill a man?"

"One who harmed her children? Think, Buddyg. If it were you?"

Buddyg's breath escaped in a long sigh. "You are right – and I would pray the good Lord's hand guided the blade."

In the midst of such uncertainty Manon learned more each day of the ways in which leather was prepared for use. She knew Bledri searched for fine dung from the town for the first pit at the tannery but was surprised when he told her, "Dog shit is the best for clearing hides of all hair." The wizened little man was making ready to row a coracle load of the harvest from Pembroke's privies and runnels. Manon shivered. She had seen how effective was Bledri's work when she first saw Gerwyn's murdered body.

At every turn Gwen made sure her mistress was aware how much knowledge Kamal had passed on to Gerwyn since the arab was given shelter. Centuries of secrets from far-off places were being used by Gerwyn's men, Gwen told her, as Nudd continued to scour the woods for tree bark

129

which seasoned and strengthened the hides. Then there was Kamal's skill with a knife, separating a good hide into the thinnest layers, each soft enough to grace the bodies and hands of ladies. His craftsmanship earned trade from as far away as Tenby and Carmarthen and Manon smiled at Gwen's interest. She had seen yearning in the dark eyes of the arab, as well as the tenderness Gwen showed him. They would make a fine pair one day.

Myrddin's visits were regular and useful, helping Manon learn the rhythm of work at the tannery. As the days passed she saw the old man's frown deepen.

"What is it worries you, Myrddin? Have there been more thefts?"

"No, mistress. The men – they work so hard and for so long each day I am fearful their weariness endangers them."

"Do you need more men?"

"Aye, mistress, but can you afford the wages?"

"Gerwyn would," she said gently and smiled, the old man relieved to see she did so and without tears.

"Then I know the very ones who will work well for you. Bledri's brother and Morgan's cousin."

"I remember them. Gerwyn liked them."

It was enough and Manon was pleased she could make decisions she knew would have pleased her husband. The disaster begun in the new castle in Emlyn had brought an unexpected increase in leather trade, beneficial to so many. She sighed as Myrddin left, and made her way to the workshop.

"Kamal, I am afraid for Nudd when he is in the woods," Manon said as a small force of soldiers passed the shop on their way to the castle. In the midst of the armoured men a threadbare wretch was being dragged screaming to his imprisonment. "Roger fitzHugh would show Nudd no mercy."

Kamal's smile did not reach his eyes. "Nudd's own hide is safe as long as he takes only bark from the trees and roots from the wayside. The shire reeve is our best customer for calfskin."

Hours dragged by, Manon filling them with work as best she could and finding comfort in her children's soft bodies as she held them close. Again and again she remembered the Gwaun valley and Nest her companion in happy days filled with sunshine and laughter. Marriage had brought them children and their lives had been as cups full to the brim but Gerwyn was gone, Nest herself a captive.

Manon centred her mind on Owain ap Cadwgan, the evil behind it all. The man's desire for his cousin had begun a chain of misery, each link forged in blood. In her dreams Gerwyn's death was linked to Owain. It made no sense but hour by hour Manon's anger grew until she could almost reach out and touch her hatred of Cadwgan's wilful son.

Gwen might not be content with the reason had she known but she was glad to see her young mistress gain colour as she took an even keener interest in the tannery and the shop. Only Non was not amused and she was a black-clad fury forcing her way into Manon's home one day.

"What are you thinking?" she demanded to know.

Manon lifted her head from the tunic she was mending for Heledd. Her unblinking gaze flustered Non. This was a new Manon, different, and Non was unsure how to proceed.

"I was told you had returned to the farm," Manon said calmly. "Why are you here?"

"The tannery –"

"Is none of your business." Manon bit the thread free of its darn.

"How dare you say that to me! Of course it is my business. My father began it –"

"And when he died it became Gerwyn's."

"May I remind you Gerwyn was my brother?"

131

"Yes, Non. Was. Now he is dead and I am the one who must make the decisions. It is not a situation I wanted but the tannery is my responsibility, not yours."

Non's features slid easily into a practised sneer. "What do you know of leather-making?"

Manon lifted her head and regarded Non, her gaze making the older woman uneasy. "Unlike you I use my eyes and ears – not my mouth. All the time we were married I listened to Gerwyn when he talked of his days spent at the tannery. He was proud of the leather he sold and ready to tell me all the details of its preparation."

"And that gives you the right to take on two more men?"

Manon stared at the unpleasantness that was Non. "I would rather Gerwyn had been alive to do so."

"My brother would have listened to me and not been so stupid. There is no need for extra men – it is a waste of money!"

Manon continued to gaze at her former sister by marriage. Once again she puzzled how Non and Gerwyn could have shared the same blood and yet be so different. "You speak as though you considered it your money. I wonder why?"

Non flushed, the redness flooding her cheeks unbecoming in such heavy features. "I am your kin. If anything happened to you . . ."

A cold smile on Manon's lips chilled the skin along Non's backbone. "Never, Non. It was Gerwyn's wish his son should have the tannery."

"Meurig? I know but –"

"Meurig will have it on his return. Until then I will use what workmen are necessary to provide this town with the leather it needs. Meurig will make his own choices when he is the master, as I am sure he will be one day. When he comes back to us he will be able to tell us all what made him leave his home, his father, his inheritance."

Non was made uneasy by Manon's words. "What are you suggesting?"

132

"Me? Nothing, Non – but it will be interesting to hear what Meurig has to tell us," she said quietly, each word burning into the older woman's mind until she sniffed her disgust and left Manon alone.

Roger fitzHugh's suffering began when the Constable sailed up river as he returned to Pembroke. The shire reeve's ears burned scarlet from the blistering Sir Gerald delivered, berating his reeve for the castle's dungeons and sheds filled with wretches guilty of trivial offences and obviously badly beaten.

"All this and yet no man to answer for the tanner's death?" Sir Gerald had bellowed for all to hear, minutes after he had arrived in the inner bailey. His list of complaints continued to ring in the cold air until the Constable stalked away to his supper and his bed.

For the younger man there was to be no relief from discomfort that night. Roger's bedspace was given over to the Constable's squire and the reeve must swathe himself in his cloak and seek warmth by the hearth in the great hall, his nearest companions the exhausted men who had sailed and rowed Sir Gerald south, lashed ever onwards by his impatient tongue. With them had come their fleas.

The new day might have augured well if ushered in with good food. In the wakeful hours of darkness Roger had thought lovingly of eggs beaten with herbs and cooked gently in foaming butter but he was to be disappointed. All eggs had been consumed by the Constable and Pembroke's reeve must settle for cold sheep roasted dry and tough. As he gnawed and spat, anger festered and he sought a quiet corner of the bailey. One face kept returning to haunt him, its beauty twisted by his hate.

"That damned whore!"

Roger fitzHugh strode to the edge of the compound where he could be alone and glimpse the river through gaps in the palisade. Tossing his bone to a skulking dog, he paced this way and that, remembering tales of Nest when she had been

133

at court, a cunning girl from the dark woods who used spells to bind a king's brother and hold him to her when he was crowned. Such a one taken against her will? The shire reeve's disdain was vented in spittle aimed at a clod of soil.

"King Henry married her off into exile and now the Constable loses her to an ignorant peasant calling himself a prince of this Devil-infested country," he muttered, careful no one could hear.

A flicker of reason was lit in the shire reeve. He had been well warned by his kinsman. 'Remember,' the bishop had said, 'the king trusts de Windsor to look after the Welsh woman and her children.'

"Her children?" Roger asked the air above him.

A seagull glided past him in search of food.

"Her children," he said again. "Is that why all the great men of this shire and all the others in Wales seek to drive this Owain to defeat and death?"

Roger remembered being told the king's whore had left court married to Sir Gerald and already with child. The young man picked at a spot on his chin. Was Sir Gerald its sire or did the babe carry royal blood before the wedding day? He wondered in silence. His kinsman had been right to urge caution. In this forgotten corner of the kingdom there was much to play for in a very dangerous game.

In the excited town, Manon was still worried by the possible theft of hides from the tannery. Myrddin assured her he had men about him he could trust to work well as he watched to make sure nothing went astray.

"At night, Myrddin? You must not oversee everyone all day and sit watch through the dark as well," Manon insisted.

Myrddin was grateful for Manon's concern. "My son, mistress. Anawrad is young and strong. May God help any thief who tries to rob us all again!"

"We have lost so much and yet the Constable has been robbed of all his treasures."

"Aye, a rich man and a Frank he may be but one who deserves our pity and our prayers, mistress."

"When does Sir Gerald leave?" she asked.

"On the morning tide, I heard." Myrddin shook his head. "Poor soul! He grieves for his family and his men say he does not sleep, driving himself hardest in the search for his lady and the young ones. Yet he has good friends. All the Franks who can sit a horse are with him as are many of our people the length and breadth of the old Dehaubarth. Be sure, Mistress, Owain will be discovered and crushed."

Spirits were high in the town. For too long the threat of a raid by Owain somewhere in the shire had everyone on edge. Now he was on the run, hunted like a diseased dog.

No thieves disturbed the work at the tannery. Good leather reached the shop and it was necessary for Manon to find another bootmaker to help Old Twm. Stock in the shop gradually grew as did sales to men who came and went in Pembroke while Sir Gerald and his allies hunted in the north.

The shire reeve returned to his duties with enthusiasm. Once again he could strut in his silks and velvets while his men ruled the roadways and alleys, farms and fields, with swords and staves, sparing no one. It was only when Roger fitzHugh heard there was in Tenby a promising lady with a wealthy father that he eased his stranglehold on Pembroke. Patrols in Pembroke were slackened as a result of his many absences, his choice of men unwilling to work unless forced.

The constant sense of unease in the town abated and talk turned again to the fate of the princess and her children. In spite of the Constable's efforts and those of his friends to pressure Owain into submission, there was still no word of the captives. Most prayers in homes or churches were now for their souls, where once the pleas to God were for their safe return.

Manon longed to see Nest again, surrounded by her children. They were gone like her own brothers and like them, until their deaths were certain, she believed them alive. Safe? When Owain had them captive, that was too much to expect even from the good Lord and all his saints.

Work absorbed Manon and kept her sane, time spent with Heledd and Dybion her only relaxation. Rhodri was growing tall, resembling Gerwyn so much it made her heart miss a beat when he came to her unexpectedly. The others in the workshop carried on their trades as though Gerwyn would walk in and examine the cutting and stitching and the high quality of workmanship in the goods she sold never varied.

Nudd worried her. While Gerwyn had been alive the boy spoke little, his words gruff and difficult to hear. Since the murder all that came from the poor little soul was a series of grunts which only Gwen seemed to be able to understand. With Manon's help Gwen saw to it Nudd was well-clothed and kept warm, his shed at the end of the yard made tight from the weather. The food he ate was the same as their own but Nudd seldom finished it at the table, taking it to his bedspace and his friend, the piglet.

The animal had grown well. It was clean, plump, docile, following Nudd as would a child. Manon had heard the little man crooning to it, just as she comforted her babies. In a strange way the small, pink beast was like a naked infant, understanding Nudd's weird utterings and trying to reply. Manon and Gwen left him alone and even the men in the workshop, as well as those who brought fresh leather from the tannery, marvelled at the link between man and beast, deciding such affection was a gift from God and not the devil. Gradually, Manon saw Nudd's grief over the death of Gerwyn was being assuaged as he lavished food, love, and

136

what passed for words on the animal with no name but 'Pig'

The shire reeve was constant in his wooing, leaving a void in Pembroke. His men had been left in the command of Brede, the lazy man who received little respect, even from his own troopers. Patrols became more random, less thorough and in the absence of a firm authority petty crime flourished in the town. Young rogues ran wild, stealing as they went. There was no one to stop them and the only defence a cudgel blow and a broken head for whoever got in the way. Increasing numbers of townspeople realised they must defend themselves to the limit and when shopkeepers and craftsmen became ruthless most would-be felons crept away to their lairs.

The exception was a gang haunting beershops and dark alleys at the far end of town. Heavy drinkers were enticed out by women promising relief. In a secret corner any with well-loaded pockets would be bludgeoned, robbed and left to stew in the mess of a runnel until the guards patrolled next morning. It was a profitable scheme, the women earning silver for very little work, their pimp laughing as he grew rich.

Not so amusing was the state of their victims. One farmer lay without his senses and no movement in his right side. Another had a festering sore on his skull and a fever no medicining could lower. A few limped away to explain empty pockets to their families after a good day at market but two men were stiff and cold by the time the troopers found them. The sergeant decided on action but he was too late to catch the procurer who had moved on to the deeper pockets for picking offered in Tenby. The women were the sergeant's only harvest from his brutal questions in the beershops. They had been the instruments the pimp had used and no one would speak against them. Furious, the sergeant had two of the women dragged to the castle to wait for Roger fitzHugh's return.

After that an uneasy hush lay over Pembroke. It sufficed in place of peace and slowly farmers and their women returned to the market with scarce food to sell, using their coin to buy from the shops and carry home items unlikely to be the target of robbers. Manon resumed her own marketing becoming aware of a subtle change in the town. Men and women spoke to her with their usual courtesy but she sensed a distancing, a coolness. It puzzled her but there were too many other matters on the mind of the busy woman.

Buddyg ran into the kitchen, breathless with haste and excitement.

"Manon! Great news! A message came from the castle for Hywel. I was in the garden and Ceinwen came out to tell me at once. The children are coming home!"

"Nest's children?"

Buddyg nodded as she straightened a kerchief disturbed by her speed. "All three of them."

Manon closed her eyes as her silent prayer of thanks went heavenwards. God did listen and answer. "Three, you said?"

"They were landed from a boat with their nurse – along the river. They should be in the castle by now."

There was an inner coolness of fear and Manon struggled to speak calmly. "Buddyg, the day Nest left there were four children with her. Her three and the other William."

"The Constable's son by Ninian's daughter?"

"I saw him go," Manon said. "What news of him, I wonder? And of Nest herself?"

Buddyg's excitement drained from her. "The message for Hywel was of Nest's three children and the nurse. Nothing more."

"Dear God!" Manon gripped her friend's hand for comfort. "Owain still has her."

138

Chapter Eight

Rhodri came running into the kitchen and Manon looked up at him, startled. "You should have been there, Mam. All the town was at the castle gate cheering and when Mistress Mabli brought the children to be seen everyone went wild."

Heledd's arms were tight around her mother's neck, a small cold cheek against hers. Manon had been kneeling to feed the fire and she turned to cradle the child in her arms. She reached a hand to her son and he helped her stand, Heledd still clinging like a limpet. God was good, she thought, Nest's children safe again.

"May the Good Lord keep you safe, Nest, and bring you home soon to your little ones," she whispered.

Her own little daughter wriggled, tickled by her mother's soft breaths. Manon stood the child on her feet and straightened, covering her belly with her hands. She was sure now Gerwyn had left her with child. It had worried her she was to birth and rear a child without Gerwyn until she knew he would be always there in the son or daughter growing in its father's image.

"You must be hungry, my chicks. There are wheaten cakes warm by the fire – and honey."

Heledd danced towards the food, Rhodri going more slowly as should the man of the house. Dybion stirred in his sleep, the wooden walls of his crib already too narrow and short for him.

"Were they good, Gwen?" she asked as the girl came from the cold air into the warmth of the kitchen.

"As gold!" Gwen took off her thick cloak and mittens. She had stopped at the workshop to tell the men there of the excitement at the castle. "Oh, mistress, you should have heard the noise when the children came out!"

Even in the depths of her kitchen Manon had heard a roaring as of surf on a sun-bright day, no harm in it.

"Little Angharad was frightened by it all and hid in Mistress Mabli's skirts. In no time Mistress Mabli had her soothed and held her up in her arms for all to see the child was safe."

"And with loving arms around her," Manon added.

Had it been Heledd, Gerwyn would have proudly held his daughter aloft but Angharad's father was in the north avenging the insult to his honour. As a Frank he was too manly to realise the needs of small children. For him it was of far greater importance to ride fast and slaughter.

There was much for Gwen to tell. "The boys were very good, straight as arrows, their heads held proud."

"A pity their father did not see their courage."

Gwen frowned. "Hard he is, to be sure. When the shouting quieted it was because the women were praying for the princess. Ceinwen was the first to kneel, bless her. Others did the same and soon all that could be heard was the murmur of prayers and the shuffling of men's feet – those who think rape is a bit of harmless fun and not a sin against women and God himself."

Manon was thoughtful. "I wonder if Sir Gerald prays for his wife?"

"And the boy still with her," Gwen reminded Manon. "The Constable's first-born."

"Indeed he is and matters greatly to his father but not all men can think kindly of a wife they may believe has allowed herself to be raped."

Gwen's mouth opened almost as wide as her eyes. "You think Sir Gerald . . .?"

"He is a man, is he not? And a proud one. It was Nest made him escape and that alone will not sit lightly with him. Now she stays away in the bed of his enemy. How can a Frank think well of her."

"What of his son?"

"Yes, his son," Manon said slowly. "The bastard boy, William. Strange he was the one kept behind. Tell me, Gwen, if Nest was willingly in Owain's bed, would there be need to hold back a child as a hostage?"

A messenger had ridden fast to Tenby and cursing, the shire reeve had left his courtship of a merchant's wealth to return to Pembroke.

"The children are well?" he asked Mabli when he reached the family's quarters.

"Thank you, yes – although harmed by the fear they have endured these many weeks."

Behind her the two boys, William and Maurice watched him, their cheeks hollowed by captivity, their eyes wary. Scrubbed clean by Mabli and in fresh tunics they were alike, Roger thought, yet had William a forehead seen on another? Circled by a king's coronet? He smiled at the boy.

"Your journey home was swift?"

William did not answer, instead he eyed the shire reeve, having learned to be cautious of all men. From behind him came the chuckles of baby David. He had been held and kissed by his sister and now amused himself by pulling at her hair. The little girl's face had aged strangely until she resembled her mother so closely the shire reeve shivered.

"I must question them, ma dame," he said to Mabli.

She was as stone. "When they are ready, sir."

"Soon, ma dame!"

"These precious young ones – and their nurse – need time, sir. Time to feed well and be at peace in their own home. I will take them to Carew as soon as –"

"No! They remain here, under my charge."

"Then it is a pity you were not in Pembroke when they were returned to us," she remarked with sibilance which angered him.

"I was encamped at Stackpole, watching with my men for spies from Ireland!"

Mabli slowly eyed Roger's lightweight boots, then up along silken hose and the length of a purple velvet tunic heavy with gold and silver stitching. "Encamped, sir? You surprise me. I would have said you had been with rich merchants somewhere. Tenby, perhaps? Instead of searching out spies or indeed, Gerwyn's murderer who still roams free. The Constable would never have rested until such a man was found and committed to spend the rest of his life working to keep fed Gerwyn's wife and children."

He flushed with annoyance at the reprimand from the woman as well as her knowledge of his recent journey. It was as stifling as being at court, surrounded by so many hidden eyes and vicious tongues.

"It matters nothing, the idle words of servants, ma dame – and you stay here with the children. That is an order!"

Mabli had his measure and bowed but not deeply. He was not worth that much deference.

A new spirit was abroad in Pembroke. Folk were still suspicious but at last there was a real hope their princess would return and with her, prosperity. Steps were lighter, smiles came more easily, coins slid in and out of pouches with less reluctance and traders of all kinds were relieved.

Manon still grieved but it lessened because of the new baby. It was something of Gerwyn for her to cherish in addition to an old cap of his she held as she prayed at the little shrine she had made in the kitchen. Gwen encouraged with hot drinks laced with honey, feeding her mistress nibbles of bread and cakes as they were baked. Gradually, the edges of sharp bones in Manon's face were softened and her skin glowed with a gentle richness.

She walked to Buddyg's as often as she could but as the length of days increased, so did the activity in the shop and her smile was needed to welcome customers. When she thanked God for her blessings, Manon realised her small world, shattered into fragments when Gerwyn died, was becoming whole again.

Only Kamal was anxious.

"Is there trouble at the tannery?" she asked him, knowing the shop and the home behind it ran smoothly.

"No, mistress, the men work well for Myrddin. There are a few cowhides from the farms – beasts dead of cold or hunger. Sheepskins come from the castle and the priory. I think soldiers and monks feed well."

Manon was puzzled. Kamal stood in front of her easing his weight from foot to foot and twisting a scrap of leather in his hands. "Can Nudd still find all the bark they need? Or is it herbs they lack because of the cold?"

"There is all they need – and more, mistress."

"Then what is wrong? The money we earn in the shop each week is good, is it not?"

Kamal nodded his head with great vigour. "The big Fleming, Ugo, is come from the north with horses and ponies. From – Cadwgan, was it?"

"He had a stud famous throughout all Wales. Cadwgan," Manon whispered and shivered as she said his name.

"The horses Ugo brings, mistress. One pull a heavy load all day, all night, no rest. Another – the bones so fine a man ride on its back like the wind. The small ones gentle, even Heledd to be carried safely."

Manon's smile was grim. "Cadwgan demanded better blood lines from his mares than for the mother of his own son, but how do these horses bring trouble for us?"

Kamal shrugged his shoulders, held the palms of his hands uppermost. "Ugo buys leather for saddles, for harness, all we can prepare."

"Surely that is good?"

Kamal nodded, yet he frowned. "From Rhos has come a Fleming who has great skill in making saddles for the Franks in the castle."

"Is that all, Kamal?" Manon said with a rare laugh. "Gerwyn always said the making of saddles took more time and skill than was rewarded in payment. If we sell the leather to the castle we make a good price. It is enough and always will be. No one else has better leather to sell in the whole shire."

Roger fitzHugh saw the hag of a mediciner walking towards the great hall of the castle, a basket of leaves and roots on her arm. He acknowledged her as he would any useful servant, irritated by the slight nod which was her greeting and the half smile which turned the twisted cheek into a fiendish grin.

"Brede!" he shouted and his ansel came running.

"Sir?"

"The tanner's death. I asked you and the others to listen for any hint of a culprit yet there has been nothing from any of you. These damned peasants watch us like hungry wolves and the murderer must be laughing his head off. I want him found and hanged!"

Brede shrugged his shoulders. "We did what we could but there was no smell of Gerwyn in a woman's skirts."

The shire reeve frowned, was thoughtful. "If he had been someone would have known – and talked – by now. Peut-être, the other way?"

"Sir?"

"A man who would be in the widow's skirts. She is free now Gerwyn is buried. Who would bed this – Manon?"

"Any man with blood and not milk in him," Brede said with a laugh, disgusting Roger with the sight of blackened and cracked teeth.

"Then get amongst the low life and find out what you can."

Buddyg came, full of goodwill and gossip. Two nights before, Hywel had fallen as he stumbled home in time for couvre feu, gashing his head badly.

"The blood, Manon! It still lies in the roadway."

"Hywel with it?"

Buddyg chuckled. "No. You may be sure Ceinwen had him inside, his head cleansed and swaddled like a baby's bottom before the Franks patrolling the town could have him away."

"Beer again?"

"Beer? Wine from France – whatever came to hand. The way Hywel drinks he proves himself a king's son."

"Poor Ceinwen."

"Aye, and poor Hywel when Mistress Mabli got word of it in the castle and came a-visiting. No need for me to put my ear to the wall, I could heard the roaring even when I raked the fire and stacked on more wood."

"Mistress Mabli was that angry?"

Buddyg held her sides and rocked on her stool, laughing at the memory. "No, it was Hywel in pain. Ceinwen told me afterwards Mistress Mabli had brought spirit as comes secretly from Ireland. There was such a din when she took off Ceinwen's careful bandaging and poured the stuff in the wound. 'To clean it,' I heard her shout at him above his roaring. 'It is the only fit use for such a liquor and any man who throws it down his gullet deserves a sore head – inside and out!' Oh, Manon, the rumpus went on for ages and Hywel has stayed safe at home since."

"Poor Hywel. Perhaps he was drinking to forget what happened to his sister. Is there still no news of Nest?"

"No. Ceinwen told me King Henry continues in a fury and Sir Gerald will not rest. He rides like a madman at every wisp of a sighting."

"I wonder," Manon said slowly, "whether his anguish is for his wife and son – or for his hurt pride?"

"Does it matter? The whole of Wales is afire and the Franks bitter for revenge because of what Owain did."

"Franks?" Manon tutted her disgust. "They are angered at the insult offered to the king's liege man but be sure our own people will never forgive Owain. Taking children as well as a woman he insisted he loved?"

"Mistress Mabli has been caring for the nurse who was with the children," Buddyg said quietly. "The poor girl can still hardly walk she had been used so badly. She tells of the princess coming to table with bruises on her neck and arms. One morning her jaw was swollen so badly she could not eat."

"Please God her agony ends soon." Manon cried for the child who had run with her in sun-dappled woods. "I hope Cadwgan is proud of his son!" she said through her tears.

"The nurse, Menna, said the old man was beside himself, begging Owain to send back all he had taken from Sir Gerald but Owain just laughed at him. I doubt there is much left to be returned, the men with Owain sharing out what was valuable. Owain had a coffer of silver as well as the princess but he had no patience with the children. Menna was ordered to keep them out of his sight but she was always being dragged away by one of his friends. Mistress Mabli told Ceinwen the girl was lucky if it was just one at a time."

"Poor soul! May she soon be returned to health," Manon said quietly and Buddyg nodded. "But what of Sir Gerald's son? I pray they left him alone and not used him for their sport."

"It was part of the princess' agreement with Owain the boy is safe. He had not been touched when Menna was returned with the other children."

Buddyg's voice went on but Manon heard little, her thoughts with Nest and the boy at such risk in the north. What threat to the other William did Owain hold over Nest?

146

His eyes? Had Cadwgan's son promised to blind young William if Nest was not soft and loving to the man who had taken her?

"Ceinwen said Menna was full of how Owain wanted to take away from the Constable all that he held dear," Manon heard Buddyg say. "Sir Gerald's new castle burned to the ground and everything in it. Just think, Manon, all those sheets I stitched gone in flames before they were ever used. Poor lady, the penalty for being rich and beautiful is very heavy."

Manon nodded. "The pile of riches is not important, Buddyg. What matters is who covets what you have. For Nest, only a live husband keeps her safe."

"They said what?"

Cynfan the baker shook with fury and flour flew from him in a fine mist, settling on the trestle at which he sat in the tavern and dappling the beer in the pot he banged so hard on the wood it broke. A small man in a torn tunic and greasy cap huddled back against the wall but Cynfan's bulging eyes were on him and he must answer.

"They wanted to know who went most into the leather shop now Gerwyn is dead."

"Everyone?"

A nod was all the pathetic little soul could manage.

"God in heaven! Is the shire reeve mad?" Cynfan asked of the surrounding drinkers. "What does he hope to find?"

The new baby was still her secret but Manon could not see the light in her eyes, the glow on her skin. Those who loved her were glad of the returning beauty but others who saw it had their own views as to its source. Whispers which had begun like the first flames of a fire in the beershops were fanned by excitement mixed with malice. All Manon knew was that every turn she was protected, Gwen watching her mistress like a hawk. It was Gwen who insisted on going to market alone so Manon was not jostled in the roadway.

147

Kamal was part of the conspiracy, ensuring all went smoothly in the shop and there was no need for its mistress to even dirty her shoes in its dust.

Comforting it may have been but as the year quickened and her baby grew, Manon became increasingly restless, stifled by all the consideration and protection. It was a bright day when she resolved to see for herself what had become of Pembroke. Gwen had taken Heledd and Dybion to the quay to see a ship newly anchored. It had come from warm seas and they would laugh at the sailors shivering as they jabbered while the gulls wheeled and screamed.

Her kerchief firm around her head and wound round her throat, sheepskin on her feet and hands and her cloak swathed snugly about her, Manon crept past the workshop and with a few steps was soon in the mass of people thronging Pembroke for market day. It was cold but the sun was up and Manon's blood rose she thanked God she and the child within her were alive.

She saw faces she knew and smiled, ready to greet and wish God's good grace on their families but heads turned away from her. A few stood and watched silently as she walked to the baker's shop. Cynfan welcomed her and asked after the children. Manon assured him they were well and wondered why he was so anxious to seem friendly, hurrying to her side in the shop and standing between Manon and his other customers. There was a flutter of fear in Manon's stomach. Was this why Gwen had kept her indoors?

Puzzlement grew as Manon walked on, buying thread from a shop, and going on through the town to buy a kerchief from a stall. All the time she was aware of the gaze of many eyes burning between her shoulders. When she turned to face the stares, the loathing she encountered stung blood to her cheeks. A man she did not know was whispered to and he glared at her, barely turning his head to spit in the dust near her feet. Manon was shocked by his behaviour. Pembroke was a raw town but there had always been courtesy carried into it from the old ways before the Franks had come and built their castle.

Manon needed the safety of her home and turned to go. A wizened old woman hissed at her in ancient Welsh Manon could barely hear, yet she could feel the hatred. With her head held high Manon walked steadily through the crowds, ignoring invisible waves of enmity flooding towards her.

"Why?" she asked Gwen as soon as she reached the kitchen.

Heledd was given some scraps to take to Nudd's piglet before Gwen settled Dybion with a wooden spoon. Only then did she look at her mistress.

"There has been talk in the town. Buddyg –"

"She knew of it?"

"Aye – and we wanted to spare you. You know Pembroke. Tittle tattle is supposed to last for a sennight but here it is only until next market day. We thought if we could keep you from the town long enough, tongues would choose someone else to destroy."

Shocked, Manon's eyes opened wide. "Destroy? In God's name, Gwen, what are they saying about me?"

Gwen could not look at her mistress and repeat the horrors she had been told until Manon took the girl's face in her hands.

"Please."

"Anyone who knows you . . ."

"Say it, Gwen, and be done."

Tears spilled from Gwen's eyes and Manon felt them trickle over her fingers but she did not release her.

"It is said," Gwen whispered, "you have a new man and that is why you look so well. There are those who will tell it loudly you wanted your husband dead."

Manon was stunned, rocking on her heels as though she had been hit. "I wanted Gerwyn dead?"

The girl nodded but in her eyes there was anguish.

Manon stepped back, her fingers clawing empty air in her distress. "Mother of God, help me! Who says such a thing?" she demanded of Gwen.

"No one knows. The shire reeve's men questioned but learned nothing of use. It was after that the worst of the talk started. I have listened, so has Buddyg, to hear the voice telling the tale. Old Twm has heard it in the beershop but by that time the words are already old and used many times."

Manon shook her head to clear it of the mist growing fast there. "Why? Why would I want Gerwyn dead?"

"It is said you long to spend your riches as you wish – live in an important house with no smell of the tanyard in it."

"Life without Gerwyn? Do any of these dogs from hell know what they suggest?"

"Oh, yes. After the shire reeve's men nosed around, the idea came as though on a breeze and it spread as a wind carries fire. Now many are sure you wanted the master out of the way."

"I am supposed to have hit Gerwyn so hard he died and then I took him to the tannery and I bundled him into the dung pit – remembering to put back the lid?"

"Not you. Some man did it for you – so they say."

Anger was creeping through Manon, dispelling the clouds of disbelief. "A man? Any man? Or has someone been named?"

"No. Yes." Gwen sighed. "Any man who has ever spoken to you, or smiled at you. Cynfan, Ithel, the Fleming – even Kamal and Old Twm."

It was hard for Manon to lose herself in dreamless sleep that night. Prayer succeeded prayer to God and all his saints, to Gerwyn, even her dead mother and sister but oblivion escaped her. She rose still tired, her features drawn and haggard. Filled with guilt for being the bearer of bad news, Gwen hurried about her tasks, glancing at her mistress when she could. An hour dragged by, two, then Kamal came to them, his dark features grave.

"Gollwyn!" he said.

Manon knew the large, morose man as a good customer, though he had come from the north and was separated from his coins with great difficulty.

"What of him?" she asked.

"Dead, Mistress Manon. A reeve's man found him by the road."

"Gollwyn has a farm in the woods above Stackpole, if I remember rightly."

"Aye, he does," Gwen said, "and sends rogues on their secret way to Ireland, if the stories be true."

Manon was more charitable. "God rest his soul, whatever his earthly sins. To spend his day here at market in Pembroke and be so dealt with on his way home ..." She shuddered, remembering the search for the lost Gerwyn and the indescribable agony of knowing he was dead.

Gwen sniffed. "Only a fool goes home unwary and unarmed carrying coins from the market."

The pig farmer's wife came into Manon's thoughts. "Drydwen?"

A deep chuckle came from Gwen. "What man would dare challenge her and think to keep his skull intact?"

"You fools!"

Roger fitzHugh was incensed by the stupidity of his ansels.

"You failed to find the tanner's killer and now he has struck again! Do you believe I want command of a town in terror of a faceless man? Anything could happen – and that I will not endure! Get this murderer and bring him to me on his knees."

The shire reeve's men scoured the town, as well as the roads and tracks leading in all directions from the castle as he sat in state in the great hall and wondered at the most recent murder. Gollwyn had been a man of no real import-ance except for his supposed trafficking with the Irish. The Constable had been so sure a spy was free in the shire. At the year's turn could he have landed at Stackpole and taken a devious way towards Pembroke, taking him near the tannery? With Gerwyn alert for thieves the spy could have suspected a trap and killed Gerwyn for his silence. Now Gollwyn had died to still his tongue.

With his couvre feu order in place and all those who lived in Pembroke shut in their homes by nightfall, searches for the killer in the town were without success. The usual drunken sots were taken to the castle and flogged but no one was of any help and Gollwyn's wife prepared him for burial.

As the first sod of his grave was dug, another farmer was discovered, this time by his wife. Ieuaf had almost reached home, dying just beyond the trees edging his farmyard. He was not a drinker and would have left Pembroke and its market with a pouch filled with coin from the sale of a cow in milk and a pig. The money must have been very tempting and Ieuaf was found bundled behind low bushes, the back of his head a bloody mess and his leather money bag missing.

Death walked as no stranger in the town of Pembroke, or on the roads, tracks, lanes of its shire. Life was hard for those who struggled to live from the soil and to this was added the danger of robbers who killed for slivers of copper and silver. The town and countryside around it for miles was rife with rumour and hearsay.

"Just like Gerwyn," Manon was told by a customer in the shop.

A small crowd had gathered outside the opened shutters. They nodded and muttered, comparing Gerwyn's murder with the two new events.

"Where has the killer been since the beginning of the year?" a farmer asked, his voice gruff with beer.

"Ireland," Drydwen announced. "All sinners go there to

save their skins." The pig farmer's wife stood head and shoulders above most of the men and no one argued with her. "Where else would there be safety after Gerwyn died and there was such a search for his killer?"

"Not Ireland," a miserable old man whined. "The place is only fit for Danes and slaves."

Drydwen flapped a great hand at him. Had she managed to reach him his ears would have rung for a week. "I say Ireland! It is why Gollwyn died. Only someone who had gone that route could know the silver Gollwyn earned from his trade with the ships sailing at night in and out of the harbour at Stackpole."

The idea made sense and if Drydwen had worked it out, so could the mysterious slayer. Men and women moved away from the leather shop, the better to spread the latest rumour and Manon decided to visit Buddyg. She had not walked the road there for many days but the horde at the shop convinced her it was safe to venture out. No one suddenly became friendly towards her but Manon sensed a warming in the air when she was near, hardly a glare or a silence marring her path.

She was refreshed by more than goat's milk and cakes hot from a bakestone in Buddyg's home. The time spent with her friend, hearing the latest news from the castle and Mabli, restored Manon's faith in the future, a future she would share with Gerwyn's new child.

Gwen welcomed her home with a smile. "See, I told you to stay inside until the whispers about you ceased."

"You mean I am no longer thought guilty?" Manon asked, a new resentment eroding the pleasantness of the day.

"No need to be like that, mistress," Gwen chided. "The master was well-thought of in the Pembroke and around. If no one can be found to answer for his killing, then people will make up their own minds. Such a deed it was! It is only right the man who slaughtered your husband should be punished for his crime."

153

"And wicked tongues may enjoy lashing me for being the schemer? In God's name, the man I loved was taken from me. Am I supposed to have been glad of it?"

"No, mistress, not when Gollwyn and Ieuaf are dead the same way as the master and robbed of the money they carried."

Manon could not believe her ears. "Gwen! You are saying two men must die to prove me innocent."

"No . . ."

"Yes! If that is what it takes to appease evil minds, then loving thy neighbour becomes a task for the saints themselves."

It was not two men who had to die. Less than a week later and the morning after a market day, the bodies of a father and his young son lay in the dust of a track leading through the woods to Carew. Ynwrig had been a good man, well-respected and devout. Once a woodsman for Princess Nest and her husband he had gashed his leg badly. Mistress Mabli had been on hand and stitched the wound with a large needle and stout thread and Ynwrig survived with a limp but no longer able to toil amongst the trees. It had been the princess herself who used his talent as a wood-carver to beautify the harshness of the castles at Carew and Pembroke.

At night in his gwennie Ynwrig had shaped animals of the forest from offcuts of wood and Sir Gerald had given permission for the man to sell such work in the market. His young son walked with him to carry the carefully wrapped pieces and play merry tunes on his whistle as he waited for his father to sell what he could. It had been Meilyr who delighted Heledd when she heard him play. That last day he lived, Meilyr's music had helped sell the carved birds and squirrels. Flushed with success the lame father leaned on the shoulder of his game little son as they walked home. No one saw them alive again.

There was no doubt Ynwrig had been struck from behind,

154

his head shattered as had been those of Gollwyn and Ieuaf. What caused even greater horror was the state of Meilyr's tragic little corpse. His arms were broken, his face bloodied and made unrecognisable as he fought to protect his dying father and then defend himself.

Every able-bodied man in Pembroke and for miles around had a cudgel or a stave in his hand, each one ready to search out the killer from under bushes, behind gwennies, in barns and copses. Anyone with unexpected coin to spend was immediately suspected of the crime and beaten before being questioned.

One unfortunate who had spent the night of the murders sleeping off a beer-sore head under a tree outside the town confessed to hearing a horse, the squeak of a cart and a strange tinkling sound. No one believed him and he was beaten again until saved by reeve's men and hauled into a corner of the castle for his own safety.

While all this had been happening, Roger fitzHugh had been wooing in Tenby and returned in a bad mood. It had seemed wise to agree to wed the girl in her native church with its low-born vicar. Having enjoyed bedding her and using her father's wealth, the marriage could soon be disallowed when he returned to court and leave him free for a more worthy wife and the rites of a proper ceremony. The plan was not going well, the lady's father unwilling to provide an acceptable dowry.

The first morning after he returned the shire reeve sat in state in the great hall and listened to tales of searching, suspicion, captures, beatings. He cast a weary eye over the men dragged before him, questioning them in his uneasy Welsh. Roger fitzHugh had not broken his fast and was beginning to long for food and wine when Ynwrig's wife was brought to him. She was a pale, tidy soul, decently covered and her kerchief around her head and throat. In her hands she held two unfinished carvings, one of a misselthrush and another of an owlet, its eyes wide and trusting.

"Why does she bring me presents? Does she think to bribe a hanging from me when I have no one to dangle?"

"No, sir," he was assured by his squire. "She wishes you to see how beautiful are Ynwrig's carvings so you may better judge the reason for the theft and murder."

Muttering curses under his breath the reeve held out his hand to the woman and she gently laid the tiny owl in his palm. fitzHugh examined the craftsmanship then frowning, held the owl at a distance.

"Ask her if her husband carves – les faucons."

The squire was puzzled, turning to question Maslin, one of Sir Gerald's men who had the Welsh tongue as well as the Frankish. The hardened soldier began describing a sleek bird with a bright eye and strongly curved beak. Roger fitzHugh nodded, pleased to be understood.

"Falcons, mistress. Did your husband ever carve falcons?" Maslin asked the widow.

"Aye, sir, but only two and they were in the satchel Meilyr carried the morning he left home with his father."

Roger fitzHugh thumped the solid wooden arm of his chair. "Tenby!" he said. "I have seen one in Tenby, only yesterday!"

He closed his eyes trying to remember what he had heard as the young lady he pursued praised the artistry of the carver who had perfectly reproduced the bird. Nothing had been said of whence it came.

"Brede! A troop of six men ready to ride!"

"Sir! What provisions –"

"None. We go to Tenby immediately!"

Excitement swept through Pembroke almost as fast as Roger fitzHugh galloping towards Tenby. The armed men with him were formidable, the rust on their mailed tunics a promise of blood to come. It was a long wait as the hours dragged by. Few wanted to wait out the time in patience and in their homes. There was little trading although shops and stalls were thronged. Only the beershops were truly

156

busy and there was time for a drunk or two to reel out into a runnel and sleep their way back from oblivion before the whisper grew to a shout.

"They have him!"

Gwen took the news to Manon who had stayed in the kitchen through the long day, busying herself with trivial tasks. Dark corners of the room had been swept, shelves tidied, while Manon prepared herself to learn the name of Gerwyn's murderer.

The shire reeve returned to Pembroke more slowly than he had left the town. His captive was bound hand and foot and sat tied to his own cart which tinkled with hanging copper pots as the soldier hurrying its tired horse whipped the fastest pace possible.

Gwen ran from the kitchen, Manon following her more slowly, hearing the girl gasp with shock when she recognised the man being brought to justice.

"Mog!" Gwen exclaimed. "Mistress, it is Mog the peddler!"

Manon could not speak when Gwen pulled her through the shop. She stared at the wreck of a man, his head bowed and bloodied as he was hauled to his fate. There would be a trial, Roger fitzHugh making sure nothing was left undone while he was in control of Pembroke. The man they held as a suspect was resigned, knowing his guilt.

"Gwen, it makes no sense."

Manon had hoped for a sense of ending. Mog's arrest merely raised more questions in her own mind. Gerwyn would never have been jumped from behind, he knew the woods and the tannery so well, a single footfall would have alerted him.

"Sense or not, mistress, he is to be tried in the morning."

Buddyg came with her girls early next day. "Are you going, Manon?" she asked, surprised to see her friend dressed in an old grey tunic, the sleeves of her undershift rolled high above her elbows as she dealt with a crock on a high shelf.

"To the trial?" Manon shook her head as she stepped down from a stool. "No. It will not bring Gerwyn home to us and the thought of spending half a day in a hall filled with so many patient only to see someone hang – the very idea fills me with horror."

"You are too kind-natured," Buddyg said and touched Manon's hand. "Me? I want to see the man who robbed young Meilyr of his life. His father's stall was near our home as you know and the lad often played his whistle for Meinir and Nerys."

Manon was surprised. "You are not taking them?"

"Why not? It is only right they see God's justice is swift and strong. What happens to Mog the peddler may stay the hand of another, saving lives and souls and keeping families together."

"Leave the girls here," Manon begged. "They will be company for us. Gwen is already at the castle, as is Old Twm, but Rhodri and Kamal stay here to protect Heledd and Dybion. We will be safe."

Buddyg hesitated. "Perhaps you are wise. A message came to Ceinwen after curfew. The Constable's young ones sailed at first light for Carew. The shire reeve is determined to stamp hard on any who murder and Mistress Mabli decided the children had seen and heard enough of death and blood of late."

"Mistress Mabli choosing to get on a boat? She hates such travelling and is always sick. Only grave concerns for the children would have made her wish to endure that."

"It is Angharad. Ceinwen says the child has bad dreams and wakes screaming, sobbing for her mother."

Manon nodded her understanding. "Rhodri slept little last night and was so pale when he broke his fast. When I suggested he stay with me and help with Heledd and

Dybion –" Manon could not stem her own tears as she remembered her son's relief.

The shire reeve was at his most pompous but he wanted the formalities of justice to be speedy. Briskly, he heard his men give accounts of the victims and their manner of dying. Mog was held upright, asked to speak and only sobbed. Disgusted by Mog's streaming eyes and nose, Roger fitzHugh decided the peddler's worldly goods be shared amongst the bereaved families and the man himself assigned to the gallows. The shire reeve strode from the great hall, leaving the crowd gathered there to erupt in excitement.

Even with the shop's shutters in place and all the doors closed and barred Manon listened to the voice of the crowd as it made its way to the castle or roamed the town. When at last she heard a roar of delight, she closed her eyes and prayed for the soul of the evil man who had destroyed Gerwyn and his family.

Very little time passed before Buddyg knocked for admittance and claimed her daughters. She would not stop for any refreshment, exclaiming over the neat sewing Meinir and Nerys had done on scraps of soft leather while they waited for her.

"Have they been good," Buddyg asked but did she not look at Manon. Instead she took off her kerchief which had been pulled awry, shaking it and carefully tying it again about her head and throat.

Manon could see her friend was ashen, greatly distressed by all she had witnessed. She asked no questions and let the little family hurry away, hearing Buddyg greet Gwen as she returned.

Gwen came slowly into the kitchen, her eyes staring with shock and disbelief. Manon did not speak to her, bending instead to freshen the wood on the fire and poke it into a blaze.

"It is finished then," Manon said and stared into the flames sculpting the sad planes of her face. "You must be cold, Gwen. Come and sit by the fire."

Gwen did not move. "May Mog rot in hell and burn for eternity!" burst from her.

"And I will be whole again?" Manon asked, an echoing emptiness in her eyes and voice.

"It was not just you, mistress. Hunydd, wife to Ynwrig and mother of Meilyr, she was there screaming for Mog to suffer as he dangled. A reeve's man would have hung on his legs and made it quick but Hunydd stopped him and the crowd encouraged her. Then the fitzHugh waved to the man to stand back and Mog took a long time to die. Even as he hung at the last he was twitching."

"Did he ask forgiveness?"

"Aye."

There was a strangeness in Gwen's soft word and Manon gazed at her, curious.

"There was a priest," Gwen said. "Mog begged him to listen to his repentance. He named the men and women he had harmed – children too. It was a long list and shocked all who thought he had just begun to kill. Never any mention of the master."

"He did not repent Gerwyn's death?"

Gwen's kerchief was loosened as she shook her head. "Not a word."

"There is more," Manon sensed. Wood crackled on the hearth and the fire almost warmed them as she waited for Gwen to speak.

"When the noose was put round his neck . . ."

"Yes?"

"He screamed for us all to hear. 'Not the tanner. I never killed the tanner'!"

Chapter Nine

Questioning the man before his trial, the shire reeve decided very quickly Mog was too low in intelligence to be the traitor, although his way of life was a most suitable cover for such an activity.

"No," he had told Brede and Rolf, "he is not the man we seek. This damned spy is still among us and I would have him before Sir Gerald returns."

"Do we still search for Gerwyn's killer?" Brede asked.

Roger fitzHugh dismissed Mog's last words as the ravings of a lunatic. "Of course the peddler killed the tanner! It was the same coward's blow from behind so let there be an end to it."

The shire reeve might be a powerful man, even a clever one, but he did not understand the gossips of Pembroke. He had begun the whispers and saw no reason why they should continue now Mog dangled at the castle gate yet quiet murmurings persisted.

It was argued in dark corners Mog had not bothered to hide his corpses, so why had Gerwyn been rolled in the dung pit and the cover put back? The tanner never carried money except to pay his men. He would not have had a full pouch late at night so why even go near him, let alone kill him? Hides, however valuable, were too big to be hidden in Mog's filthy clothes or in his cart and he was a man who

161

liked to travel fast, not encumbered by weighty leather which might be difficult to sell. Rumours, opinions, disagreements seethed and rumbled for one day, two, like slowly boiling porridge.

Manon was unaware of her name being bandied again between stalls, in beershops and alleyways. Nor did she realise Gerwyn might be dead but he still had good friends who knew the love and trust between the tanner and his wife. Her supporters were many and they defended the widow stoutly, talking of her great loss and no hurry to attempt to fill the gap left in her life.

"The shire reeve is right – for once. It was most likely to be Mog," was the accepted verdict as the latest tale which began to circulate involved the shire reeve's sergeant, Brede, running away from an angry husband, his tunic and boots in his hands as he fled from a sharp knife aimed at the parts of his body causing the worthy merchant offence.

The sun was bright, the air crisp, as Kamal stopped the cart in front of Buddyg's house. They were waiting, Buddyg and her daughters, and Heledd squirmed with delight in the bed of the cart as the two little girls were lifted in, their feet warm in sheepskin boots.

"Dybion?" Buddyg asked.

"Sleeping. Gwen will see to him and let him beat a pot with a spoon all day – when she is not feeding him tasty morsels to fatten him up."

Buddyg climbed in beside Manon, the mothers wrapping the children's warm cloaks around them before they made themselves comfortable for the journey. Many stopped to watch them, the red of Buddyg's cloak warm against Manon's soft brown wool, the small girls wriggling and giggling.

"Is there news from the castle?" Manon asked as the last of the houses were behind them.

"The princess?" Buddyg held Manon's arm to console her. "She is not yet free . . ."

Manon's eyes were large, anxious. "Is there hope it will be soon?"

"Always. Ceinwen had it from Mistress Mabli before she left for Carew with the children. The search goes on and Sir Gerald barely sleeps. The big Fleming must keep fresh horses for him wherever he goes."

"Are Nest and Owain still in Ceredigion?"

"No. The Constable was told of Owain's men who went further, to Arwstli and Maelienydd, thinking to hide in the mountains. He would have followed but news reached him. All who raided with Owain in Emlyn were destroyed by the men of Maelienydd."

"How many?"

Buddyg shrugged her shoulders. "A handful."

"It would be some revenge for Sir Gerald."

"Too small for such an angry man. He heard of others nearer here, who sought to hide in Dyfed. He had them hunted down and captured, then dragged to Carmarthen for hanging."

Heledd and Nerys were squealing with delight as the branch of a tree flicked at their passing.

"Oh, Buddyg. When will Nest be free and home again to hear her children's laughter?"

"Ceinwen asked the same and Mistress Mabli was so sure. 'The King may be in France', she said, 'but he will not rest while my lovely child is held against her will'. She knows King Henry well, does Mistress Mabli. 'With God's help', she said, 'he will use every man and woman within his reach'."

"Please God, it may be so," Manon whispered.

Soon the only sign of busy Pembroke was the track deeply rutted by many wheels and scarred by the hooves of horses and cattle. Along the way odd scraps of rags dangled from thorns, left where they were ripped from clothes. High branches were still bare and only ivy climbing twisted trunks gave any colour.

Buddyg's sigh was of deep content. "It is so good to be out of town for a while."

"A morning like this we are the first ones to breathe the air, it is so fresh."

"Aye, when the market is at its height who knows what humours spread in the gush of staleness coming from so many. I fear then for the children."

"As I do!" Manon turned an anxious face to her friend. "Buddyg, am I wrong to keep Heledd in the house so much – and Dybion? I feel the constraint myself but it would be worse if they sickened and . . ."

Buddyg hugged Manon. "We are all in God's hands but it does not hurt to thwart the Devil and all his ways. Besides, you need your children near you."

"Because of Gerwyn?"

Buddyg leaned against Manon, letting her sense warmth and comfort as the cart trundled on. The road they followed took a wide sweep away from the town and the monks on a hill nearby before it curled back towards the woods. Kamal edged the horse to the right, along a narrow way leading towards the river they could see glinting through naked trees.

"Is this the first time you have been here since . . ."

Manon nodded and looked at Buddyg, tears held back with effort and a determined sniff. "I had to come. Myrddin needed to talk with Kamal and the weather was good. It seemed right. Please God it may be so."

Buddyg's arm was around her friend's shoulders and she squeezed hard. "It will be. The girls can run in the woods as we have always wanted for them and we shall go home tonight, ready to be safe and cosy in our little town nests. These babies of ours will sleep more soundly than they have done for a while."

In spite of the reassurance Manon was anxious as Kamal jumped from the cart to lead the horse down a slope and into the busyness of the tannery. She looked at the sprawl of it with new eyes, the low hut near the water, wood-lined

164

troughs along the slope of the hill and at the top of the yard, the dung pit. A great shivering began in her and Manon clutched her belly with her mittened hands as if to console the new child.

Only when Kamal had stopped the cart and steadied it with a weight of wood against the wheels, did he lift down the mothers and then the children. The little girls squealed their excitement at the smell of woodsmoke, the sight of dripping trees and a stream coursing and bouncing down its rocky rab bed from the hill behind them as it flowed towards the river.

Heledd pulled at her skirt. "Mama, can we play?"

"Of course, cariad, it is why we are here. Now, stay in sight at all times and if a grown-up tells you to come away from somewhere, you do it, quick as you can. Promise?"

Heledd nodded, her eyes wide. She leaned her head against Manon for a moment and was off with Meinir and Nerys, Buddyg following them when she saw her friend needed solitude. Manon walked alone to the dung pit. In the place where he had ceased to live, she was lost in her love for Gerwyn.

"Dear God, let it not be the end of him loving me. I can bear all you want of me if I still have Gerwyn's love – and yours."

She was aware of someone approaching and turned to see Myrddin hobbling towards her.

"A good day to you, Mistress Manon. Am I disturbing you?"

"No, Myrddin – and I thank you for your courtesy."

"It has been hard for you coming here?"

Her tears answered him. "It had to be done," she whispered.

"Aye, a festering wound must be opened if it is to be healed."

They talked of the tannery, of Kamal's knowledge proving a Godsend, the new barks Nudd had found.

"All who work here are held in low esteem because of the smell they carry to their homes." Myrddin laughed, a creaking sound, as his chest rumbled. "Not all are as willing to use the clay and the river water to go back to their wives as fresh as Gerwyn always insisted."

It was difficult for Manon to speak but for Myrddin's sake she made an effort and he was pleased to see her wan smile. His arm swept in a great circle.

"All this is good, mistress. It was not the tannery killed your man, nor one who works here. Whoever came that night brought the evil with them."

"The man who was hanged. Do you think he was the one?"

"Mog?" Myrddin was unsure and shuffled from foot to foot. "I watched him die, the man they said killed the master." He sighed and shook his head. "Why should he deny that deed and not any of the others which must have weighted him?"

"If he did not . . ."

To them came the laughter of children as they played in and out of the trees, chasing Buddyg.

"I always trust in our sweet Lord, mistress. If Mog was not the evil one destroying here, then the truth will out – one day."

She lifted her chin and gazed at Myrddin. "You know it is said of me I conspired to have Gerwyn killed?"

The old man did not look away, facing Manon as he nodded.

"Am I the black one – in your eyes?" she asked him.

The old man smiled gently. "Never, Mistress Manon."

The relief almost made her swoon but she stiffened, proud to have his trust.

"A man so old, I have seen many women turned to widows," he said gently. "A few have been joyous at the change and soon looked for another man in her bed – if there was not one hiding there already." Myrddin talked of men he had known, husbands and fathers so brutal their deaths were a gift from God. "Most women grieve a while, then knot their kerchiefs about their throats, roll up their sleeves and do the work left undone."

"I remember," Manon said slowly. "After raids from the north that was all that could be done – children to feed, wood to be cut, homes to mend."

"Then there are women like you, lady. Grief is their shadow and in sunlight or in the gloaming, it never lessens. Only for their children do they feign pleasantness and contentment. One day, with God's help, it becomes a habit." He lifted a hand towards Buddyg, hiding behind a tree to catch Heledd as she passed. "She is as you are."

"Myrddin, you tell me your eyes are weak but I think you see too much." She smiled at him, a strange sage with his lined cheeks and white curls above the sheepskins around his body and legs.

"From my Betsan I learned about men and women. Many a time we starved together but she never lost her spirit or her smile."

It was chill, shaded by the trees on that bright day. Manon hugged herself to keep warm and Myrddin's hand was on her shoulder.

"Aye, you miss your man's arms around you, as I miss my Betsan against me – and in my bed." He chuckled and it became a fit of coughing. "You young ones," he said at last, "you see us as old. My Betsan had her wrinkles and her hair was as white as a snowfall, yet her body fitted mine and our lusts warmed us to the end."

"God was good to you, Myrddin," Manon whispered.

"We had his blessing. Your man has been taken from you but you are comely and you have wealth. There will be men who want to fill the space he has left."

"No one can."

"You speak true. Yet I can tell you there will come nights your body betrays your heart and makes you long for the blessings of St Dwynwen."

Manon knew what he said would happen in time. She cradled her hands against her unborn child and prayed it would not be soon.

"Beauty and riches, mistress, they can bring great blessings with them as they did for you." He frowned and she saw his concern for her. "Best not forget they are seen as great sins to those with ugly faces and crippled minds."

When they returned to Pembroke, Buddyg and her sleepy daughters were unloaded at their door, Ceinwen coming from her home to hear of the adventures of the day. The cart creaked on through the town and it was Manon who longed for her bed and oblivion. At the leather shop Heledd ran in to tell Gwen all that had happened since morning. Manon followed more slowly, seeing her home with new eyes. Sturdy walls, a wide hearth, a solid roof. There was food in the crocks on a shelf, flat bread on a bakestone ready for the evening meal which simmered over a fire. A rowdy banging was Dybion sitting up in his cradle and pounding on the carved wood with a spoon as he greeted his mother with a wide, toothless smile, then lifted his arms to her. She picked up her little son and buried her face in his neck, breathing in the smell of him.

"A good day then?"

"Aye." Manon smiled at Gwen. "Aye, it was."

Gwen was relieved. Her mistress had begun to find a kind of peace until Mog was hanged then the haunted look had returned to her eyes. Whatever had occurred at the tannery that day had brought with it a new serenity.

"It was so strange, Gwen. At every turn I heard 'Gerwyn was my friend'."

"Who was it spoke?"

"First it was Myrddin. He works so hard and yet his legs are so stiff and his coughing . . ."

"He has no need to work. His son, Anawrad, would keep him – and willingly."

"I know. Myrddin told me again it was he should have

168

been at the tannery that night, with Anawrad at the wedding but Gerwyn insisted he take his place, it being too cold for Myrddin to stay on watch all night. Gerwyn told him if the thief knew all the men would be at the wedding, it might tempt him into coming out of hiding. Gerwyn wanted to be the one to catch the devil. 'It should have been me, mistress', Myrddin kept saying, 'but Gerwyn was my friend'."

"Nothing but God's truth. You said yourself your man was uneasy, waiting for trouble at the tannery."

"And it came." Manon made a supreme effort and pushed aside her misery. "Myrddin was right. 'A friend to so many' he said of Gerwyn. One by one the workmen came to me and asked of my health. Each one bowed his head as he claimed Gerwyn as a friend."

"A hard day for you, mistress."

"In many ways – and yet . . . ."

"A weeping wound hurts when it is cleaned –"

"Then heals and leaves a scar," Manon murmured.

Gwen busied herself with the basket Manon had taken. "The cold and the sunshine made you all hungry."

"So it did," Manon said with a smile. "I have never seen Heledd eat so well – and Buddyg's girls too."

The flask was lifted from the basket and shaken. Gwen was puzzled. "Hungry they may have been but what did they drink? Running in the woods makes a child thirsty – if I remember aright."

"A boy came with goats and milked them to fill our cups. I would have rewarded him but he refused. 'It is little I can do. Gerwyn let me graze my goats here, on his land. He was my friend', he told me."

"The Lord's hand has been with you this day, mistress, your man helping to guide it to its mark."

"I felt him with me, Gwen. All the kindnesses he had done, they were coming back to warm me."

Gwen bustled away to nag Nudd into washing and Kamal to fetch Old Twm and Dyfrig, the new man from the workshop. Rhodri needed no reminding, his belly growling him into the warmth and good smells from the kitchen.

Manon washed her hands and dried them slowly. "Myrddin was right," she whispered to herself. "Gerwyn is still with me. I have him as a friend but oh, how I long for him as a husband in my bed."

Father prior continued to write, his fingers crabbed with cold and slow. He had been aware of the shire reeve's entry, the young man standing near the one brazier the cleric allowed himself as he worked.

"May God be with you, my son," came at last as the prior laid his pen down carefully and waited for the ink on his letter to dry.

"And with you, father," Roger fitzHugh replied. "I came as soon as my duties would permit after I received your summons." It was a relief for the young shire reeve to speak the familiar French of the king's court again.

"I am grateful."

The prior waved the young man to a chair and Roger reluctantly distanced himself from the glowing charcoal, its frail heat having little effect on cold air bounded by thick, rough stone and a low roof of wood and thatch.

"You have been diligent, my son. A sinner with many deaths on his conscience captured and answering to the greatest judge of all."

The cadence of courtly words was as music to the shire reeve. "We may all sleep more soundly now, father."

"May we? I wonder. There is still the puzzle of the tanner's death."

"Killed by the same blow as the peddler's other victims? I think not."

"There are those in Pembroke town and its countryside who would disagree with you, my son. Perhaps they are wise to do so?"

"Father?"

The prior slid his long fingers inside the sleeves of his

habit and smiled benignly at the unsavoury youth. The fool was dressed for court and not the rigours of a cold day's work in a primitive environment.

"We may not be of the world, here in the priory, but be assured we know all that transpires outside our walls. The seeds of rumours started by your men have found fertile soil amongst the mischievous and the envious. Whether or not she is guilty, there are many who hold the tanner's widow responsible for his slaying."

"That was not my intention –" Roger began but the cleric stopped him with a raised hand.

"I am sure it was not, my son, and I will acquaint Sir Gerald with that fact when I next speak with him. No, it is another matter I wish to discuss. The tannery is not far from the priory. It would be simplicity itself to dam the stream and install a mill wheel – should the land ever be part of this foundation of St Benedict."

It took a moment for the shire reeve to realise what the prior suggested. "But the dung pit, the troughs –"

"What of them? Easily dismantled by willing helpers, the land with the stream running through it could be used for a more worthy purpose – milling grain for bread to feed all the hungry gathered at our gates. Do you not agree it would be a change which might benefit so many?"

"Of course, father, but –"

"The land is not yet ours," the prior commented and waited for the slower wits of his companion to savour his meaning.

"No, sir, and it would need –"

"A licence from the king? Yes, it would, or one from the Bishop of London in King Henry's absence."

Roger was stunned by the scope of the prior's plans.

The cleric waited. "I believe you have the ear of that fine man and good churchman, the bishop?" he said smoothly, not expecting an answer. "As to the tannery, the way your men are working, Gerwyn's wife might soon be persuaded to relinquish the land to the priory."

"I do not understand, father."

The prior's smile had all the smoothness of a practised courtier. "Oh yes, my son, I think you do," he said softly. "The townspeople will use their tongues on her and condemn her."

"But if she is not guilty?"

"These unlearned ones have their own laws, do they not? If enough of them decide she should pay for her husband's death . . ."

Roger fitzHugh was left to imagine the outcome. "You want the land," he said at last.

"As well as a licence for a mill."

"But the tannery! Sir Gerald expects it to deliver him the best of leather."

"Then it may go nearer the town. The stream to the west of the palisade should suffice."

The young man was not at his ease. He knew he had been outwitted by the sharpest of minds. "What is it you would have me do, father?"

"Nothing, my son. All I will do is pray the hungry may be fed and a rich woman will cease to benefit from her husband's murder."

It had become Kamal's habit to go down to the quay each morning, seeing for himself the goods arriving in Pembroke. His sharp eyes saw any new leathers as well as the uses to which they could be put. Carried to the castle they might have been but within a week there would be copies on sale in the leather shop at a price Pembroke people could afford.

The ship docked that day had a full cargo of wine from France. The best was lifted carefully on to the backs of sure-footed ponies. One would trudge the long way round to the monk's town for the prior as the rest made their way up the steep hill and through the castle gates to be rested before it was served at high table. Lesser wines went to the shire reeve's men and the guards, any liquor too rough even for their gullets being sold on to the taverns in the town.

Gwen was in no doubt what would happen. "That new wine, be sure it is harsh enough to scour privies. Men too witless to know better will fill their bellies and addle what wits they have. Curfew or not, tonight there will be trouble!"

"Nothing new in Pembroke," Manon said with a rueful smile.

"Aye, you are right, mistress. There'll be broken heads in the morning, you mark my words."

Many nursed aching pates next day but the only talk was of Euron, a woman who lay with men for her bread. Her body was discovered at the far end of town, in a nook hidden from any lights from the hovels nearby. A worn tunic, once green, was pulled up over her head, huge bruises and bites to be seen until a kindly soul pulled her rags into a semblance of decency. Gasps of horror greeted what was exposed, a once-comely face mottled and purpled, bruises such as made by long-nailed fingers encircling her neck.

"Look!" The woman who had pulled tidy the tunic pointed to Euron's outflung hands. Her fingers were curled, their nails broken and bloody. "Whoever did this, she marked him."

Two of the reeve's men bent to the corpse, their moods and words foul from their share of the new wine. Matted hair hung from their chins and dangled under their helmets. They might have looked impressive in their jerkins studded with beaten metal had not each been bedaubed with badly wiped vomit. Questions in atrocious Welsh were shouted at the bystanders but achieved only sullen faces and silence.

"Who knows her?" Brede demanded of the crowd.

Sannan pushed gawping men aside. "I do."

One of the armed men would have dragged her nearer but she glared at him and his hand dropped to his side. Sannan was not easy to look at in the early light. Her creased and grubby tunic had faded from its original colour. It might once have been red and it was stained, its edges mired. Hitched up at the waist by a broad belt it revealed muddy legs ending in boots once worn by a man. Sannan's kerchief was tied round her hair, its dull brown strands draggling against the greyness of her neck.

Kneeling by the body Sannan touched the closed eyes and murmured a prayer, many around her protecting themselves as well as Euron's soul with the sign of the cross. Sannan's gentleness hushed the crowd around her and made its members see the corpse for what it was, a woman who had endured much and met a violent death.

"Her name is Euron," she told the reeve's men, "and she would have fought to stay alive." Sannan began feeling along the length of the dead woman's tunic, shaking her head. "Euron always carried a knife – I have seen it many times. Look, the sheath is still in place," she said and showed the soldiers the gap in the seam of the torn tunic and shaped leather on a linen belt against the skin. "The bastard must have taken the knife from her – but I swear she used it on him first."

"Is there anything more missing?"

"Her kerchief. It was a clean one."

"Next, you will be telling me his name," the taller of the two men said and earned a ripple of laughter from the crowd.

Sannan was not amused. "Aye. There is one who likes to sink his teeth into any woman he can afford. Cedifor – lives like a dog on the road past Lamphey that goes to Manorbier."

"Is that all you can tell us?"

"He will be sore, his head aching from the wine, his eyes scored deep by Euron's nails and with marks from her knife. She would not have died easy – and may God make him suffer all the torments of damnation before he rots in hell!"

174

To a chorus of 'Amen' the hunt began. The onlookers guessed this was another crime the shire reeve would want cleared away quickly before the Constable and his bad temper returned.

There was difficulty rounding up all the soldiers suffering after too much indifferent wine but by mid-morning they were riding along the tracks Sannan recommended. A weak sun was at its zenith when Cedifor was discovered. He was lying near a stream in the shelter of an old gwennie, its walls giving him some relief from the cold.

As Sannan had predicted, Cedifor was a marked man, one eye so scratched it was swollen and closed. Nails had scored deep tracks in his face and on his hands. When his arms were dragged away from his body to be tethered, blood oozed around a once-clean kerchief staunching a great wound in his gut, from which jutted the leather casing of a knife handle.

"Is this it?"

Roger fitzHugh held the knife out to Sannan when his men returned to the castle with their captive. She examined it carefully, the short blade keen and its handle covered with stitched leather.

"Aye. Gerwyn, the tanner, did that for her and made no charge – nor did he want to lie with her in exchange. He was a good man."

Manon carried her basket towards the market stalls. At every turn she heard gossip of the dead woman and Cedifor, the man ailing from his stabbing.

"May the Good Lord keep him safe for his hanging," said one man flushed with drink and ill humour. "When he dangles he should stay there a sennight. Euron was a good lay, God rest her soul."

Manon was disturbed by the way in which Euron was so easily dismissed. Whatever her life had been she was a woman and must have longed for a warm home, a decent man to provide for her and protect her. Perhaps she had even yearned for children.

"Shameful!" a clean and respectable woman declared as she lifted the thick blue wool of her tunic clear of the mud from thawing soil. "Such a slut wild in the town! With her ways she harmed us all."

"Not you, mistress," An old hag cackled with glee from a nearby stall. "Euron saved you many a busy night from your man. Old he may be but we all knew he had lusts younger than yours!"

Hurrying on, Manon heard loud whispering and turned to see who it was. Two women who were often in the leather shop had their eyes on her and their heads together so no one might hear what they said. There was a coldness between her shoulders and Manon knew it was of her they gossiped.

Was it starting again? Had Mog been believed when he had screamed his innocence of Gerwyn's murder as he dropped on the end of a rope? The questions haunted Manon as she finished her marketing and walked home, arriving there listless and pale.

Gwen advised her to, "Pay the witches no mind, mistress. Any who knew the master and who knows you, hears only lies from those hussies."

Cedifor was tried on the day he was found. When a helpful reeve's man pulled the knife from Cedifor's belly, blood gushed until the helpless killer paled and swooned. Roger fitzHugh knew justice must be swifter than usual if a living man was to be hanged and Cedifor was dragged to the castle gate and had his neck stretched with great speed.

A crowd had gathered at the gate and cheered as Cedifor swung his last, blood dripping slowly from him to land on the stones beneath his feet. A stray dog attracted by the smell, dodged and pushed through a forest of legs, licking the blood to assuage its hunger. There were cheers for the animal until a gesture from fitzHugh had the dog kicked away and decency restored. It mattered little. Cedifor's blood had long gone and the trickle stopped as he ceased to breathe.

Sannan echoed Gwen's words next morning when she pushed aside puny men and marched into Manon's home.

"Take care, mistress. There is talk in the town — bad enough for me to slap a few heads."

Manon was not dismayed by the woman's forceful entry. She took Sannan's hands in hers. "Please, Sannan. What is being said of me?"

The big ungainly woman gazed at Manon, then nodded to herself. "Best you know. The tale is that damned-to-hell Mog was right, Gerwyn's death is not laid on his soul. Whispers say another man hit Gerwyn and put him in the dung pit. A man you paid with your body to kill that fine man, your husband."

Manon gasped, breathing with difficulty as does a sleep-walker drenched with ice-cold water. From across the room Gwen screamed abuse at Sannan and raced to beat at her.

"No, Gwen," Manon said as she held Gwen's arms. "You did your best to warn me but it is only right I hear the worst being said of me. Now I know. I thank you, Sannan. You have done me a kindness."

"How can you say that," an angry Gwen needed to know.

Manon smiled at her. "Bless you, Gwen, you have been my good friend in all ways but I must hear to my face all that is whispered behind my back or hissed at me as I pass." She turned to Sannan. "Mistress Mabli told me once this was what she must do for Princess Nest in the English court. They had only the Welsh when Nest was first King William's hostage. Frankish words came very hard but Nest insisted they learn quickly and know what was being said of them. Nest must sit amongst the Frankish ladies and Mabli in the kitchens. Together they understood which of the smiling faces hid enemies. Now is the time I need to know who are my enemies. Can you name them, Gwen?"

Slowly, Gwen shook her head.

"Sannan?"

"No, mistress, but there is a stirring going on. Before, it was the reeve's men asking questions but they are silent. Now it is a murmur here, a whisper there, then beer or wine to muddle where the rumour starts. I will find the evil one if I can."

"You are truly kind, Sannan. Why would you do all this for me?"

It was a rich, rollicking noise, the laughter from Sannan's belly. "I am called every bad name – in the old Welsh as well as the new. I have a hide thicker than your good man ever tanned – and a sight thicker than yours," she said gently to Manon. "You have always spoken fair to me and there are not many like you who will."

"You know the worst said of me and yet you do not believe it. Why?"

"If you were the kind of cunning bitch the evil tongues say you are, Gerwyn could never have loved you as he did."

Tears flooded Manon's eyes. "I thank God for you, Sannan, as I do for Gwen. Only those who are like you have helped me since the year was new. The Lord knows I did not want to lose my Gerwyn. When he died a part of me went too."

"She was near to losing her reason," Gwen told the big woman.

"So I was told – but anyone with eyes to see could tell you pined. Take heart, mistress. I have big ears and I will hear who is the cause of all the distress you are being caused. Until then I must listen – and bang a few heads together, for your sake and for Gerwyn. He was a good friend."

178

Chapter Ten

Winter was dying and there was an itch in the air. Women shook fleeces and blankets, lessening fleas and lice. Brawls were more frequent in taverns and beershops. Urchins dodged faster, were more daring, as they jostled and thieved, while a growing pack of dogs barked and ran wild.

Roger fitzHugh was pleased with himself. The Constable might have been away many weeks in pursuit of Owain and Wales was in uproar but Pembroke remained quiet. The shire reeve's grip on the town and its surrounding country-side was tight, tight enough to force even the most compliant man into silent resentment.

True, there had been complaints. He admitted only to himself one or two of the men under his command had been over-zealous in their dealings with the scum of the town and of course there had been murders. On his return Sir Gerald would have little fault to find in that quarter, Roger decided. Once he had found Mog in Tenby, still in possession of the youngest victim's carved whistle, the arrest, trial and hanging had taken but two days.

As for Cedifor, the latest to swing, his justice had occupied less than a day, a necessary urgency when the man was half-dead already. Roger fitzHugh frowned at the memory. It had been difficult to get the wretch's head in the noose, unconscious as he was. The festering sore that was his gut stabbed by the dying harlot, had given off such a stench the hangman himself had turned his head away to throw up bread and meat.

Pleased with himself, the shire reeve was unaware of the intense bitterness in the air of Pembroke, released as constant bickering among neighbours, arguments over prices charged at market, the slapping and punching of whores in taverns and alleyways. Such women were not slow to retaliate and three of them had been flung into the reeking security of a cell in the castle.

Only tongues enjoyed freedom and their owners used them to lash victims and achieve a momentary illusion of justice in a harsh world. Little was needed to rouse up a storm of words and it was not long before Manon realised she was becoming the outlet for a building resentment. When words flung at her became spittle, then stones, she ventured out only when neither Heledd nor Rhodri were with her.

With the noise in the town at its shrillest next market day, Cynfan the baker pushed his way through from the shop, brushing aside Kamal as he came.

"Leave us!" he ordered Gwen and at a nod from Manon she did so, but not out of earshot. "Mistress Manon, it is time for you to get away from Pembroke."

She held he head high, proud. "You are a good friend to be so concerned and I agree it is not pleasant but it will pass. It did so before."

The big man was restless, ill at ease. "This is different, mistress, believe me. I have no proof but I would swear someone has loosed the hounds of hell to bay for your blood."

His earnestness frightened her. "But who? Why?" she asked, her eyes wide with the beginnings of fear.

"If you wait to find out it will be too late. Let me take you and your children to safety," he urged. "I have silver hidden and I have a trade. There is always need for bread so we

180

could live well in Tenby, say. Or Carmarthen? That far away the king's rule holds and you would not be hunted."

Manon had paled at his words but she was spirited still and shook her head. "No, Cynfan. I thank you for your concern and your desire to help my family but the children are God's gift as well as in my charge. We stay here." She had not realised as she spoke, her hands shaped a shelter around the curve of her belly.

Cynfan was no fool. "You carry Gerwyn's child?"

"Yes," Manon said quietly and lifted her head to smile at him.

"Then let me take on Gerwyn's duties to you and the unborn one."

She was shocked. "It would not be right!"

"If we married there would be no difficulty." He did not wait for her reply. "I beg you, Manon. I would give my life, let alone my name, to help you and the little ones. Rhodri, Heledd, young Dybion, they would be as my own – and the new babe would know no other father."

She held out a hand to him and he held it gently in both of his. "You are kind, Cynfan, but such an action would confirm what my enemies suspect. It is said of me I used a man to end Gerwyn's life that I may take another husband. You would hang with me."

He began to protest and would have pulled her to him but she stopped him with a gentle shake of her head.

"No, my dear friend, it must not be as you wish. There is hate for me and I do not know its face."

"That damned sister of Gerwyn's?"

"I think not. Her strong dislike of me is clear for all to see but one thing I know of Non, when she wishes me harm, she enjoys the task too much to share the pleasure with anyone – nor would she ever allow any man to usurp her rights, as she sees them. I know of no one daring enough to risk Non's spite. Sannan has felt the evil as it springs and she swears it is from a man."

"You believe Sannan? A whore?"

"Why not? She is a good woman in her way and she has been kind to me. Oh, Cynfan, whatever is ahead of me I must face it alone. For the sake of my children – and Gerwyn."

In the home which had held so much promise, Cynfan knew there was nothing more for him. The big man was desolate but he summoned his dignity and bowed to the spirit of the woman he loved.

"Then may God help you, Manon," he said softly.

Next day it was Ithel who appeared. He came very early, as Kamal and Rhodri took down the wooden slats which secured the front of the shop through the night. Newly combed silver hair shone in the bright early flames of the fire and once again Gwen was waved away. Manon greeted her visitor as she cut bread for the first meal of the day.

Ithel smoothed the black velvet of his sleeves. "Many men and women work for me one way or another, and I hear of everything that passes in the town. There are many like me, Mistress Manon, honest folk who admire you and defend your name." He hesitated, seeking time to choose his words carefully.

Manon put the bread on a wooden platter before she looked up at Ithel. "There are others?"

"Indeed there are – and they will stand in shame before their maker when the time comes for them to answer for their sins."

"As we all must."

Ithel stepped closer to her. "I would not have that come too soon, Mistress Manon, but there are those who would have it so."

It was early in the day but Manon was tired. "Who is it wants me dead, Ithel?"

He was surprised she said it so calmly. "I have as yet been told no name. Rumours are in the air and to grasp the truth in them is like trying to catch a handful of mist as the breeze rises."

Manon nodded. "Even a spider can be held by its unseen thread but the man who would see me hang leaves no such trail. Why should he be so treacherous to me?"

"A man? Not a woman?"

"I am assured the talk starts when only men are gathered."

Dybion had cried in the night, his gums reddened with new teeth and there had been little sleep for his mother. She made herself stand tall and smiled at Ithel, grateful for his concern.

"You are a good man and a good friend."

"Then let me be a better one." Ithel moved closer, feeling the heat from the fire on his cheek. "Sir Gerald's interest is in Emlyn now he has been deeded land there. One castle may have been burned but he is a stubborn man and another will rise on his land in the north as soon as he has his wife back and Owain dead. The castle here in Pembroke is important to King Henry and he must keep it filled with men who can defend the coast against rebels or against invaders from the sea. The haven of Pembroke will always be useful for trade but with Princess Nest gone, the English king's patronage will move elsewhere."

Manon was angry. "But Nest will return. She must!"

"If God is good to her, then it will be as you say. Yet as a wife used for so long by another, her marriage to the Frank will be cooled. He will keep her close and watch her well. It can never be as it was before, mark my words, mistress. You will see the stream of coin into the coffers of the town's merchants become a trickle."

Manon was horrified by his words. "You talk of Nest's agony in terms of money?"

"No, indeed I do not but I watch the flow of life in Pembroke. I hear of the bartering, the gleaning of silver and copper. While Sir Gerald ruled here and his lady was in Carew with the king's blessing, there was a certainty in the air. Sir Gerald is no weakling and with him as Constable the entire shire of Pembroke thrived. You know yourself the fine surge of trade in the town as he equipped himself and his family to live on the banks of the Teifi in Emlyn. With him gone there, fewer traders come, fewer stalls open at the end of town."

"There must always be a market. Farmers and their wives have nowhere else to get such a good return for their produce. Do you suggest they trudge all day to get to Tenby?"

"No, Pembroke will always have good food for sale – the land here is so rich. I ask you to think of the journeymen who haunt any place where money flows freely. What of workers in leather and metal with belts and brooches? Potters with bowls and flasks? Bards and jugglers who entertain?"

"Surely they have little effect on the merchants in Pembroke?"

"You are right, Mistress Manon, but when they come it is a sign of health. Last market day there were but two traveller's stalls open. No, with Sir Gerald and his lady gone, so has the smell of wealth which attracted many to come here."

Manon was puzzled. "I understand what it is you say but what has it to do with me?"

"There are those left in Pembroke with naught to do but wag their tongues."

"It will pass, God willing."

"Aye, it will, but not before someone has seen to it you are taken from us and hanged."

A wave of fear rushed through her and Manon closed her eyes, her hands resting on the child she carried.

"I am sorry, mistress, but you must see the danger which threatens you. There is no safety for you, or your children, in Pembroke." A sudden redness suffused his cheeks. "In God's name, Gerwyn is already dead! Of what use are you to your children if you follow their father to the grave?"

Struggling to breathe normally, Manon clutched the wool

184

of her tunic, the better to still shaking fingers. "What would you have me do?"

Ithel drew near and bent towards her. "Leave this place."

"How can I? The shop is our livelihood."

"Let me take you far away. Somewhere you can live in comfort and safety."

It was all horribly familiar. "Tenby, I suppose. Or Carmarthen?"

"Even further. Cardiff we could soon reach by boat and be too distant for Pembroke gossip to harm you."

"Cardiff?" she whispered, appalled by all she had heard of the vast, unknown sprawl of a town.

"There is good money to be made there, once we are established. I have silver put by and with the sale of your properties –"

Quietly, Manon reminded him who would own the farms and the tannery. "The stock and goodwill of this shop have been promised to Gwen and Kamal – should I have to leave here for any reason. The rent they will pay should feed Gerwyn's children."

Ithel's face was as white as his hair and Manon had it in her heart to pity him. She had known he had a softness towards her because of her youth but he was always a man to heed above all things, the jingling of a pouch.

"It was kind of you to think of leaving all you have here to help me. Now you understand why I trust in God – and God alone – to help me stand against my enemies and protect Gerwyn's children."

"You are a strong woman, Manon," Ithel said gently and bowed to her. "May the Good Lord himself help you in the hard times to come."

"Sir, a ship is coming upriver."

At the steward's words Roger laid down his spoon reluctantly. The cooks had at last managed to prepare a dish as he ordered and now it would cool.

"It is heavily laden, sir, and carries Sir Gerald's emblem on the mast."

"Laden? Cargo?"

"No, sir. Men. Some are lying on the deck."

"Wounded – that is all I need. Send a messenger to Carew."

The steward turned to go.

"By boat. Four rowers. They are to return immediately with the mediciner, Mabli. Go with them and do not return without her."

Attending to sick men was not part of his duties, the shire reeve decided and gave his attention to the rabbit simmered slowly in wine and herbs before the freshest cream was added. He was right. The dish had cooled and men he deemed injured in pursuit of the king's whore, as he named her, were loudly condemned to further suffering.

His meal completed, Roger changed his embroidered shoes for strong boots and was swathed in his cloak by an anxious squire.

"Ma chambre," he began, then realised the boy was puzzled. It infuriated him the child was of de Windsor's training and used only the local tongue. "The place I sleep, guard it well. No one is to use it, comprends-tu?"

The boy gulped, guessing experienced soldiers senior to the shire reeve would be in the castle grounds within minutes.

"No one!" Roger shouted and marched off to reduce to a minimum the chaos entering his life.

Men wounded in skirmishes while searching for Princess Nest were lifted carefully from the ship. Buddyg had the news from Ceinwen, who had it in turn from Mistress Mabli, ferried in haste from Carew to take charge of the healing of the injured.

"Any of them who could speak told of Sir Gerald driving himself and everyone else without cease. He has been ruthless with any enemies captured, or indeed those who have seen or heard aught of the devil, Owain."

"Had any seen Nest?" Manon asked.

"None who have been returned to Pembroke but there are stories of those in the north, well into Ceredigion and beyond, who glimpsed the pair. Owain was his usual self, charming when it suited – but impatient."

"Nest?"

"One man was said to have talked of King Rhys' daughter. It was the usual tale. This time her face was bruised and she held her head stiffly, closing her eyes when she could."

Manon bent her head as she prayed for her friend. "Sir Gerald?" she asked Buddyg.

"At first he seemed glad to hear of her wounds, then it was as if Satan was in him. He had the men saddle up before sunrise, breaking their fast as they rode at a Devil's pace for God knows where."

Gwen was puzzled. "Why should he be glad his wife had been beaten?"

"A willing bedmate need no beating," Manon said and Buddyg nodded her agreement.

"So, it was rape?" Gwen asked.

"Does Owain know of any other way of lying with a woman?" Manon remembered the raid on her home in the Gwaun valley. "For sure, his father's men did not."

Activity in and around the castle took attention from Manon's supposed sins and she was grateful. Mistress Mabli had been shocked at the sight of the wounds the men bore and hurried to remedy the neglect. Immediately, she sent out a cry for maggots.

Winter's grip still held under the trees and the white grubs were rare. Nudd went into the woods, his nose helping him trace rotting carcases. Children followed him, fighting with Nudd and amongst themselves so as to be the ones who carried maggots to the castle and be paid for them with food.

187

Opinions raged along the rows of houses, stall, shops, while market days had an extra buzz of noise. Using maggots to clean wounds was not uncommon but the idea of so many being laid on deep gashes which had festered for so long had the good and bad people of Pembroke delighting and shivering in equal parts.

All this gave Manon the privacy she needed to put into practice what occupied her waking hours through the long, dark nights.

"Will you have them in your care?" she asked Buddyg.

"The children? They are welcome in my home, you know that – but why should you be so afraid?"

"I wish I knew," Manon told her as she twisted her hands in her lap.

Buddyg covered her friend's cold fingers, the warmth easing terror a little. Manon reached into her tunic for a small pouch which jingled.

"Keep this ready."

"Manon, no! Your children –"

"Please, Buddyg. If they do come to you, there is no knowing how long they must stay."

Buddyg tried to hand back the pouch. "There is no need."

"Indeed there is. My mind will be easier."

"Then I will keep your money and hand it back to you when happier days return."

"May God make it soon, Buddyg. The enemy I am unable to see – he will not rest as long as I draw breath."

With Gwen's help Manon put her house in order. At the tannery and in the shop Kamal prepared for difficult days to come. Manon's blood chilled as she saw leather goods ready for sale stored not in the shop or the workshop but in the yard, buckets of water ready in case of fire. Nudd helped, his bent form scurrying wherever he was needed. More water stood by doorways, only food and necessary tools were in sight and no valuables could be seen. From the roadway nothing appeared altered to anyone passing.

There was a warm welcome for one visitor who limped into the activity. "Myrddin! It is good to see you. You are well?" Manon held out her hands to him, her smile wide and handsome, then her eyes narrowed. She was disturbed by his obvious concern. "What is amiss?"

"If it sits well with you, mistress, I will come each day before curfew."

"We will be glad of your company, be assured of that, but you have a reason, I think?"

"When there was stealing I watched the tannery through each night until the awful one when Gerwyn took pity on my aching legs – and died for it. Now, it is little enough I can do to keep watch while you and your children sleep."

"I am grateful, Myrddin, as Gerwyn would be."

"Then that is enough for me, mistress."

Brother Paulinus hurried from the priory gate. He had been dealing with the destitute as well as hopeful traders, listening to endless woes and pleas as well as overhearing gossip tossed back and forth. He coughed gently, trying to attract the prior's attention.

"There is a difficulty, Brother Paulinus?"

"No, father. Cynfan the baker has sent loaves and the cauldron of soup will be enough today."

"That is good, my son. You have thanked Cynfan?"

"Of course, father, but he is an angry man."

The prior raised thin brows in surprise, his pale eyes alert. "Cynfan? Did he say why?"

"The widow of his friend, Gerwyn."

"Ah, yes. The tanner so brutally killed."

"Cynfan says she is being persecuted in the town and the shire reeve is content to let such discord continue."

"Then brother, we must pray for God's help."

The young monk followed his superior into the strength of stone walls and low wooden roof, to the altar illumined by its candles. The prior sank to his knees and gazed at the cross before his eyes.

His companion paused before kneeling, impressed by the clean, sharp lines of the prior's face. The older man was intent on the cross, his lips moving in a silent prayer. How good he was, the monk thought and was humbled.

Myrddin had only one peaceful night before the mood of the town worsened. Earlier that day Manon had tried to visit Buddyg but had been jostled and covered with spittle until she resigned herself to confinement in her own home.

"Those women should be whipped!" Gwen said viciously as she scrubbed at Manon's cloak and tunic. "I will soon have these clean and dried but what passes for their evil tongues needs more than clay and a twist of sticks to rub them raw and make them sweet."

"It is getting nearer, Gwen."

"What, mistress?"

"The day I see my traitor. Then, with God's help, I will know what to do."

"You have no idea?"

"None. It could be any man in the crowd out there."

"Because of Sannan you are still sure it is one man?"

Manon nodded. "And Cynfan, Myrddin too. They feel no woman has a part in this."

"Yet it is a woman's way, twisting the truth and forging it to her liking."

"And there are men who would make good women."

Gwen's healthy laughter cleared the air. "Aye, and some are too timid to be either," she said and stretched Manon's clothes to steam by the fire.

While Manon smiled and nodded she kept her thoughts to herself. She had long wondered why her foe did not merely shove a knife between her ribs and be done with it.

Was it just the risk of being caught that stayed his hand or was there a deeper, darker reason?

It was an hour before couvre feu when the old man came to her.

"Mistress, is there wood enough to strengthen your doors and shutters?"

Manon did her best to appear calm in front of her children. "Of course, Myrddin. Kamal and Nudd will help you." Heledd, sensing danger, stood against her mother and gazed up at Myrddin with huge eyes. "Will you sit and have supper with us first?" her mother asked the old man.

"Later, mistress. I will enjoy your bread and meat but I must earn it first," he said and grinned at Heledd, bending to tickle her chin until the child giggled.

The men went in search of suitable wood and Rhodri was sent to fetch the goat.

"You want me to bring her in here, Mam?"

"Yes, Rhodri – no need to go outdoors to milk her."

"What about Pig, Mam? Does he come inside too?"

Nudd's pet was almost full grown but as tame and docile as any household animal.

"Nudd has a little space for him inside the woodpile. Pig will be safe there."

It had all been planned. Without saying a word Gwen damped down the fire so disturbed flames could not leap and destroy. She kept the children busy, Dybion sitting in his corner, clapping his hands in delight at the bustle and excitement in the air. Manon watched the men pile planks and logs against the front walls. She helped carry from the shop the last of the stitched goods to be stacked in the yard. The pile was protected when Kamal piled on it branches topped with wet fleeces to deter fire.

Old Twm was not to be hurried, his knife slicing the ends of staves to murderously sharp points. "Keep 'em by the wall at the back, mistress," he advised.

She was puzzled. "What are they for?"

A wicked glint in his eyes, gums empty and wide in a grin, the old man's chest crackled as he laughed. "Shove 'em in if they try to get over. Only try it once, they will."

Manon returned to the kitchen, pausing at the door to bend her head in prayer. Her pleas to God were for her children and the workers who had become kindred spirits.

"Sweet Lord, let them not be harmed because of me." The baby she carried kicked and in Manon there was a lift of hope. "We are all in Your hands," she whispered and pushed open the door.

Gwen had Heledd and Rhodri setting out slabs of bread on the table she ladled a rich stew into bowls. The smell was enough to summon hungry men and the meal was eaten in silence, every ear alert for danger.

It was as emptied bowls were being gathered, crumbs and crusts swept to the floor for the goat that a wave of noise hit the front of the building. It was quickly followed by blows on the wood from flung stones, some of them splintering the shutters on the shop front.

The men in the house scattered, each standing by buckets brimming with water. The walls at the front held and Nudd stabbed at any hands or heads rising above the back wall by the river. He was rewarded by shrieks of pain and fewer bodies ready to scale the palisade.

From the roadway, assailants continued to hurl abuse and stones in equal quantity and Manon could hear women's voices urging the men to, "Go in and kill the bitch!"

The bitch they spoke of knew it must end soon. The shire reeve was in Pembroke and would not allow any breach of his Frankish law of couvre feu while he was so close at hand. Almost as the shutters finally gave way there was the sound of horses, the clattering of iron and the deep-throated bellowing of huge men.

Stones ceased to rain on the leather shop and screaming was muted to an unpleasant murmuring. There was more pounding on the door as Roger fitzHugh demanded entrance. Myrddin, flanked by Kamal and Old Twm carrying staves, opened the door and pulled it wide.

Behind the shire reeve and his men, the roughest of Pembroke townsfolk pushed and shoved to get into Manon's home or at the very least, see and hear what was going on in there. Orders were shouted for a strong guard to stand with swords drawn at the entrance. Only when that barrier was in place did Roger fitzHugh march towards the light and warmth of the kitchen where Manon waited. She held herself proudly, convincing him she was unashamed by any guilt and trying to assure herself she was unafraid.

"Ma dame," the shire reeve began, "I regret the disturbance you have caused." His accent was strong, his words a mixture of Welsh and French.

"I, sir? I have been here with my children, troubling no one."

"No, ma dame? If my men were not in front of your door, I say this house and shop would have been wrecked and looted by your fellow countrymen."

"They have no reason to do so."

"Then why do so many of them tell me the wish is for you to pay for your husband's murder?"

"I had no part in Gerwyn's death – except to bury him and grieve day and night for the loss of him."

"Are so many wrong?"

"Yes, sir. In God's name, I am the one who must endure life without Gerwyn. As the good Lord is my witness, I am the one who weeps for him, who holds his children as they cry with longing, yet there are those who whisper my guilt and persuade men – men drunk with beer and your Frankish wine – that I am evil. Why do you not search out whoever it is causes me such agony? He is the one who throws the king's peace to the winds."

"Enough, ma dame! It is past the hour of couvre feu and I will have Pembroke silent!"

Roger fitzHugh spoke in swift French to Brede and Rolf. They reached for Manon and grabbed her arms. Gwen flew at them, beating at the steeled leather of their jerkins with angry fists. Myrddin blocked the way and was thrust aside.

"Gwen! The children, remember!" Manon cried out as she was dragged away.

There was no time for more. Nudd lifted Manon's cloak from a hook on the wall and her sheepskin boots from a dark corner. He ran after the soldiers, pulling at them until one took the cloak and boots.

Kamal held Nudd at the door of the shop, preventing the boy from rushing out into the crowd. They watched from behind two armed guards, Nudd crying and knuckling his eyes as Manon was led towards the castle. After the dimness of the passageway and the shop the light from a multitude of flares and the acrid smoke flurrying towards her stung Manon's eyes. Gripped tightly, she could not lift a hand to shelter her eyes, nor wipe the tears which streamed from them.

Horsemen used their destriers to hold back the crowd, howls telling of unshod feet trodden by massive hooves. The animals served their purpose. Had they not done so Manon would have been pushed to the ground by the crowd, there to beaten and kicked until she died.

Even with the protection around her she found it difficult to stand upright and walk. She stumbled along as best she could, being dragged when her steps faltered. Smells of greasy leather, unwashed bodies, foul breaths from her captors made breathing unpleasant and the little stew she had eaten at supper was kept in her stomach with difficulty.

As the castle gates closed behind her, Roger fitzHugh and his men slowed their pace and Manon could walk more steadily. She had come such a short distance but her world had changed. Around the bailey groups of men stopped to watch her by the light of flares raised in sconces on the walls and she could see she was being led to a small hut built of hewn wood and solidly roofed.

194

"With you safely locked here, ma dame, the town will be silent. In the morning I will decide what must be done with you."

The shire reeve waved her in with an impatient hand and a strong push had her tumbling to her knees in the darkness. Cloak, boots, were flung in after her and the door swung into place. Immediately, a wooden bar fell in slots ready for it and in Manon rose a choking fear.

Tears were a relief and flowed steadily as she crawled around the stinking floor, searching for her clothes. A finger touched clean wool and she swirled the cloak around her body, wrapping it tightly and not knowing if it was only the cold which made her shiver so violently.

Boots were harder to find but Manon persevered and slowly pulled them on her feet, brushing away straw she was sure had been nibbled by rats. One corner of the tiny cell had few draughts and she huddled there, caressing the movements of the child within her and crooning to it. As if in a dream Manon imagined herself at home by the fire, Heledd, Dybion, Rhodri sitting nearby while in the background the shadowy figure of Gerwyn watched over them all.

Praying, crying, occasionally sleeping for fitful moments, the hours passed until she could see the door outlined by the faintest of lights. Slowly, it grew bright. Manon stood and stretched aching limbs as she begged God for the strength to face the day to come.

Chapter Eleven

No one came.

There was barely light enough for Manon to see the prison she paced in short steps. One corner was filthy and foetid, to be visited only when she needed relief. The rest of the hut was bare walls, a draughty roof, and ancient straw mixed with indescribable rubbish. She leaned an ear against a gap between door and wall. Outside, the castle was busy with noises. Men hawked and spat, shouted oaths, roared with laughter. Horses chewed bits, shook their heads and harness jangled.

Time passed and she could smell cooking fires, hear good-humoured banter as bones were gnawed and thrown to growling dogs. The thought of food was no help to Manon, her gorge rising as she waited for someone to come to her but she waited in vain. Horsemen, four she thought, clattered past and there were creaking sounds she had learned was the main gate opening and closing.

Men passed nearby and shouted. She thought she heard a woman cackle in response but it was all too far away for Manon to hear what she said. Nearer, a blacksmith began work, cursing a boy who yelped when he was kicked. The hammer blows of the workman pounding metal beat a rhythm into Manon until she was shaking, longing for peace, but there was no end to it. She was exhausted, lying on the straw and resigned to misery.

It was hard for her to know the hours she spent alone but at last the wooden bar scraped as it was lifted from the door. Manon blinked in the light streaming into her prison and saw Gwen carrying a basket.

"Dear God, cariad!" Gwen hid her face and her tears as she placed the basket carefully on the floor and tried to hide her agitation at the sight of her mistress.

Manon started up and rubbed at eyes sore in the sudden light. "The children?"

"They are safe and well and with Buddyg. I took them there this morning as soon as it was light and already her girls are spoiling Dybion and Heledd."

"Rhodri?"

"Bless him, he is being too much of a man for sport with little girls."

The thought brought tears and Gwen knelt by the stricken woman. She held Manon, rocking and crooning to her as she would a distressed child. When the shivering and crying lessened, Gwen took off her own cloak and wrapped it round her mistress. Then, with the linen cloth which had covered the basket, she made a seat for them on the filth of the floor.

"Come now, cariad. You must be hungry – and thirsty." Gwen reached in the basket for a cup and a covered jug. "Milk fresh from the nanny, it will hearten you."

Manon tried to sip but her teeth rattled on the cup. "Oh, Gwen!"

"You can do it." Gwen's strong fingers surrounded Manon's and helped her become steady. Careful sips became gulps and the milk was drunk quickly. "Good. Now you must eat."

Manon pushed away the fresh bread and cheese Gwen had ready for her.

"Yes, cariad, a stinking hole like this sickens you but that babe inside you needs to break its fast and must do so through you."

Wearily, Manon laid her head on Gwen's shoulder and was fed, crumb by crumb, until half the food in the basket had gone.

"There." Gwen smiled at her mistress. "You will be stronger now and can eat the rest later."

"Tell me what is happening out there."

"In the castle? Very little. Men are snoring when not working or marching this way and that to look important."

"At home?"

"All is quiet. Two of the reeve's men guard the shop. Dyfrig returned this morning. He helped Kamal and Myrddin put right the damage from last night and Ithel the moneylender sent a man to help. Cynfan came early and brought the bread for you. I did not see him, I was with the children."

"Tell me about them."

Gwen saw the hunger in Manon's face and talked of rousing the young ones, dressing them, wrapping fresh clothes in bundles to be carried.

"Myrddin came with us, Rhodri trying hard to match his steps."

Manon smiled at the thought, then tears came as she remembered Rhodri doing the same thing with Gerwyn, not so long ago.

"And you are sure they are well?"

"Yes, cariad, I am sure," Gwen said softly and felt Manon relax against her. She talked of the house and the shop, the men tidying the yard, sorting the stock.

"You have fed the men well?"

"As I was allowed."

Manon lifted her head, struggling to see the expression on Gwen's face. "Who would stop you?"

Silence grew and was made stark by the noises outside the hut.

"The black she-devil," Gwen said at last. "She came mid-morning, full of plans."

"Non?"

In the dimness Manon saw Gwen nod.

"So soon? How could she have known?"

"Bad news travels fast – and she has big ears."

"How did she get into town?"

"Her man brought her but he did not stay. At least he will get a little peace while she haunts Pembroke."

"She has not been near the children? Please, Gwen, tell me she has not harmed them!"

"Hush, cariad, your little ones are safe with Buddyg. The lady Ceinwen, is helping her and if the black witch goes near she will get Prince Hywel roaring at her like the dragons of old. Good at the roaring he is, that son of King Rhys."

"Why did she come? What is it she wants?"

"Everything you have, cariad – but she finds nothing." Gwen chuckled. "I wish you could see her hunt. The children denied her tongue, she began in the shop. Kamal she ignores because he is an outlander and the new man is so shy he hides away in corners. As for Nudd and Old Twm they gaze at her as though she is from another land and have her well confused. She tried ordering them about but Myrddin is bigger than she and he bellows at her – good as Prince Hywel sometimes. 'We will get all in order but we will not take down the shutters and trade until the mistress returns to us' he told her and she was so angered I feared the apoplexy for her."

Gwen had tried to make her voice as gruff as Myrddin's had been and was rewarded by Manon's faint smile.

"Non does not take kindly to being thwarted."

"No she does not! The house has been gone through like Owain ap Cadwgan's men on a raid."

"Has she left us anything, Gwen?"

"Even she may not take what is not there to find," the younger woman said with a sly smile.

Manon was puzzled by the hidden meaning in Gwen's words. "Of course, the money! So, she did come after it?"

"I must wear my kerchief across my face so she does not see me smile. Every corner has been poked and disturbed."

"The hearth –?"

"Was the first place she searched. Burnt her tunic, knocking apart the wood as it heated water for washing. I was sent out while she dug but I peeped through a crack in the door and watched her reach the stone under the fire. You should have seen her face as she tried to lift it! Blowing on her fingers, she was, and spitting on them until she reached for the long poker and prised up the stone."

"She found the box?"

"Aye, and was burned worse in her haste to get it open."

Manon was weary but even she laughed at the thought of Non's face. "She was angry?"

"Satan himself never had such a temper. That was when she started going mad – like a whirlwind she was – and no corner of the house left untouched. I asked her what she had lost and was sent to hell for my courtesy. All I could do was tidy behind her. That riled her and I was tempted to tell her where you kept your riches, cariad, just to see her face."

"No!"

Gwen hugged her mistress. "I did not. Better to keep her good and mad then like the Devil, she will disappear in a puff of smoke."

"Thank you, Gwen," Manon whispered.

The silver under the hearth had been dug up two days before. Hidden in a basket and covered with some of Nudd's sage and rosemary, it had been carried by Ceinwen. She had taken it to Mabli for safe keeping in the castle.

Nibbles of bread and cheese shortened the hours yet Manon was still uneasy when summoned before it was dark to face the shire reeve, sitting in the hall in a frowsty blue velvet tunic. For someone so young he had the colour of a man whose stomach sat uneasily in him, Manon thought. She saw his frown, an unwanted sprout of beard and decided he was in a foul mood.

"I have been kind, ma dame," he growled at her in his usual mix of Welsh sprinkled with French.

Manon's chin lifted defiantly. "Kind, sir? You have surely been over-courteous. Against my will I am taken from my children and my home. Then I am locked away in filth."

"Enough! Remember, because of you the town is – en derangement – and there is rebellion."

"I am not the cause, sir."

"No? I remove you and all is – tranquille."

"So, it was for you to have peace I must be taken from my family and housed as a common felon?"

Roger fitzHugh's skin darkened. "There is much talk, ma dame. Your husband is dead."

"That is my grief, sir, and my children's."

"Grief, you say? It was your plot to kill your husband."

"No!"

"Oui, ma dame. All the talk is of your – conspiration. Justice demands a trial."

"Why should I be tried when I have done no wrong?"

"Others will decide if you live or die. I have been too – facile – with you. There is much talk in the town you are couched too soft and private for a murderess." He turned to his sergeant "Take her away."

Manon could scream her innocence but it had no effect on the armed men who dragged her to a far corner of the bailey and unlocked a door in a squat, stone building. A barred space in one wall allowed in light, enough for her to see what had once been straw on the floor. Shapes moved and there was rustling.

"Please God, no," she whispered, dreading the rats which must infest the place.

Like a death knell the door slammed shut and was locked behind her. Almost at once she was aware of something hideous approaching. Her tunic was tugged and a face rose, appearing in front of her like a spirit from another world. Manon stifled a scream as wispy grey hair around a mass of wrinkles and naked gums loomed near.

"Old Myfi means no harm," a voice called from under the window.

Manon was becoming accustomed to the darkness and she began to distinguish pale blobs which gradually took the shape of dirt-streaked faces. She struggled to remember. Myfi was a name she had heard. A destitute old woman who stole crusts from houses and picked over dead men's clothes. Then there had been gossip of two whores taken by the shire reeve's men to make beershops and taverns safe for drinkers.

Sinking down on the rotting straw Manon realised the degradation to which her unknown enemy had brought her. Why? Surely no other woman had been so ill-used and for so little reason? She had not knowingly harmed a soul yet she must be made lower than a leper. Even Nudd's Pig had a better life.

As Manon despaired thoughts of Nest came to her. "Was it like this for you?" she whispered into the darkness.

Nest had been held by the Franks as a hostage when she was too young to be a woman. She had survived the harshness of Frankish courts to live at last in contentment at Carew. Her husband's ambitions had taken them north to Cenarth Bychan in Emlyn and it was cruel Nest should be a prisoner again. This time she was the captive of a ruthless man who used her body at will and called it love. How she must have struggled to free her children. They had been returned and Nest must live in hope Sir Gerald would not rest until he reached her and his son.

"But Gerwyn is dead," Manon whispered into the foetid air. "How can I survive – and my child with me?"

She pulled her cloak warmly about her and curved herself to protect the baby, longing for the peace of her home and the sound of Dybion breathing nearby. Tears relieved the misery and Manon stayed huddled in her corner, time having no more meaning.

The door was kicked open. "Hot food for the lady who kills husbands," the guard jeered and dumped a basket at Manon's feet.

The door was closed and barred again before Manon could see what it was Gwen had carried for her. The smell of stew and fresh bread brought from their corners all the waiting animals on two legs and on four. The basket was snatched away and Old Myfi tugged Manon's cloak from her as she rose to defend the supper her unborn child needed.

Fingers pulled her hair, long nails scraped her face and fists pummelled her until she fell. All she could think of in the darkness was the baby and Manon curled into a ball, letting kicks rain on her head, her shoulders, her back. Pain soared, taking with it her wits and flooding her with darkness.

Manon could hear a faint voice coming from afar, a voice she knew.

"Where is she? In God's name what have you done to her? If she dies I will see you all hang!"

Past caring, Manon floated away again to a place of shining peace. Hands grasped her and shook her body, refusing her the comfort and serenity which was so near.

"Cariad, speak to me! Tell me you live!"

After a night of oblivion Manon was as rigid as death with cold and pain and her groan was quiet, almost unheard.

"Thanks be to God!" said the voice and there was movement. "You! Call yourself a guard? Fetch Mistress Mabli this instant – or hang alongside these bitches for the murder of this sweet lady."

A man rumbled an argument and Manon slid gently towards the light waiting for her. It was peaceful, inevitable, welcoming, but the noisy voice went on. It berated Manon's companions, promised the guard eternal damnation, pleaded with Manon to speak. Her sigh was tiny, a regret she could not drift into the haven she had glimpsed.

Gwen pulled the thick cloak away from Old Myfi and wrapped it, fleas and all around Manon, cradling her in an attempt to revive an almost lifeless body.

"You are not to die on me, do you hear? Your children need you. We will get some good food inside you, then you will be yourself again."

Manon longed for quiescence but she was shaken.

"Cariad, please," begged Gwen. "Please stay with me."

A warm face was against hers, warm air breathed into her nostrils. Hands were rubbed and Manon felt gentle tears on her skin. As from a distance she knew they were not her tears.

Rustlings and murmurs were ended by firm fingers on her wrist, her brow. Manon was soothed by calm words and a woman's gentle pressures. She was lifted and carried from darkness. Cold air stung her and she coughed.

"Good," said the calm one and brisk orders were given.

Too tired to wonder where she was going, Manon surrendered to the moment, glad to be alive and cared for, even as she mourned the light and serenity experienced and lost.

Again, there was darkness, this time of high walls with pools of light from flares propped in brackets. Motion ceased and she was still, in a quietness of space, away from the bustle and racket of the castle. Manon struggled to open her eye fully and saw the jewel colours of tapestries covering walls, a fire heaped with logs which crackled as they burned and gushed heat. Nearby was a brazier with Mistress Mabli bent over a pot heating there.

Manon's clothes were lifted away and her limbs rubbed gently, firmly, with coarse linen. Gwen talked endlessly, refusing to let Manon's attention slip away. When her whole body was tingling she was raised and warm liquid spooned between her lips, Mistress Mabli encouraging every swallow.

"There, little one. Good broth you have in you to make you strong again."

The baby?" Manon whispered and Mabli loomed closer. "I have not felt it move."

"Then you must await God's will, cariad," Mabli said and gently stroked Manon's face. "Gwen told me you wanted no one to know about the child you carry. Why?"

Manon turned her gaze to the fire. "I longed to tell everyone but its growing would be all the proof my enemy needed that I was unfaithful to Gerwyn."

"He did not sire this child?"

Mabli saw Manon's ravaged features enlivened by a glorious smile. "Oh yes, it is Gerwyn's. It was his gift to me before he died."

"And you were afraid for it – and for you if the Pembroke gossips decided you had lain with another?"

"Who would believe me?"

"Anyone who knew you, cariad," Mabli said and leaned to lay her lips on Manon's forehead.

Manon was beginning to look around. "Where am I?" she asked.

"Why, in my lady's chamber – as these Franks will have it called. She would want you to be here."

"Is there no news of Nest?"

"None, but we all pray for her return. Now cariad, you are safe and you must sleep."

Tiredness dragged at her but pain would not let Manon rest easily. As feeling returned to her hands and feet a violent tingling occupied them until she cried out and Mabli dosed her with poppy juice. Gradually, the discomfort dwindled and there was agony where Manon had endured blows by fists and feet. Even those aches were defeated in time by the medicine and sleep drew itself over her, dulling even the grief for her baby which must now be dead.

"La veuve – she lives?"

Mabli did not answer immediately, instead she slowly studied the shire reeve from the embroidery on his shoes to his petulant expression.

"Yes." Eyes in the disfigured face glared at him. "Had she died in your care you would have had to account to the Constable for two more deaths."

"Two?"

"Manon's – and the babe her husband sired in her before he was felled."

Roger fitzHugh almost smiled. "You are so sure it is his?"

"As you would, had you not spent so long at court where it is rare for any child to be certain of its sire."

Her words had a hiss to them, a suggestion, and the shire reeve flushed. "Do not talk to me in such a manner!"

"Why not? Pembroke is in uproar. You and your men are unable to control the hotheads and because of that a grieving woman is near dead with her child." Mabli's expression hardened, was shrewd. "You do nothing to stem the rioting. Nothing! In whose shadow do you walk, sir?"

When Roger did not answer, Mabli raised a hand in disgust. "I do not have the time or patience to bother with you now," she said and turned from him to go about her business, dismissing him as she would a careless servant.

The day had been well-aired when Manon woke.

"Come, cariad. Time to be clean."

Flanked by a servant girl carrying a steaming bowl, Mabli brought clean towels into the room. Swiftly, gently, Manon was stripped of her covers then bathed and dried. Bruises were probed for signs of hidden damage, grazes anointed with a healing ointment and the red mounds of flea bites treated with a balm which stung, then soothed.

206

In a fresh shift and wrapped in a shawl, a linen towel about her shoulders, Manon was settled by the leaping fire. There was the sting of spirits and the sharpness of herbs and wormwood as her hair was repeatedly dressed and combed until Mabli was satisfied all fleas, lice and their offspring had been dealt with.

"The Franks are not like our own people, Manon. They are not as clean, nor do they mind the odd bite, but I have seen too much sickness following the paths of the little beasts. You can rest easy now, cariad. You are safe."

"Safe? Until I am tried and hanged," Manon said and was limp in her chair.

"What nonsense!" Mabli said briskly as she cleared away her pots and combs.

Wearily, Manon shook her head. "Roger fitzHugh does not think so. In Sir Gerald's absence he would have an obedient Pembroke. As long as I live he is sure there will be rioting and discord. My death must pay for his ambitions."

Mabli leaned close, the twisted cheek adding to the grimness of her expression. "You leave that young man to me!"

Mabli startled the shire reeve as he sat at meat in the great hall.

"I have time now for a word with you – sir."

He waved the bones of a chicken's leg at her, swinging his knife in the other hand to show himself at ease in the presence of a formidable woman.

"Now – and in private, if you will," she insisted.

Grudgingly, he laid his supper on the table and wiped his hands and chin on a greasy napkin. Without a word to Mabli he strode off, expecting her to follow and match his pace. Resting and healing amongst Nest's treasures, Manon did not hear the exchanges between Mabli and the reeve. The rest of the castle's inhabitants made sure they could and revelled in the battle.

207

Roger fitzHugh was determined not to be outmanoeuvred by a mere female mediciner. "Ma dame, I was displeased at our last meeting to understand you had taken charge of the prisoner – my prisoner. You will return her to me at once."

"To you, sir? And why should I do that? Manon is a good woman and has been part of no crime. I doubt even the brothers in the priory could accuse her of committing a sin, yet you had her thrown in amongst hardened women who beat and kick her to death's door."

"Faux! She passes a night with women as bad as she is and –"

"And is near to dying for it."

The reeves fleshy lips shaped into a sneer. "There are those, ma dame, who would count it a more pleasant end than to swing by the neck from a rope."

"As you will, you young clod, if you proceed along your chosen path."

Roger fitzHugh turned on Mabli, the pustules in his cheeks rampant in the redness of his anger. "Have a care, ma dame! I control the garrison in Sir Gerald's absence – and I control the town. Control, ma dame, not dance to the tongue of an old witch useful only for her medicines and spells."

There were hidden squires and maids who swore Mabli drew a huge breath.

"And your use, sir reeve? You strut about while your men harry the townspeople at will. This castle and this town are at the frontier of King Henry's kingdom. A strong man is needed to hold fast and to lead, yet you are lashed this way and that by a slimy tongue of Satan. Why, you even skipped to his tune by keeping secret from me Manon's presence in the castle."

"You have been brought here from Carew to tend the wounded," he blustered.

"I have done so and at the will of Sir Gerald's princess I care for her friend," Mabli shouted at the shire reeve.

"Silence!"

"The truth hurts? Good. It means there is still a conscience hiding under all that bravado."

"Yes, there is and my conscience, it says to me the town will riot again and again I use the swiftest way to settle all."

"The Frank way? With a sword and a rope?"

The shire reeve was uneasy. "No, ma dame, I follow Sir Gerald. He would have us all use the – justice – your people understand, a murderer staying alive to feed the family of the one he slaughtered. I have decided there will be a trial where all may speak and I – yes, I, ma dame – decide what will be done!"

"In God's name, a trial?"

"Yes, ma dame. A trial – and soon."

"You realise that should Manon be declared guilty of her husband's death –"

"She will be hanged for it, I assure you."

"As sure as I am yours will have been the hand used to murder her."

Mabli's voice had dropped to a sibilant whisper, the secret listeners hard-pressed to hear clearly what she said.

"Me? Murder? You make no sense, ma dame."

"No? You were not in Pembroke at harvest. Manon was poisoned and I fought for her life, day and night. Yes, I saved her but she lost the child she carried."

"This woman eats bad meat and you must make it a matter of life and death?"

"That is not what happened. The poison was in a cup of milk. I know the hand that put it there but not the mind that planned it."

There was silence. Roger fitzHugh rocked in his chair, the joints creaking.

"Someone wants her dead?"

"They do. Last time they used Gerwyn's own son, persuading the boy the liquid would merely discomfit his stepmother."

"Where is he, this boy? He must be made to talk –"

"Fled to Ceredigion."

Roger fitzHugh cracked his knuckles as his thoughts raced. "You have no idea who plots death?"

"None that makes sense. Gerwyn's murder may not have been part of the intrigue until it was realised you might hang Manon and save the hidden killer any more effort."

If she was right and he wrongly hanged the tanner's widow it would go hard against him, the reeve decided. As he gnawed at his lower lip Mabli saw his unease and breathed more easily.

"It must be known who it was killed Gerwyn," Mabli insisted. "Until that matter is dealt with the townspeople will not rest. Think back to the night he was slain. Because of your curfew nothing moves in the town when it is dark. In daylight there are ships from all corners at anchor here, their sailors free to roam. Journeymen, farmers, craftsmen, thieves, they flood Pembroke on market days, disappearing when the guards impose curfew. Any one of them could have struck the blow which killed Gerwyn."

At last Roger fitzHugh realised his own danger. Manon dangling at the castle gate could solve his immediate problems in the town but when Sir Gerald returned with his lady? For an ambitious man it could be the end of all hopes. He restlessly pulled at the loose end of a silver thread as he pondered his way out of an impasse.

"Bien sure, it must be someone close to this Manon?"

"It would be easy if it was Gerwyn's sister but her mouth reveals all she thinks. She has not the cunning to scheme all this, neither has her man."

The shire reeve was restless, not knowing which way to turn. "There is a murdered tanner who was well respected and must be avenged."

"True, but if Manon is hanged for that . . ."

"I will be doing someone's bidding." Roger fitzHugh could see no way he could escape blame. "There must be a trial," he said at last. "I have given my word."

"Well, sir," Mabli said quietly, "is not a trial to decide innocence as well as guilt?"

The bakeshop was filled with those who wished to buy bread as well as some who would steal and others standing in the heat escaping from the oven. Cynfan was tall enough to keep all who entered under his eye and hurried towards a hesitant figure at the door.

"Mistress Ceinwen, what news?"

"Oh Cynfan, how can we help her?"

"Manon?" the baker asked and at the woman's nod he pulled off his apron and threw it at a journeyman, leading Ceinwen to the privacy of his kitchen.

Ceinwen was always simply dressed, her tunic immaculate, her headdress neatly tied but today there was about her a sense of dishevelment. "I have just come from the castle. The poor girl is well but weak and Mistress Mabli has her in the best of care. She is even nursing her in the princess' own bed."

"Then what concerns you so much, mistress?"

"A trial. The shire reeve has insisted."

Cynfan's jovial face became grim. "When?"

"The day is not yet decided but it must be soon. Cynfan, what can we do?"

He thought for a moment. "If your man can spare you, get back to Mistress Mabli."

"The guards may not let me in again so soon."

The baker did not answer, going instead to the door and shouting to his journeyman for a basket of loaves fresh from the bakeoven. "Not too heavy, mind," he added, then smiled at Ceinwen. "They will pass you through if you carry food for the wounded and a message for Mistress Mabli concerning the herbs she needs."

Ceinwen sighed with relief. "Of course. Is that all I can do?"

"No. Persuade Mistress Mabli to do all possible to delay the trial. Make out Manon is not yet able to stand –

211

whatever comes to mind. The old woman is wise and she spent long enough in the English court to know how to scheme and lie."

"And you?"

"Me? My business will be with Gerwyn's friends. He is owed a favour or two – and I will see they are paid in full."

In the priory the shire reeve was impatient. He had answered the prior's summons and must now await his pleasure. Should such a man of the church indulge himself in pleasure, Roger asked himself as he paced the beaten earth floor of the small room. The cleric was certainly taking more than a passing interest in this wretched woman and her hanging.

At last the door opened and the shire reeve bowed. "Good day to you, father."

"And to you, my son." The prior's pale eyes gleamed in the dimness lit only by one candle. "Tell me, is it true the tanner's widow sleeps in the best bed in the castle and is nursed by Sir Gerald's own mediciner?"

Once again Roger was surprised by the local knowledge the prior acquired in his complete seclusion from the world.

"Mistress Mabli insisted, because of the friendship as children between the widow and the Constable's wife."

"No matter, my son. It will help our cause – the good of the church and the starving souls in our care."

"I will try her in a day or so and then it will all be over."

A slim, finely boned hand gleamed in the fitful light from a flickering flame. "Not so hasty, please. We need the good people of this town so angered they will be satisfied only with what they conceive to be justice. It is time for patience, reeve, during which I am sure your ansels amongst the guards can let slip to the right ears all the comforts the widow enjoys? Remember, when the Constable returns,

212

with or without his wife, the outcome of the trial must be totally convincing. I am sure you understand?"

In a chair covered with skins, her hands cupped over the motionless curve of her child, Manon grieved. The baby had been still for so long it would be born as dead as its father. Across the room Mabli and Gwen gossiped as they inspected the cleanliness of a whitened shift, a russet tunic, a linen kerchief, for Manon to wear.

"Before he rode away the big Fleming heard of your encounter with the shire reeve," Gwen said. "Ugo told Kamal the horses were ready and he must get them to Ceredigion. He will tell Sir Gerald what has been happening in Pembroke."

Mabli sighed. "The Constable's first duty is to find his wife and bring her home, yet poor Manon has a sad need of friends."

"She knows we will aid her. Kamal has made new sheepskin boots for her."

Mabli looked up, seeing Gwen's full mouth tightened into a hard line. "Something is wrong?"

Gwen said nothing, glancing instead at Manon who was intent on her baby and her misery.

"Sweet Jesus, girl! Any fool can see you are angry. Who has made you so? Kamal?"

"No! Not Kamal."

"Someone in the town has spoken out of turn?"

Gwen's attention was centred on a small patch of mud at the edge of Manon's tunic. With spittle and rubbing she cleaned the tightly woven wool.

"Tell me, Gwen. Who?" Mabli insisted.

"Who else but the black witch!"

Manon lifted her head at Gwen's bitter outburst but the girl was so furious she never noticed.

"She knew it meant everything to him and could she wait to butcher it?"

"Who was butchered?" Manon's words were very quiet but they reached Gwen.

The girl was reluctant to answer but under her mistress' steady gaze, she surrendered her will. "Nudd's Pig."

Even Mabli was shocked. "The beast he raised from a runt? Why, it was his pet – almost his familiar."

"Non knew it," Gwen said. "When the master was alive he made it plain to her Nudd and the pig had his protection."

"And then mine," Manon added.

"Aye – and much good it did yesterday. She sliced the beast's throat herself and drained the blood for a pudding. The carcase went on the spit but the smell of it sickened me. Even Old Twm was turned. Only the she-devil ate meat for supper."

Manon was distressed. "Non wanted it slaughtered when she first saw it and I refused her."

"So she told us." Gwen's face was as dark as a thundercloud. "Said you had done her a favour, the pig so well cared for the meat was at its best. That was when Myrddin went for her."

Mabli was surprised. "Myrddin?"

"Aye. Told her what he thought of her." Gwen licked her lips, pleasured by the memory. "It took him a long time to say what a pathetic excuse for a woman she was. Then she screamed he was finished as a workman for the family but he said that you were the master now," she told Manon. "Only you could put him off. That was when the she-devil stormed off into town."

"Nudd?" Manon wanted to know.

Gwen was crying but she faced Manon. "He had already gone."

"Gone where?"

A shrug of her shoulders saved Gwen words. "When Non brought in the bowl of blood he cursed her in the old Welsh, made a sign at her and went. It was strange," Gwen said thoughtfully. "I have never seen him walk so well."

"What sign?" Mabli wanted to know.

Gwen pointed two outer fingers at her own eyes and then turned her hand to point at an imaginary Non.

Mabli was shocked. "Dear God! If Non is a believer she will not sleep this night – or any other."

Manon was stirred to action. She pushed aside the skins covering her and reached for her shift and tunic. As she donned them Gwen hurried to help, Mabli following with the kerchief.

"Well, cariad, apart from the bruises which are beginning to show all the colours of the rainbow, you look well. My sweet Nest would be pleased to see you recovered and here, in her chamber."

"How I wish she was here! I miss her – as you must."

"All we can do is pray for her, child."

"I do, that God be with her, Mistress Mabli, and with us all."

"Amen to that. You are pale, come to the fire."

Manon shook her head. "For so long I have been waiting to know my enemy and have been helpless. Because of my weakness this wicked, wicked woman who calls herself my sister has murdered the one thing Nudd loved above all. It is too much!"

"You are frail yet, cariad," Mabli decided. "Sit by the fire as I asked you. I have broth warming and it will strengthen you."

"Ready for the birthing of my dead baby?" Manon twisted her fingers together in her anguish then pulled them apart, holding them out, begging. "Why, Mistress Mabli? So much death because of me – I should hang and be done with it!"

"Enough of that, my lady!" Mabli held Manon by her shoulders. "You have three fine children who need you and they need you alive, not walking meekly to your gallows."

"But how can I put an end to it?" Manon cried and beat at Mabli. The older woman tightened her hold and Manon began to sob. Mabli gathered her in her arms and held her as the tears poured and released despair.

As suddenly as they had begun Manon's cries ceased. She raised her face to Mabli who saw the younger woman's eyes were filled with wonder.

"It moved! Mistress Mabli, it moved!"

Mabli tightened her grasp, ready for the agonies of a useless birth to begin. Manon pushed her away.

"No, truly. The baby moved." Tears dried on Manon's cheeks as her fingers caressed her belly. "There! A kick, Mistress Mabli. Feel it! It was a kick – and there again."

Gwen busied herself drying her own tears as she watched Mabli sink awkwardly to her knees, lift the tunic and put her ear to Manon's belly. There was as long moment then Mabli smiled.

"I hear it, Manon. The babe's heart beats strongly. Now, will you fight?"

Chapter Twelve

With the care of Manon added to her other duties, Mabli had little time to rest. She was determined the wounded men shipped back to Pembroke from Ceredigion be returned to full health while loudly lamenting the loss of Nudd's skill at finding the plants she needed now in such abundance.

"Where can the boy have gone to?" she asked Gwen.

The girl was tired, her life in the home beyond the leather shop made impossible by Non's constant suspicions. "Who knows with Nudd? He is safer alone in the woods than anyone I know but I miss him."

Mabli was sympathetic. "Has the black one given no sign of leaving for her own home?"

"None. Kamal is very patient with her tantrums and Old Twm just shakes his head and pretends to be deaf. Dyfrig is afraid of her and stitches the boots and buckets in his gwennie until she has gone."

"Why does she stay?"

Gwen had no doubts. "To give us all a taste of hell. She still searches for silver where there is none and daily nags Kamal to open the shop and sell what he can."

"He refuses?"

"Always courteous is Kamal," Gwen said, the weary lines of her face softening to comeliness as she spoke. "He knows all she wants is the coin he might earn to find a nest in her pouch."

"Not a good woman," Mabli decided and turned her attention to Manon, wrapped in skins and dreaming by the fire. "Now, my lady, it is time for my special tonic."

Memories of the tincture and its horrid taste made Manon hesitate. "Must I?"

"Yes, cariad. Until you are yourself again I will dose you three times every day."

"Then I believe I am well again this instant!"

Mabli smiled. "See, it has done its work but you will have some to be sure."

A knock at the door heralded a servant. "Mistress," he said to Mabli, "a message from the shire reeve. The prior is here to speak with the tanner's wife."

"The prior? What business has he with the Mistress Manon? The priest who ministers in the town, he is the one hears her confession."

"The shire reeve insisted the prior be allowed to meet with the tanner's wife privately."

"She is not well – " Mabli began but the boy was anxious and raised a hand to stop her saying more.

"Mistress, the shire reeve ordered it!" he said and fled Mabli's wrath.

"What is that ridiculous man's game?" she stormed as she paced Nest's room. "I warned him how he might suffer if the trial went against you," she told Manon. "Is this his way to escape the penalty of his foolishness, inviting the prior to intercede?" Mabli snorted her disdain. "If this is another attempt to make himself appear blameless, it is the ploy of an idiot." She bent over Manon sitting in the chair by the fire. "Be warned, cariad. When two ambitious men like the shire reeve and the prior conspire, only they will benefit."

Mabli was uneasy as she allowed Gwen to help Manon tidy herself. It was only ten years or so since the Benedictines arrived in Pembroke to build a priory near the castle at the urging of Arnulf of the hated Montgomeries.

Founding the priory and planning to escape to the peace of holiness after a life of violence and cruelty had not saved Arnulf. When his brother Robert, the infamous Earl of Shrewsbury, defied the new King Henry, Arnulf had been dragged into treachery until Henry threatened his life. It was Sir Gerald, then Pembroke's castellan, who had saved his master, finding him a wife, safe passage to Ireland and a quiet death there. It was far away from the haven Arnulf had planned for his immortal soul in Pembroke.

Mabli sighed. "So many deaths," she said softly before turning to Manon. "You will be well, child?"

"I will, thanks be to God – and to you." Manon's smile was a welcome sight. "The good Lord has kept my baby safe from harm and now I must do the same."

Mabli laid a gnarled hand on Manon's shoulder, squeezing it gently. "As I told you, have a care with the prior. He has great guile."

Manon had not long been on her own when there was a knock at the door and it opened. A short, round monk stood aside to allow in the tall, austere figure of the prior. He bowed to Manon.

"God be with you, child."

"And with you, father."

The squat monk with a pudgy face below his tonsure and eyes set close above a blob of a nose, hurried forward to move a chair close to the fire for his superior.

"My companion is Brother Paulinus. He has good Welsh and will help me if I have any difficulty."

Manon bent her head to acknowledge Brother Paulinus, busy flicking his glance in all directions and missing nothing. When his eyes met Manon's she read in them contempt for her. She watched the prior settle himself in a carved chair and steeple his fingers in a semblance of piety. Strange, Manon thought, he is a true member of his order and yet the folds of his habit fall like thick silk. She surveyed brother Paulinus, seeing coarse wool and a rasped neck where his habit had rubbed against flesh. Her gaze returned to the older man and she saw the weave of the cloth he wore in humility was of the finest craftsmanship. Mabli was right.

"I have been concerned for you," the prior said in stilted Welsh. "Gerwyn was a good man and an excellent worker at his trade. His earthly body is sorely missed by us all but we must be consoled to know his soul is with God."

Tears rose unbidden and in her weakness, Manon let them fall.

The cleric twisted a large jewelled ring on his finger. "There are those, I understand, who would mark you guilty of his death?"

Mabli's warning came to mind and Manon chose her words carefully. "Friends assure me there is but one man who stirs up gossip against me. He is unseen and unknown. If he had the courage to accuse me to my face I might begin to see the reason for his lies."

"Is it a lie?"

The prior's pale blue eyes were like twin daggers of ice piercing her very soul but Manon was unafraid.

"As God is my witness, sir, the gravest of lies."

The cleric pursed his lips primly. "You realise, when the trial begins, I can be of no help to you. The king, in the person of the shire reeve, must have his justice."

Sensing danger, Manon was silent and the prior frowned at her stillness.

"Should you put yourself in my hands – the hands of the church – it might be possible to avoid a trial and you would not hang for your husband's murder."

She waited.

"You have fine children. Three, I believe?"

Manon bowed her head in assent.

"It would be possible for them to be placed in the care of good Christian families and the boys be educated by the brothers in the priory."

Manon was annoyed but she kept her features serene. Only the baby kicked at the plan but she soothed it unob-

220

trusively with a gentle hand. "And where would you place me, father?" she asked courteously.

"There is a sister house of our foundation."

"I have not heard of one near Pembroke."

"It is in France."

It took a breath or two before Manon realised what the prior offered. "So, I am to be exiled for life and my children raised by others. Forgive me, father. I sense a price for all this generosity."

"There always is, my child," she was assured in silken tones. "In return for taking you to a place of safety and giving your children opportunities they could never hope to have in the household of a mere tanner, it would be necessary for you to sign over to the priory all your properties and monies. You have, I believe, two farms, the tannery, the leather shop – and whatever silver you have stored or amassed through trade."

It had been good to be forewarned and Manon made a supreme effort to be as smooth as the prior. "Your searches have been very thorough, sir."

"Brother Paulinus is diligent in his work for our foundation. This has been his suggestion."

Brother Paulinus looked suitably smug until he saw red battle flags unfurl in Manon's cheeks.

"You and your monks have been too kind, Father. Were I guilty of the crime you would have me own, I could be tempted. How sad Brother Paulinus' diligence has been misplaced."

Watching the faces of the two men pale as she spoke, Manon explained who had title to the properties they had assumed she owned, free and clear. Father Prior was no stranger to disappointment and had learned to hide it well.

"You and Gerwyn are to be congratulated on the generosity of your disposition," he said. "However, you still own in your own name the shop and house in Pembroke and any silver you have saved."

221

Manon held a lip between her teeth to ensure she did not speak in haste. "What would that buy me?" she asked in a carefully pleasant voice.

Brother Paulinus whispered to the prior who covered his mouth with an elegant hand as he thought and decided.

"You might still go to France – but as a menial sister."

"I would cook and clean instead of pray?"

He bowed his agreement. It was a courtly gesture but it angered Manon. She made herself breathe steadily.

"My children?"

"They would be cared for."

"The boys tutored?"

"Ah!" The prior raised his hands and placed the tips of his fingers together. "The homes found for them would be with families not quite so well born."

With the baby's kicking beginning to match her fury and with Mabli's cautions ringing in her ears, Manon gripped the arms of her chair until her knuckles were white.

"You have been generous to a fault, father, but I must refuse your offer."

"Think on it well, daughter. It is your life I offer you."

"Which I should lose if I am guilty? To agree with your terms is to admit to the world – and to God – I conspired to have my husband killed. I did not. I loved Gerwyn with all my heart and soul and I have been deprived of him and his love, as have his children. Now you would have me agree they should lose their mother as well? You ask too much of an innocent woman, sir!"

The prior was startled by her vehemence but he recovered quickly and waved a hand to encompass the luxury and richness of Nest's quarters.

"It is known in the town how you are living when the law demands you be held in a cell with other felons –"

"You threaten me, sir? You would aid the faceless one who wants me executed?" Manon forced herself to be calm. "If I hang I do so because the king's justice is at fault but then it would be you who was guilty before God, not me.

Think on that, father prior, and pray for your own immortal soul!"

"I see you did not bend to the prior's will," Mabli said when she returned to a Manon still seething with fury.

"How could I? I was to surrender myself, my children – and what he thought was my wealth. For the benefit of the church, of course."

Mabli studied Manon, angry and flushed, with her hands on her unborn child.

"Your wealth would have brought him great glory before his bishop. He must have been so sure you were guilty."

Manon pounded the arms of her chair. "Then he is as big a fool as the meanest tongues in the town – him and all his brothers with him!"

"Hush, cariad. Men are ever the best gossips, and what else are they to do for harmless sin in a priory?"

"Harmless? When they would lock me away in the silence of a convent, strip me of all I had and take my children to be the playthings of idle Franks?"

"He meant well."

An exclamation of disgust was all Manon had for the prior's motives as she rose and paced from wall to wall. Mabli watched until Manon slowed, exhaustion overcoming the angry spirit.

"Time to rest, child. The girl is bringing you fresh meat and you must eat well. Strength you will need in abundance when you face your accusers." Mabli smiled her twisted smile and lifted a hand to touch Manon's cheek. "You have found in you the will to resist. That is good. On the appointed day you will be ready for the battle against your enemies – whoever they are."

News of it came too soon.

Roger fitzHugh stormed into Nest's room and glared at Mabli standing guard, then at Manon. "You would have been advised to heed the prior."

"Pembroke at peace in an instant? That is your choice, sir. For me, the price was too great."

The shire reeve looked around the room at the furnishings, unwilling to meet Manon's gaze. "Price? What price, woman?"

"The one demanded. My children torn from me and my body delivered to France – but no new death to add to the long list held at your account before God, sir!"

The reeve's skin reddened as he threw out a hand towards Mabli. "You should not listen to this woman. She does you no favours."

Manon shook her head. "Again, you are wrong, sir. I listened to God and to my heart. There is no guilt in me and I will not let my children be fouled by false claims so you may sleep easy!"

By now Roger fitzHugh's noise was a rich purple. "Have a care, ma dame! Remember, whatever is said, I am the one who will decide your fate."

"You would take that duty from God, sir? Indeed, you are a brave man if you can face his wrath."

Roger fitzHugh spluttered, too angry to speak. He made the effort to control himself, looking around the room as he did so. "Like the prior, I am satisfied the people will be enraged to know you are living soft in the Constable's own quarters."

Manon knew now Mabli had been right. The shire reeve and the prior were joined against her.

The older woman put a hand on Manon's arm as she took a step towards the fitzHugh and it was Mabli who moved to confront him. "You should be relieved it is so, sir, but then, you have never seen the princess in a temper. Such a roasting she would give me – and you – when she returns, had the friend of her childhood not been housed so."

"She will return?" There was no doubting the unpleasantness of Roger fitzHugh's manner. "After so long on her back in another man's bed, I doubt Sir Gerald will allow her the standing she once had."

The tortured muscles of Mabli's right cheek were a white scar in the red of her fury. "Once had, sir? Never for a moment forget she is the daughter of King Rhys and Queen Gwladus. Both her parents were of royal blood, older by centuries than that of your Conqueror. You may hold sway here while Sir Gerald seeks his lady. He in turn may have power from King Henry to make decisions of life and death for us all but Princess Nest is the real heart of this place and its people."

"Carew –"

"Carew is but part of the kingdom which is hers by blood right and is her escape from the world. When she returns to us you had better be sure you have done all she would approve. Remember, she has long had the ear of the king and will continue to do so."

"You truly believe, because of the Constable's wife, King Henry will concern himself with the fate of a nobody? A tanner's wife?"

"I know the king well, as you do not. If your actions offend Princess Nest, the king will be angered. Ask Robert of Bellême, the Earl of Shrewsbury, brother to the Montgomerie who first built this castle. Ask him how swiftly the king acts when he is angered – and then say your last prayers."

Roger fitzHugh was a desperate man. The mediciner had made it clear what would result if the tanner's wife was executed. Then news had come from Pembroke town, a promise of rebellion if no neck was stretched for Gerwyn's death. The prior's offer had seemed a Godsend. For a long moment the shire reeve hesitated, the solidity of his neck a dull red. He glanced at Manon and no longer saw the bewildered woman who had been dragged before him. She returned his stare as would an unforgiving carving in stone.

"I will see the king's justice prevail!" he blustered.

"So will I, sir. So will I," Mabli promised.

*   *   *

How news of the trial travelled through the countryside no one could explain. On the day appointed by the shire reeve, a horde gathered at the castle gate. Roger fitzHugh insisted only men and women who had a real interest in the outcome were to be admitted. His orders were carried out by his men with great use of foul language, both Welsh and French, as well as many blows and a very small measure of common sense.

With no time for Manon to see her children again, she was led from Nest's room by two silent and heavily armed men. A small door opened and she was pushed into the great hall of the castle, hearing the hubbub of excitement from the crowd gathered there. Immediately in front of her was a raised dais on which was a massive table and a huge carved chair. Being nudged in the back by the hilt of a sword had Manon walking around the dais and into the full view of those assembled.

A surging roar greeted her appearance and she turned her head aside, the better to become calm. Now she could see the Constable's chair and sitting in it was Roger fitzHugh garbed in a tunic of purple velvet which was heavily embroidered and almost clean. Carrying a stool, a scribe climbed nimbly on to the dais and took his place near the shire reeve.

Manon breathed deeply and faced her fellow townspeople with an assumed serenity. In a dark blue tunic, a white linen kerchief wound round her hair and throat, Manon was proud, defiant, as she gazed at her accusers.

The prior sat near the dais but apart from the smell of ordinary folk, Brother Martin at his shoulder. Across the hall from him was Non in new black, the sleeves of her tunic as rich and full as those of a noblewoman, her linen kerchief as fine as silk and draped with great care. At first Manon could not see Iolo, then she glimpsed his slight body being jostled by townspeople eager to creep nearer the dais.

It was hard to hide the fear and desperation she felt.

Manon clenched her fists inside her sleeves and looked at the crowd, this time seeing friendly faces. Myrddin was one, as erect as stiffness allowed and as close as he could get to Manon, Gwen sheltered by him. A few paces from the prior was the tall figure of Ithel, the velvet of his clothes gleaming almost as brightly as the silver of his hair in the light of flaring torches.

Others she recognised and was deeply grateful for their presence. Ceinwen, her features tranquil, her eyes closed as she bent her head in prayer. Beside her was Cynfan, silent for once and grim. Looking past the shire reeve and his scribe Manon saw Mabli, her back against the wall, a smile of encouragement lighting her eyes. She could see no sign of Nudd, nor of Ugo, the big Fleming, and Manon had a sense of emptiness.

There was no time for more. The shire reeve lifted his hand for quiet and when it was slow in coming, his men cuffed those closest to them who were talking. Only then might Roger fitzHugh be heard. Words boomed and faded around Manon's head and she forced down nausea that she might hear.

"– too much suspicion and gossip in the town, causing discord which is a danger to us all. Today will be heard the facts. Only from them and not from rumours, will I decide what must be done in the king's name."

"Hang her!" came from the back of the hall, the cry taken up and repeated again and again, until the great hall and Manon's ears echoed with blood lust. She was near to fainting but steeled herself to be steadfast as she gazed back at the crowd.

Men-at-arms beat about them and order was restored. As Roger fitzHugh prepared to speak Manon realised the prior stared at her, his face a mask, his eyes unblinking. In a moment she knew his thoughts. A deal had been struck with the shire reeve. Should the verdict not be in her favour, her children and her wealth would be forfeit to these two men. It was doubtful she would be on the next ship to France, the hangman's noose saving the cost of her passage.

Roger fitzHugh had been talking for some time before Manon was aware of his words. He was telling again all that had been done to find Gerwyn's killer, the men dragged to the castle and beaten, revealing no hint of who it was struck the fatal blow.

"She could have paid anyone to sneak out after curfew!"

The voice was unknown but it set off a rolling tide of noise and silence was hard to establish. The shire reeve must fume and try to contain his anger patiently until he could be heard.

"Soon after the tanner died news came from the north, the Constable's castle burning and his lady taken. Before Sir Gerald sailed for Emlyn, he left me accountable for the safety of Pembroke's castle and town. A spy had been reported her, in this shire, and my men were even more vigilant than usual."

Whispers grew into shouts of revelation but Manon was bemused. It was the first she had heard of a traitor. A spy amongst them? Was he working for Cadwgan? For Owain? For the Irish?

"When so many men rode from here to search for the princess and the children, Pembroke was at risk of a raid from the sea as well as from Ceredigion," the shire reeve said. "Every night, as darkness fell, my men patrolled the town, watching every door, every shadow. After couvre feu, extra men watched the walls and the approaches to the town, determined to catch the spy if he moved as a shadow in the dark. Whoever killed the tanner did not go from Pembroke to commit his crime."

Manon tried to think against the noise deafening her. Gerwyn might have been killed by a spy? A face came to her and she closed her eyes, the better to see it. The man who was watching Nest and her children walk to the quay. He had been there some time, she remembered, eyeing the boxes Kamal had made and which were carried with such care to the ships because their contents were precious.

"Dear God," she breathed as she prayed, but no one heard her. "He was the man in the shop with Meurig!" Manon's thoughts raced. The man had kept his back to her so he could not be recognised. Why did he fear her knowing who he was? And what business could the spy have had with Gerwyn's son?

She saw Non rise to speak and fear rose in Manon. A black sleeve was a graceful draping as a long, white finger pointed at a hated sister.

"That woman is rich enough. She must have paid well to have my brother killed, the plans made long ago –"

"No!" Myrddin was pushing his way to the dais, determined to confront Non. "If a death was ordered that night then it must have been mine."

He had to wait a long time until excitement stilled and Roger fitzHugh nodded for Myrddin to continue.

"A man died at the tannery because of stolen leather. Only that day, when Gerwyn came to the tannery, did even I know he was to take my place. It was cold – bitter and raw. By the time most of the men had gone to their homes, ready for the wedding, my leg was agony. Gerwyn, good lad that he was, sent me home to a warm bed."

"Why was I not told this?" the shire reeve demanded to know.

"I tried – dear God, how I tried, but no one would listen." He cast a look of scorn at Roger fitzHugh and the assembled crowd. "You did not want the truth – any of you!"

Myrddin was questioned at length over the stolen hides and fleeces, the crowd becoming ever more restless. Eventually, all were diverted by shouting outside the huge door at the entrance to the great hall. It opened and to Manon's surprise, Nudd walked in but it was not Nudd as she had known him. Growths and warts still encrusted his face, his hair was as straw-like as ever but he stood straight. Though his gait was odd it was that of a man, not the boy he had been.

Nudd was followed by a shambling figure wrapped thickly in layers of old clothes which covered all but his eyes and nose. "Leper," was a word bouncing from mouth to mouth but the man's grime was a healthy covering of soot and he carried with him the smokiness of smouldering wood.

Manon listened as Nudd told the shire reeve this was the charcoal burner whose hut was deep in the woods but not far from the tannery.

"What has he to tell us?" Roger fitzHugh wanted to know.

Nudd held the man's arm and urged him to speak. The charcoal burner gazed fearfully at the mass of bodies assembled around him and he was clearly terrified of being among so many shuffling, murmuring people. Nudd leaned close and whispered. He put an arm round the man's shoulders, comforting him as he would Rhodri.

Eventually, the charcoal burner pulled the scarf from his mouth. There was dirt but no sign of disease to be seen as he gazed at Manon. "Let God be my witness, mistress, but I could not save him. I was in the woods – too far away. It was all so quick."

The only way Manon could reach him was to step up onto the dais and walk across to Nudd and his companion. She smiled at Nudd and knelt in front of the charcoal burner, holding out her hands to him. The timid man lifted a mass of bindings from which protruded fingers blackened only by his work. Manon grasped them and they might have been alone, so intent were they on each other.

"You were there?"

He nodded.

A hush grew in the great hall, every ear hanging on the charcoal burner's words.

"Please tell me," Manon begged, "I need to know. Did Gerwyn suffer?"

The man shook his head. "It was too fast for that, mistress. Gerwyn was arguing with someone and another man came from the bushes behind them. He had a piece of wood in his hand and struck Gerwyn once. Hard."

In a stunned silence the charcoal burner withdrew his hands from Manon's. His left hand he hooked in worn leather doing duty as a belt. With his right hand and arm he described a swift, vicious blow.

"Forgive me, mistress. I would have given my life for Gerwyn. He was my friend."

Manon smiled through her tears. "As you are mine." She turned and was surprised to see Nudd's eyes on a level with hers. "Dear Nudd, you are such a good man. How did you find him?"

"I was living in the woods and came upon his new hut. We talked," Nudd said, surprising Manon with the clarity of his words.

They realised the shire reeve was banging on the table and glaring at the strange trio, Manon with two creatures usually despised and ignored.

"I will have the truth!" Roger fitzHugh thundered. "You, charcoal burner, they tell me . . ."

The bluster of the shire reeve fizzled to nothing. He recognised intelligence peering from the bundle of rags. Here was a man who regarded him, the king's officer, as a monstrous being from another world.

"Sir?" Even the voice was not that of a stupid man.

"You saw who killed the tanner?"

"Aye, sir."

"Is he here?"

The charcoal burner looked carefully at the crowd, section by section. "No sir, he is not."

"The other man, the one who argued with Gerwyn?"

"He was the one I saw push Gerwyn's body in the dung pit and pull over it the cover? Aye, sir. That man is here."

Chapter Thirteen

Terrified by the storm of shouting which erupted at his words, the charcoal burner cringed against the dais. With Nudd's help Manon persuaded the man to step up, away from the pushing bodies. They stood there, Nudd holding him firmly, Manon clutching the rags round his hand, each soothing him as best they could.

Apart from them, Roger fitzHugh was scarlet faced as he flung his arms about in calls for order. His men worked hard, one of them swift enough to bar the door at the back, while his colleagues were drenched with sweat before the shire reeve could be heard demanding of the charcoal burner the culprit be identified.

Slowly, the man searched the quietened crowd, then he raised a hand and pointed. The mass of bodies parted, moving away from the finger of accusation, until a slight figure was exposed, cowering against the wall.

"Dear God, no!" Manon breathed, unable to believe the man she had dismissed as nothing had been party to Gerwyn's murder.

A cringing, whining Iolo was dragged forward, many hands beating at him.

"No! No!" he screamed as he was held upright at the edge of the dais to face the shire reeve.

Manon looked across the seething mob towards Non and

almost felt pity for her. Gerwyn's sister was white with shock and it was obvious the revelation had come to her as a thunderbolt on a clear day.

Roger fitzHugh began his questions. Few could hear the answers and there were shouts for Iolo to, "Speak up like a man." With his cap pulled from him, the pale skin of his head shone like that of a bald baby with a beard, its eyes and nose running freely.

"Gerwyn was not meant to die!" he said and it echoed up to the rafters above a silent crowd, avid for truth. "I watched Myrddin go home and thought no one was at the tannery."

"You were always the thief of the leather?"

"No – yes. In a way."

"Yes," Roger fitzHugh decided. "Who was your accomplice?"

The sorry little excuse for a man clamped his mouth shut and kept it that way. He was thumped by the soldiers guarding him, screeched at by the shrillest of his neighbours, but no word passed his lips.

Manon swayed and Mabli ordered a man-at-arms to take the girl a stool before she collapsed. Even when she was seated on the dais, Manon could see Non was as rigid as if carved from stone.

"Sweet Jesus," Manon whispered but only she heard. "Is this what it takes to still that tongue?" Tears rose and ran down her cheeks, fresh grief for Gerwyn. Only Mabli noticed.

The shire reeve was struggling to use the best Welsh he could manage when the rushlights on the walls flickered in the draught and there was a roaring from the far end of the great hall.

"Let us through!"

All heads turned, the newcomer easily seen, he was so tall. Ugo pushed his way through a mass of gawpers as he towed a thin, scruffy individual towards the dais and the shire reeve. Manon's spirits had lifted when she saw the tall

233

Fleming but it took her some time to recognise his companion. The size of a large child he was thin, dejected, his eyes always downcast but Manon knew him.

"Meurig!"

There had not been such excitement in Pembroke since the last raid by Cadwgan and Owain when the entire town, livestock and all, had packed into the safety of the bailey. Manon was close enough to hear the exchanges between Ugo and Roger fitzHugh but she had little of the Frankish tongue. Amongst the words she could make out were 'Gerwyn' as well as 'quickly', 'north' and 'son'. Then 'fear'.

As Ugo spoke urgently, the shire reeve listened and the prior sat erect, waiting with eternal patience for the outcome. The delay gave Manon time to study Meurig. Gone was the plumpness of boyhood when he had fed at her table. Gone too, the resemblance to Gerwyn, his son's cheeks drawn and dirty, the black curls so like his father's muddy, tangled, flattened. Only his eyes were the same but filled with shame and regret when at last he stared at Manon. She smiled at Gerwyn's son and saw the dawning of hope in him.

"Meurig ap Gerwyn, you will answer me truthfully, as God is your witness," the shire reeve said, frowning as he spoke.

"Aye, sir. I will."

A susurrance of 'Sh' ensured everyone might hear what was to come and Roger fitzHugh waited until there was silence.

"I am told you have been brought here from the border with Ceredigion and that you have been serving Cadwgan ap Bleddyn and his friends. Is that true?"

"Aye, sir."

Necks were craned, the better to see and hear.

"This is the encampment on the north bank of the Teifi river, near to the sea?"

Meurig nodded. "Until the eisteddfod ended and we

234

journeyed to a manor of Cadwgan's close to Aberystwyth. We had been there two days when Owain ap Cadwgan rode in with Princess Nest and her children."

Gasps of horror were quickly silenced when the shire reeve raised his hand. "How long did the woman and her children stay there?"

The boy hesitated, his brow wrinkling as he tried to remember. "It was almost morning when they came. Owain and his men fed well, then he took the princess away from the hall . . ."

There were few present who did not guess what followed.

"And then?"

"The next day Cadwgan came and demanded his son. Owain would not obey at first but soon he came to the hall, pulling on a tunic. Owain was angry at being disturbed. He was heavy with wine and shouted at his father."

"They argued?"

"Like wolves over a lamb."

The shire reeve leaned forward. "What did Cadwgan want from his son?"

"At first, he said everything stolen from Sir Gerald was to be returned. Owain just laughed and said it had been shared out amongst his friends. It was then Cadwgan stormed at him and said the lady and the children should be sent home. He was in fear of losing all he owned to the anger of King Henry."

"Owain was not willing?" the shire reeve asked.

"No, sir. He drank more wine and pushed his face against his father's. 'She is mine', he said. 'I have taken her again and again and the blood in her from Hywel Dda shall mingle with mine and not that poisoned Frankish brew which moves those brats of hers!'"

"Cadwgan was not happy with his son's words?"

"'In God's name, Owain', he shouted. 'She was the king's woman and Wales, north and south, will be set on fire if she does not go from here – and the children. Gerald is sire of them all and what father would see his sons in the hands of his enemy? Be certain the Constable will be on us as soon as he has gathered men to destroy you'."

"Cadwgan could not persuade his son?"

"No, sir. The rages were terrible to see. Owain would not surrender to his father's will and he ordered the horses saddled, the princess to be thrown up on the first one, its reins tied to his mount."

"The children?"

"Each was in front of a man, the nursemaid too since it pained her greatly to sit on a saddle and she swooned."

Women throughout the hall understood, clucking and tutting in sympathy.

Once again the shire reeve raised a hand for silence. "Cadwgan – what did he do?"

"We had only just come from the eisteddfod so everything useful was already packed. Cadwgan knew the manor would be the first place Sir Gerald would seek Owain, after the camp on the Teifi. By nightfall he made sure the manor was deserted and sent us all away."

Roger fitzHugh pulled at his chin. "Why did you go to Ceredigion when you left Pembroke?"

Meurig was tired, sagging as he stood. Ugo stepped up on the dais. With the shire reeve's permission he beckoned a servant to bring a cup of wine for the boy. Meurig gulped down some of the liquid and was heartened, colour flushing his thin cheeks.

"A man I met here in Pembroke, suggested I could be useful at the eisteddfod," he said. "Cadwgan was to host it at the mouth of the Teifi."

"This man – how did you come to know him?"

In a silence that echoed, Meurig told of the pleasant stranger talking to him as he left the castle one day. The man was interested in leather and the boy boasted of his father's work, how the new way of tanning skins made quality goods available to any with silver in their pouches and coffers. Seated in a tavern and drinking wine for the first time, Meurig had answered questions on the caskets he had taken to the Constable, what sizes had been made, what they were to hold.

It was then Roger fitzHugh would have had Meurig taken away and hanged as a traitor but Ugo persuaded patience. There was more to be learned from the boy.

"This man's name?" Ugo asked him.

"In Pembroke I knew him as Elystan but when I saw him again at the eisteddfod, Owain called him Osfael."

Whispers grew, everyone convinced only a spy needed two names. Roger fitzHugh showed his annoyance at the interruption and the voices dropped away, then he glared at Meurig.

"What was he like?"

Meurig faced the shire reeve, telling of the man's height, stature, his thinning hair and trimmed beard. When he mentioned a stiffened left shoulder, Manon gasped. Meurig had described the stranger in the shop, the one who had been careful to keep his face from her. She was not the only one to react.

"That was him," said the charcoal burner, "the one who struck Gerwyn. His right arm was free and powerful but his left arm hung useless at his side."

At last Gerwyn's murderer had a name and Manon was weak with relief. She gazed at Meurig, chastened and penitent inside his dirt.

The crowd was restless and Roger fitzHugh impatient. "What became of the spy, Osfael?" he shouted and everyone held their breath to hear the answer.

"He was one of the men Owain took with him when he raided Sir Gerald's new castle in Emlyn."

"A wise move since, thanks to you, he knew all that was there to be thieved."

"Not just Meurig," Manon called out and the paleness of a myriad faces turned towards her. "That man, Osfael, was in the shop one day and I saw him – but not his face. I saw him again the day Sir Gerald and the princess sailed from the quay. He was watching everything loaded into the boats."

"You are sure it was the same man?"

"Yes. As someone tried to push him away and get a better view, he heaved them back. It was then I saw his left hand was hooked in his belt, the arm stiff and not used."

"Did you see his face that day?"

"I did – and thought it familiar, yet he was a stranger."

Roger fitzHugh turned back to the boy. "Where is this – Osfael – now?"

"He went with three others. They rode fast horses and were to hide from the Constable in Maelienydd."

For some of the listeners it was merely a place far away in the north. To others the word 'Maelienydd' was whispered like a ripple in a dreadful stream which flooded the hall with horror. Many crossed themselves and murmured prayers for souls lost in hell. Those in ignorance had the facts told them. Soon after Princess Nest had been taken, news had come from the north that all of Owain's teulu seeking sanctuary in Maelienydd had been slaughtered by its people.

"Ah!" The shire reeve sat back in his chair against the best of Pembroke's carving. As the crowd continued to whisper and murmur he scratched a spot on his cheek, pleased the spy was named and had died unpleasantly, yet disappointed he had no murderer to hang at the gatehouse.

The prior was unmoved by the turn of events. True, he had lost the gift of the tannery but there would be other ways, other people he could use to benefit the church. He flicked a glance at the shire reeve who frowned as he stared at the men and women before him. Most were intent on their gossip but one, Iolo, was crouching, bent over in his distress.

"Bring that fool here," Roger fitzHugh ordered.

It was a distraught man the guards held upright in front of the shire reeve.

"A spy dies as he deserves and you wail for him. I would know the reason?"

Iolo was an unlovely sight. The weepings from his eyes and nose were hideous and his arms were so tightly shackled he could not wipe his face.

"Osfael was my brother, sir. Only now do I know he is dead."

Gabbling rose unhindered as Roger fitzHugh tried to decide what to do. In the commotion Manon looked for Non. She saw cheeks even whiter than before, a rigid body arced in pain. Only Mabli moved. She went to the shire reeve and spoke in his ear until he nodded, then commanded a silence it was hard work for his men to achieve.

Mabli stepped to the front of the dais and confronted Meurig. She spoke to him clear and direct so all could hear. "Last harvest time your mother, Manon, was gravely ill and like to die. There is no doubt she was poisoned and I believe, by you."

Voices started to annoy and she scowled the chatterers speechless.

"I must know – we all must know – who it was gave you the poison for Manon."

Meurig, ashamed and contrite, looked at his father's wife. With a nod and a half-smile Manon encouraged him to speak.

"It was Elystan – Osfael. I had been complaining my father let Manon have too much say in the shop because of her wealth and he promised me a potion which would quieten her." Meurig turned to Manon. "I never meant real harm! It was just to make you sleepy and keep you out of the shop."

Manon guessed then it had happened after she had caught him stealing but she said nothing.

Mabli had no such hesitation. "Why did you run away?" She asked the boy.

"It was my father, mistress. He was so lost when Manon was ill, so unhappy when she slipped the baby."

In the stuffiness of the great hall the gasps of surprise made even the flares flicker.

"Was that all that concerned him?" Mabli wanted to know and those assembled were quiet, waiting.

"No," Meurig said. "My father was afraid Manon would die. He kept saying – 'so like my mother'."

"Ah, Gerwyn's mother could have been poisoned. Who did you think might have done that evil thing?"

"Then, I did not know. Osfael said he got the vial from his brother."

All eyes swung towards Iolo, cringing under the attention and the hate centred on him. The shire reeve pounded the table and dismissed Mabli with a wave of his hand, then waited until a mouse could have been heard squeaking.

"Iolo, look at me."

A guard used the back of his hand to urge Iolo upright and attentive to a shire reeve who was in no mood to be patient.

"Did you dispose of Gerwyn the tanner's body after your brother, Osfael, struck him?"

Iolo sighed and gave up all hope. "Aye, sir."

"Was he dead when you rolled him into the dung pit?"

Iolo drooped until cuffed upright by one of his guards. "Osfael told me to. He is one of Owain's men and knows how to kill swiftly."

Horror rippled through the crowd. If it was possible Gerwyn was still breathing when dropped into the stinking stew of his own dung pit, then Iolo was as guilty of the murder as his brother. In the time it took to quieten everyone Manon was able to lose herself in prayer, turning her thoughts away from Gerwyn's last moments.

Roger fitzHugh had not finished with Iolo. "Your brother who was a spy, did you give him shelter in your home?"

"No, sir. Never."

"You surprise me, Iolo. He was your kin and never slept under your roof?"

Iolo straightened a little and cleared his throat. "Osfael

240

always refused me that – he said Non's tongue was too dangerous for him, always flapping as it did."

Laughter rippled around the great hall and eased the grimness of the moment until the shire reeve raised his hand for silence.

"Did you provide poison which was meant to kill Manon, the tanner's wife?" he asked.

Iolo nodded and drooped.

"Speak up, man!"

"Aye, sir."

"And did you give poison to the mother of Gerwyn, causing her to die?"

Only those closest to the miserable wretch caught the mumbled answer.

"Say it!"

"Aye, sir."

Roger fitzHugh sat back and wriggled against the carving to scratch relief. Before a mass of Pembroke people he had an admitted murderer to dance in the air. He saw the tanner's wife stand and seek his attention, earning a frown for herself.

"Mistress?"

"May I ask Iolo a question?"

Impatiently, the shire reeve waved assent and Manon got as near to Iolo as she could.

"I believe you did not wish Gerwyn dead."

Wariness was in the eyes lifted to her and it took many heartbeats before he had the grace to nod his assent.

"Why was I to die?"

Iolo took a long time answering until a hefty nudge with a hauberked elbow persuaded him. "You had what she wanted," he spat at her.

Manon was surprised. "Non?"

"Aye." Petulance had replaced fear and despair. "She never stopped. Day and night she kept on and on how she could do things better than you with the riches your father left you. Would you let her when she tried? Not you, you

241

bitch! You sent her back to the home you always reminded her was your brothers' and not hers. She was beside herself and there was no rest for me."

"So I must be poisoned?"

"Why not, if it was the only way I might get some peace?"

His listeners were divided between exclaiming their surprise and straining to see Non.

Manon had more questions. "Gerwyn's mother?" she asked.

"Her? Another silly young whore like you. We had nowhere to live but with Gerwyn and his father and Non could run the household better than that stupid girl who birthed Gerwyn. She was a pretty little bitch as took the old man's eye and he would marry her when she bore him a son. She was no use in the house. Non was better at it – she kept telling me so."

"You made sure Non had what she wanted? Even if you had to murder young mothers?"

"Why not? A quiet life is my right – like any other man."

So that was all it had been, Manon thought as she sank on to her stool and noise rose around her. With the help of his brother he had been stealing the best hides from the tannery for Owain, the spy killing Gerwyn when he caught them thieving. After that there had been no clever, devious mind at work, merely the simple pettiness of unthinking spite behind the poisonings and the vicious gossip. Iolo had always been less than a man and always in Non's shadow. Who would have noticed him in a crowded beershop as he slid in the dangerous words which were his weapons of death?

Manon could feel pity for such a pathetic creature but Roger fitzHugh was not so generous. He pointed at Non, glaring furiously at her as he did so.

"Your tongue has murder to answer for, ma dame. It is right you should hang beside your instrument."

Manon leapt to her feet. "No! I beg you, no!" she pleaded with the shire reeve. There was no way she could watch Non led to her death, Gerwyn would not have wanted such an outcome. Manon sought Mabli's help but her begging must be silent in the shouting of the crowd. Mabli thought for a moment, then leaned close to the shire reeve and whispered in his ear. Waves of sound lessened to an ebbing tide and the people of Pembroke waited.

Roger fitzHugh gestured towards the prior. "I understand, father prior, you have need of a menial novice for a sister house in France?"

The cleric nodded. "That is so."

"Then you may have this woman," the shire reeve said, pointing at Non. "The rest of her life in silence and on her knees will be some recompense for the slaughter her tongue has procured."

Cheers, whistles, shouts, greeted the decision. Iolo was battered as he was dragged in one direction, Non hissed and spat at as she was forced from the hall in another.

Mabli rescued Manon and hurried her away to Nest's room and peace. Manon was shaking with exhaustion and relief, trying very hard to breathe steadily.

"The children —?"

"Gwen has gone to Buddyg's house to tell them you are free and safe. They will be home when you get there."

"I must go now!"

"No, cariad. Listen!" Mabli's strong hands grasped Manon's shoulders. Even in the quiet room the hubbub from the great hall could be heard. "The rest of Pembroke is at the gate. Trust me, child, they would have the skin off your back in that crush." Mabli saw her words reach Manon's understanding and she relaxed her hold.

"Why are they waiting?" Manon saw Mabli's fingers sketch the sign of Christ's death. "Is Iolo to be hanged today?" she whispered.

Mabli nodded. "It is only just, cariad. In Maelienydd his brother paid for Gerwyn's death – aye, and many others, I have no doubt. Iolo's life will end here and it is a small recompense for the murder of your children's grandmother."

"Mared," Manon said softly.

"What was that?"

"She was called Mared and Gerwyn loved her. He was only eight years old when she died."

"Old enough to remember so much but Gerwyn's soul can rest easier now she is avenged."

"Oh Mabli, I hoped when I knew who killed Gerwyn it would bring peace." Manon's cheeks were pale, her eyes huge and full of tears. "Now I must live with the knowledge of how much Iolo hated me – the dreadful things he did to us all."

Mabli cradled the young woman, soothing her as she would a child. "Come now, cariad," she said when Manon's sobbing eased to a spell of quiet hiccups. "You are tired and you are hungry. I have good bread and cheese you would not touch when I wanted you to break your fast. Eat it now little one, while I heat some broth."

Slowly, the crumbled bread was eaten, cheese nibbled, until Manon's natural hunger was tempted and she ate heartily. Mabli spooned into her soup enriched with scraped venison, allowing no rest until the bowl was empty. With a sigh, Manon felt tiredness drag at her limbs. Mabli stroked Mabli's brow, persuading her to lie back and rest.

"I heard talk of the prior in the kitchen," she told the young woman. "He has made it known he wants a mill near the priory, the dues it would earn greatly enriching the foundation."

"Near the priory? But that would be . . ."

"Aye, cariad. The land and the streams of the tannery would have suited him well as a gift."

Manon shivered. "I have been in the way of so many ambitions."

244

"Think instead of the dear souls who have fought for you and your children."

"Of course!" Manon struggled to get out of her chair. "I must go home, Mabli."

"In good time, cariad. It has been a strange day for you – so many hard things to learn. When you walk in to your home you need to be calm – and happy."

"Happy? How can I be so without Gerwyn?"

There were more tears and Mabli sprinkled poppy juice into wine, waiting until Manon had drunk it all and was asleep.

"Manon – cariad," a voice whispered.

It was hard for her to waken, the habit of fear still holding Manon in its grip. Mabli's face loomed into view and her gentle, twisted smile reassured.

"The day is almost gone, child. Gwen is waiting with a fine stew for you all."

Manon struggled to sit upright but her limbs were heavy, useless.

"Your children are well and there is someone here who needs to speak to you."

From behind Mabli crept Meurig. He had been vigorously cleaned and tidily clothed in a borrowed green and brown checked tunic too large for him, scuffed boots on his feet. Bare of dirt he could not hide his anxiety. Manon held out a hand to him and he rushed forward, falling on his knees before her.

"Can you ever forgive me?" he whispered.

Manon's answer was to hold the boy's face between her palms and kiss his brow. With a sob, he buried his head in her lap and all Manon could see was his cleaned hair springing again as had Gerwyn's She stroked the curls until he quietened, then lifted his head.

"As God is my witness, Manon –"

Her finger across his lips stopped more words. "You were used, cariad," she said. "All your life you had known Non

245

and you believed her – why should you not? She loved you in her way and long ago perhaps, she did mean well."

"What would you have me do?"

Manon smiled at the boy. "It is very simple. I would have you like your father. Many saw him as 'only a tanner' but he was good at his trade and dealt honestly. Because of his nature he earned many friends, such friends who would have only the truth for him, no matter what cost they might bear."

There was time for Meurig to reflect on Ugo who had ridden hard into Ceredigion and dragged him back to Pembroke to face the justice of the court in the castle.

"You want me to be a tanner?"

"Is it in you to be a good one?" Manon asked gently.

The boy thought long and carefully. "As a child I hated the smell of the place but my father was always clean when he came home to us. Is that what you mean?"

"Many men work at tasks in God's fresh air, yet they carry the stench of corruption with them always. Even straight from the dung pit, it was something your father never did."

Although thinned to skin and bone, Meurig had begun to have the look of a man about him. "I used to hate the tannery, knowing when I was older I must spend all my days there."

"And now?"

"Seeing Owain and his father, Cadwgan, has made me think of God's will in a different way. Owain, born one of the cracach in the north, was as drunk and vicious as the worst of the sots in Pembroke town." Meurig leaned nearer, his mouth to Manon's ear. "The day after the princess arrived, I saw her when she was taken to her horse. Her face was bruised and her body was as sore as that of the nursemaid but she would not swoon. Can one man be as coarse and brutal as a dozen?"

It hurt Manon to think of Nest's suffering but the boy

must be answered. "When there is much of Satan in him, yes, Meurig, he can."

"Then I will labour in the stink of the tannery and cleanse myself as my father did. Even then I may still not be worthy of your trust."

"Why not? Gerwyn saw you as the successor with the skins – and Kamal will be there with his advice."

He clutched at her hands. "Will you help me, Manon?"

She smiled at the lad's eagerness. "Aye, I will that. It is time for us all to start afresh. The tannery is too far from Pembroke. With a buyer for the land we could close the workings and begin again nearer the town walls. There would be less danger from thieves and the Constable's men can guard it for us at night. What do you say?"

A wide grin in the haggard young face told Manon all she needed to know.

"Go then and find Kamal. You can begin to plan."

When he had gone it puzzled Manon to realise how sleepy she was. She could have curled up on the skins by the fire and slept, it had been such a long, strange day. Greater, was the longing to have her children's arms about her and the promise of her own bed where she could dream of Gerwyn.

"Iolo?" she asked.

Mabli shook her head and made the sign of the cross.

"So, that was why you wanted me asleep?"

"It was best you rested until the crowds had gone –"

"And Iolo had been hanged?"

"Aye, cariad, it is over."

Mabli was not as sombre as Manon expected her to be, the older woman was almost light hearted.

"There has been news to cheer you?"

"Oh, Manon, hope at last! A messenger came while you were asleep. The king is greatly angered my lady is still not free. Punishing Cadwgan has not changed Owain's heart – if he has one – and the king's man, the Bishop of London, is at Shrewsbury. From the king he has offered great power to

Madog and Ithel, the son's of Cadwgan's brother. All they must do is seize Owain or drive him and his father from Wales. With the cousins the bishop has sent Llywarch ap Trehaern who is desperate to avenge the deaths of his own brothers by Owain's hand. These are strong men in the north, cariad and they are gathering great hosts of our people to drive Owain into the sea – or his grave!"

"What of Nest? Will she be safe?"

The twist of Mabli's cheek tightened. "I have no doubt Owain has pleasured himself with my sweet child's skin but he is a coward and will run in the face of so many enemies. The only skin he will take to safety is his own."

"He will leave Nest behind?"

"Aye – and Sir Gerald's son, if it saves Owain's neck. Soon, my Nest will be home with her children. It is where she belongs, as you do with yours. Now, take that babe of Gerwyn's you carry and see you both feed well before you sleep."

Manon embraced Mabli. "How can I ever thank you?"

"Not me, child. The good Lord looks after us all and he has dealt justly this day."

There was a gathering at the gate but it was a small one, the time of couvre feu fast approaching. Most of the towns-people were already within doors but there was still an air of excitement, of celebration, after all they had witnessed.

Two of the shire reeve's men escorted Manon, ready to deal with any who would hinder her return home. As she neared the gate she was surprised to see Ugo, waiting there with Meurig.

The big Fleming bowed to her. "With your permission I will make sure you reach your home safely."

The gate swung open for the little group and ragged cheers greeted Manon's appearance. It gave Ugo time to walk beside her, one arm pointing to a sight in the distance. Only Meurig recognised it was a ruse to prevent Manon seeing the body hanging still and limp from a noose at the side of the gate. The boy's face whitened, had a greenish tinge, but he walked steadily onwards, talking of the children and hoping Rhodri would forgive him his past harshness.

"You must be patient, Meurig," Manon told him. "It will take time for Rhodri to learn to trust you again. The good Lord has brought us all through such horrors but if we have faith, forgiveness will become familiar to us all."

"Manon!" Cynfan, cap in hand, was in front of her. His face which had become drawn and haggard was now shining with relief and happiness.

She put out a free hand to him. "Gwen has told me all you have done, Cynfan. God knows you have been kind to my children, and to me, when we needed you most. I thank you with all my heart."

The burly man bent to her hand and kissed it, Manon feeling the dampness of his tears.

"Forgive me, Cynfan, I must go to my little ones."

In the short walk to the leather shop there were many who stopped Manon, thanked God and wished her well. Ithel was in his doorway and bowed to her across the heads of those between them. As she walked, Manon could see the familiar sights, smell the roasted meat Cynfan's oven boys had cooked for the hungry folk roaming Pembroke after the trial. A Frankish hanging made many men hungry, she thought. The Welsh way was to make a murderer work the rest of his life to keep fed the family of the person he had killed. With the coming of the Franks had returned the blood price for a death and the lust for executions all could see.

The roadway cleared a little and Manon could see the shutters of the leather shop were in place. She knew Gwen was waiting inside, Dybion in her arms. Heledd would be jumping up and down in excitement while Rhodri would be still, silent, his eyes huge as he longed for sight of her and the reassurance she brought him. She began to run but Meurig stopped, dragging her to a halt beside him.

"Manon, look!"

She raised her eyes, following the pointing finger. On the roof of her home Manon could see a raven perched, its head tilted to one side as it watched the approach of the little group.

"Do you think . . .?" Meurig began in a whisper.

"Oh Meurig, if only it were so," Manon said, her voice filled with yearning. Longing for Gerwyn was unabated but dare she take the raven's appearance to signify her husband's spirit waited for her return?

Ugo was curious. "This bird, it is important?"

Her gaze did not leave the glossiness of the raven, the brightness of an unblinking eye following their movements. Ugo repeated his question and Manon tried to answer him, seeking words to help Ugo understand.

"The old ones believed the souls of great men – and women – come back amongst us in the bodies of ravens."

The tall Fleming did not scoff. Sunk in his own misery in a far-off land he had longed for such a sign. "Gerwyn was a man who should live on," he said gently. "I can see the bird protects this house and all who live here – the family Gerwyn loved, his friends who fought for you."

Manon held out her hands to him. "As you did, sir, and I thank you and God for it."

Ugo bowed and watched as Manon walked into her home, Heledd rushing to hide herself in her mother's skirts. A Rhodri who seemed to have grown was carrying Dybion, the baby laughing and holding out his arms to her while Gwen and Kamal held hands and cried, leaving Nudd to close the doors and give the little family the peace it needed.

Alone outside the shop Ugo looked up at the raven. "If you are Gerwyn you know your murderer is dead and you are avenged. Your wife is freed of all guilt, Meurig has returned to grow into a man and the poisoner who orphaned you hangs from the castle wall. Yes, your sister

250

lives – in silence. Is that what you wanted us all to bring about?"

He was sure the raven nodded to him as it tossed its head and cawed, a proud, raucous sound.

"I will wait with you, Gerwyn – until you fly away." Ugo smiled. "I am a patient man."

Princess Nest

Easter, 1093. King Rhys lost the battle of Aberdare, the southern kingdom of Wales and his life. With his grown sons dead or captured, his widow and baby son safe in Ireland, only his daughter, Princess Nest, remained. Little more than a child and speaking only Welsh, she was taken hostage by the English king, William II. Terrified she may have been but Nest was not only very beautiful she was a determined survivor, eventually becoming the most favoured mistress of the king's brother, Henry.

August, 1100. King William dies 'accidentally' and Henry claims the throne. He takes a Saxon wife and Nest is married to Gerald who had been born in Windsor, the son of its Constable, Walter, and a good friend of William the Conqueror, father of Henry I. The newly-weds return to Pembroke, Nest with the gift of lands at Carew, near Pembroke, and Gerald is soon appointed Pembroke's Constable.

January, 1109. Nest is with Gerald at his new estate in Emlyn, in the north of Pembrokeshire. The castle Gerald built is attacked at night and Nest raped by her cousin, Owain, before being taken captive by him, together with four children, three of them hers. Wales is in uproar at the crimes and, as a beautiful woman whose abduction caused war, Nest earned the title 'Helen of Wales'.

May, 1169. To help the king of Ireland free his country from the Danes then ruling from Dublin, a fleet sailed from Pembroke with an army led by Strongbow de Clare. Of the knights under his command, most were related to Nest by blood or marriage. After a successful campaign, her descendants settled there, giving modern Ireland its first fitz-Geralds, fitzStephens and fitzHenrys, through Nest's sons by her two husbands and by King Henry.

After a long life it is not known when or where Princess Nest died but in the chancel of Carew Cheriton's church, and honouring remains buried in its wall, is a small effigy of a woman holding a heart in her hands. Nest always loved Carew. Perhaps her heart is still there?